AISHA

Copyright © 2001, by Angela Catramadou-Parker, Phoenix, Arizona

All rights reserved. No part of this book may be reproduced, in any form or by any electronic or mechanical means, including information storage and retrieval systems, without permission in writing from the author, except by a reviewer, who may quote brief passages in a review.

Library of Congress Card Catalogue Number 00-14320

ISBN 0-9660449-3-2

Published in the United States by Cosmos Publishing Co., Inc.
P.O. Box 2255
River Vale, NJ 07675
Phone: 201-664-3494
Fax: 201-664-3402
E-mail: greekbooks@worldnet.att.net
Web site: greeceinprint.com

Printed in Greece

ANGELA CATRAMADOU-PARKER

AISHA

A Spellbinding Novel With A Sence
Of History In The Making

To my Hungarian friend with love & best wishes

Angela C. Parker

9/13/01

COSMOS PUBLISHING
RIVER VALE, NJ

This book is dedicated to my son John Paul and daughter-in-law Lisa who introduced me to my first computer, and my precious grandson Joshua Winston Parker with love always.

I would also like to dedicate it to the memory of my mother Maria, and my beloved sister Theodosia, the two women who truly loved me and believed in me.

I offer my thanks to God for granting me the guidance, the creativity and the patience to accomplish this...

And to the Egyptian people who for centuries offered refuge, freedom, friendship and hospitality to millions of foreigners like myself, my gratitude.

This is a work of fiction except for the names of historical personalities and places all other characters are imaginary.

For a lifetime I've been obsessed about the subject and the historical events I have witnessed until I realized that very often the subject chooses the writer and not the other way around. **Aisha** is my obsession.

The author

CHAPTER I

Aisha knew the threat of death was always present. At the end of her solo dance that night at the "purgatory," as the working women referred to the cabaret, the audience applauded her warmly. This happened often and it always surprised her, considering the patrons consisted entirely of soldiers who had come to Egypt to fight a war on the desert front, desperate men who felt no obligation to respect local laws or any civility in any form.

From the beginning, the women at the night club had advised her to avoid, if possible, the company of Australians and South Africans who, after a few drinks became violent and very hard to deal with. She had heard many chilling stories about barroom brawlers, and until that night she had managed well, she thought as she headed to her dressing room.

After she changed from her exotic costume to an evening gown, she was heading toward the bar when suddenly from behind she felt a strong grip on her wrist that sent a stab of terror into her heart.

She whirled around and saw a blond South African towering over her. His eyes were bloodshot, and he looked as if he had not shaved or slept for days. His face was haggard and his clothes rumpled.

"Please, let me go," she pleaded helplessly. "You're hurting me!"

He smiled, a smile as thin as a razor slash. "What the bloody hell's the game?" he asked and looked at her wildly. Then, with a vicious swing of the hand, he forced her into a chair, pulled up another for himself, and clapped his hands for the waiter.

"Two bloody whiskeys!" he croaked.

Halil, the waiter, looked at her and with a gesture of despairing fright, he whispered in Arabic, "Aiee, Aiee! He's a swine!" Then she saw him talk to madame, gesturing in her direction.

Madame hurried over at the mere hint of violence. As she approached, she was shaking her head as if to reassure Aisha that it was not serious and not to worry. She could handle it.

"How's my boy getting along? Enjoying yourself?" she asked with her thick French accent, trying hard to sound friendly and cheerful.

The soldier's face turned green.

"Bloody cow! I'm not your boy, and I'm not enjoying myself!"

A sudden expression of savage resentment passed across her fat made-up face. Her eyes glittered and the blood rushed to her cheeks.

"Le salaud!" madame whispered. "But why? We try to offer service and superb entertainment."

"Rubbish!" he hissed, and spat on the floor. "Bloody roughhouse!" He emptied his glass with a gulp. "Entertainment? Ha! My ass!"

"Well, well, darling —"

"Don't darlin' me, you old goat!"

She stared in utter disbelief. *"Mon Dieu!* He's vulgar!" she said in French. Then she called, "Antoine, *cheri.*" And gave a quick over-the-shoulder look in her husband's direction.

The angular old man came leaping like a frog. He put on a brave front, but Aisha knew he had no stomach for fist fights.

"Here, Antoine! Why don't you get a drink for this soldier. Yes, a drink on the house." Then, in French, "he's a beast. Call the police before it's too late. Then, in English again, "Hurry, *cheri,* hurry!"

Meanwhile Aisha eased out of her chair and was ready to run but he jerked her back and forced her to sit.

"Where d'you think you're going?"

"To the girls' room," she lied.

"You take me for a bloody fool?" His laughter was a lion's roar. His eyes were without a grain of sympathy for what they saw. They were not eyes, she thought, they were razor blades. His mouth twisted with sarcasm and hate.

"Smart pigeon, eh? As if I'm a bloody fool. Well, you ain't goin' nowhere. You're staying right here, then you'll come with me. That's why I spend my goddamn money!" He pulled out a hashish-loaded cigarette, which he lit. "Want one?" he asked, his eyes half-closed.

Aisha spat on the floor disgustedly. "You keep your shitty filth," she said, and tried again to get away.

He reached out a hand and caught her, jerking her as if she were a doll. "You're not going out — not while I'm here. You're gonna do what I damn please."

"You lousy coward!" she screamed. Out of the corners of her eyes, she looked at him and saw the ominous flicker of his jaw muscles.

He ignored her insult and yelled for another drink.

She stared at him, longing violently to reach over and rake her nails across his blond cheek until she drew blood.

Madame's purple face stared at her, and she gave an open-palmed gesture. She opened her mouth as if to say something, then changed her mind. She apparently decided talking was not helping. As Aisha watched her, she noticed how ridiculously fat she was.

"Drink this," the soldier hissed. "Bloody bitch!"

"Damn you! I wouldn't touch your poison," she said savagely, and flung him a vindictive glance.

He met it with cold contempt, impervious as stone.

Madame pressed Aisha's hand with sudden firmness, a kind of promise of help, and left.

Anger choking her, Aisha sat back and waited. She prayed the soldier would fall asleep, that there would be an air-raid, a heavy bombardment, or something.

But nothing happened. The orchestra kept banging away and no policeman, local or foreign, showed up.

He looked up at her, a cold half-smile on his lips. "You're not any better than the rest of your bloody people, filthy beggars the lot of you, in a rut-filled hole you call a country, with a fat pot-bellied king."

Filled with humiliation, she tried to say something to defend herself and "her" people before he interrupted her. "A chap I know says you local women know how to please a man, a real man, I mean."

"Like you?"

"Bloody right. You learn early here don't you?"

"Why sure! It's all in the blood, the animal instincts and the hot climate," she mimicked ferociously.

The soldier gave her a thuggish look. "We'll find out soon enough," he said, sweat beginning to pour down his face.

Panic-stricken, she looked around. *Where the hell are they? Where is the police, somebody, anyone?*

Of the working civilians in the club, no one dared come to her rescue. They knew the soldier was armed. So while the Arab waiters heaved their curses in Arabic, madame added hers in French from a distance, and no one seemed able to do anything.

Meanwhile the soldier drank, his eyes half-closed. She knew she had to do something. Somehow, she had to get out of there. Desperate, she looked at the main entrance of the cabaret, only few feet from where they sat.

She calculated her movements. Suddenly, she leapt to her feet and dashed for the door. He reached out and caught hold of her skirt. She jerked it free, hearing it tear, and smashed both fists against his chest.

For a second, he reeled backwards in genuine surprise. In the suspended second, she snatched a chair and threw it at him. The chair landed on his head and he let out a wild scream. "Damn you!"

Trembling, she pushed chairs and tables right and left as she dashed for the door. She heard two shots fired and people screamed.

Without turning to look back, she touched her chest to see if she had been shot. She couldn't tell, but as long a she could run, she did. Eventually, the loud voices that echoed down the alley slowly receded. After a while, they subsided completely.

Exhausted, she stopped and leaned against a wall, gasping for air. She wiped the perspiration from her forehead with the back of her hand and took a deep breath. Everything was still. Then she heard the clank of a soldier's boots coming down the street. He must have followed me, she thought, half-crazy with fear.

She tried to think. There was no one about, not a taxi to be seen. She had to hide fast. She knew if he caught up with her in the dark alley, he would kill her. Taking her shoes off, she raced and hid in the shadowy doorway of a building.

The hollow ring of clattering feet roused her to act. She pushed the door. It opened with a creaking sound. She started to climb the stairs. When she reached the first floor, she stopped and strained her ears in the darkness. She heard footsteps moving inside the building. She continued climbing until she reached the roof, only to realize that instead of a shelter, she had found herself in a trap. She had to get out of there fast. But where and how, she wondered as she surveyed the square, flat, open terrace with no place to hide.

She scurried to the side of the parapet. The wall that separated the roof from the adjoining building wall was not very high. Without a moment's hesitation, she threw her shoes over, pulled up her skirt and jumped the wall, only to find herself in another flat terrace and another open trap. What if that door was locked? What then?

She reached over. With trembling hand she turned the handle. It opened with ease. From somewhere, a blue lamp threw some light on the staircase. She strained her ears, but there was no sound. Without making the slightest noise, she went down the winding stairs of the second building. In the lobby of the building the Arab doorman asleep on a wooden bench by the door. She tiptoed past him and slipped outside, leaving the door ajar.

For a moment she stood in the darkness of the doorway and anxiously inspected the length of the ill-lighted street with its sleepy houses.

The alley was empty and everything appeared quiet. I must have lost him, she thought, and for a second, the hope halted the beat of her heart. She took a few more steps and then stopped to breathe. The sweat was coming down like water. She knew that if she could get to the end of the road and managed to cross the boulevard, she would be safe.

Cautiously, she walked to the end of the alley. She was ready to cross when two iron hands grabbed her by the shoulders and nailed her to the ground.

A scream escaped her dry throat. She screamed again.

He cursed and hit her hard across the mouth. She folded on her knees. Her face burned like fire. The pain brought tears to her eyes. Fear paralyzed her, and she had no strength to move.

"Filthy whore!" he groaned like an animal in pain and jerked her. "Did you think you'd get off so easily?" He laughed. Then with a powerful hand he whirled her around to face him.

Half-blind from the tears, she managed to take a fleeting glance at him. His youthful face was ugly from hate, and his eyes burned with a beastly passion. She felt his powerful grasp on her arm, tight like an iron claw, and she knew there was nothing she could do. She had neither strength nor resistance left in her, and she let him push her forward.

"Walk!" he ordered hoarsely, "and walk straight or I swear I'll kill you!" He gave her a look of complete contempt. His eyes glittered, his nostrils flared and he was breathing fast. His forehead was damp with sweat. She forced herself to walk.

When they reached the boulevard, he stopped a passing taxi. He opened the door and with a powerful push and a belly laugh, he tossed her, head first, to the other side of the cab, then he came and sat by her side. He lit a cigarette and laughed again, seeming to enjoy a good joke.

"Drive on," he ordered the Arab driver.

"Where to?"

"Just drive. I'll tell you when to stop."

The car sped down the boulevard and turned on to the Grand Corniche. She noticed the moon was up, shining on the calm sea. She could not feel any pain. She was numb all over. The car traveled fast on the dark streets of the silent city. She leaned to the side and began to cry.

Then the coldness that had gripped her began to ease. It was as if fear had been raised to such a high pitch that it killed itself. If it's written, it'll be, she thought with total resignation, and the muscles of her body began to relax.

Suddenly the car halted with a powerful jolt and she was hurled flat to the floor. Panic-stricken, she looked up. Like a flash in the dark, she saw the driver lift a heavy cudgel, which he brought down heavily upon the soldier's skull.

She heard a thump, then a loud groan that tore out of his throat like a short gasp. The cigarette fell from the soldier's lips, and his eyes glazed over as he dropped to the floor, folding up. Then there was silence.

"Are you all right?" she heard the driver ask.

Stunned, she stared at the motionless uniform, then at the driver. She brought her hand to her mouth to suppress a scream while shaking.

"I knew it was you!" the driver stammered. "My name is Hassan."

She wracked her brain to think.

"I guess you don't remember me," he said, "but unless I'm wrong, you're Aisha, aren't you?"

She nodded and mumbled, "But, I don't know anyone around here in the city."

"Not that it matters, really. I would have done the same for any other woman, Arab or not. But we're from the same village, Aisha. Now you're a famous dancer. We taxi drivers know what's going on in the city. I'd know you anywhere. It infuriated me to see this beast push you in the car the way he did. They haven't left us a shred of dignity. How did you get in this mess? Why?"

"For a loaf of bread, my brother. For a loaf of bread." She wept silently.

The driver left his seat and came around to check the soldier.

Horrified, Aisha asked, "Is he . . . dead?"

"He's stiff all right. I didn't mean to kill him. I only wanted him out of action. But that bastard was drunk, and carried a loaded gun. How was I supposed to handle him? There wasn't much else I could do. But don't worry, I'll take care of him."

He pulled the gun from its holster and threw it on the floor of the cab, then he went through the soldier's pockets. They were empty. The driver started to laugh, little spurts of laughter.

"You know," he said, "that son of a dog would have killed me too, at the end. He had no money for his fare. He was broke! I wouldn't have believed him, of course, and I would have demanded my fare. They've killed Arabs for less than that. Taxi drivers are easy prey!"

"It's all my fault," Aisha protested.

He shook his head. "Relax. It's not your fault and I won't get in any trouble. I'll dump him somewhere, an empty alley, I guess." He pushed the body of the uniformed man on the floor. "It was either him, or us."

The driver scratched his head. "I was back at the village a couple of weeks ago to visit my old mother," he said, as if forgetting for just an instant the circumstances. "My mother was telling me how everyone there is so proud of you and how you've made a name for yourself." He stopped, and looked at her in perplexity. "They also know how much you're helping by sending money to your uncle Youssef and your friend Foula who, as I'm sure you know, now has two small children. Yes, the villagers remember you, and they're very proud of you."

Aisha blinked back her tears and looked at the young man in utter disbelief. "I'll never forget your kindness, my friend," she whispered.

"Forget it. Tonight we both could have been killed. So as

long as this bloody war and blackouts are on, I'll be outside your workplace to make sure you get home safe." After a brief pause, "I think I'll keep the bastard's gun for protection," he said as he pushed the gun under the driver's seat.

Impulsively, Aisha moved to the far end of the seat and covered her eyes with her hands.

"You can ride in front, if you wish. I'll take you home safely." The driver came around and opened the door for her.

As she stepped out of the taxi, she felt the first rain drops on her face. In seconds, the rain came down hard, as it often did before dawn.

On the way home the whole picture became clear in her mind. How could she have imagined that she could have changed her village life and find freedom, love, and prosperity unless she accepted that her past life at the village, with all its deprivations, was part of her destiny and the plans that shaped the woman she had become.

For the last few years in the city she had tried to put her past life and the village behind her. She had tried so hard to erase it from her memory, as if it had not existed. Now, it all came back with nostalgia and a renewed understanding that she had never felt before. The memory of her life at the village returned with vengeance to haunt her, and she knew that unless she released the anger she harbored in her heart, she would never find peace and speculate and hope for a brighter future.

By the time she had reached her apartment, the rain had stopped and the stars shone again in the clear Alexandrian sky.

CHAPTER II

The Village, late 1939

The muezzin from the minaret was calling the faithful to prayer. Aisha picked up a rock and threw it in the river. As she watched the ripples spread, she spoke to the water.

"As you increase in depth, may I increase in strength!" She repeated the words three times. After a momentary pause, and as an afterthought, "Please God," she whispered, "help me change my life, my destiny. Don't let me live like my mother, and her mother before her. We are at the bottom of the heap. No one can endure deprivation without hope of prevailing. Please." Then she stooped, filled her palms with cool water, and moistened her neck and temples. She felt refreshed.

Surrounded by silence and stillness, she felt she was not alone. She turned around, tossed her hair back, and took a few steps. She saw him leaning against a palm, a half-smile on his lips, a bottle in his hands.

"Terrific speech," he said. "I'm impressed."

Taken by surprise, Aisha stood for a second feeling awkward, embarrassed, angry. She glanced around. "I didn't see you. I mean —"

"You thought you were alone. And you are, my dear. Don't mind me. It was a great pleasure watching your performance.

You are the most beautiful sight I've seen in some time." He laughed, raised his bottle, and took a deep swallow.

"Strange that we should run into each other again, and here of all places," she said.

"Not strange at all, Aisha," he said without hesitation. "I followed you."

"Why?"

He shrugged. There was gentle amusement on his strong, handsome face, an expression that had so strangely affected her each of the last two times she had briefly seen him.

She had never met anyone like him before in her life. In his twenties, perhaps, he wore European clothes like the first-class train passengers, but she knew for a fact, and from the villagers' gossip, that he was a native, one of the sons of the powerful and wealthy land-owner Abdel Latif, who derived his wealth from the village land and the natives' cheap labor. However, the Basha lived in the city when he was not visiting or gambling in the fashionable European centers and was raising his children with the best European education his money could buy.

Aisha knew all that — she had to remind herself each time the Basha's son tried to stop and talk to her during his rare visits to the village. She knew he was the son of a Basha. And yet, as he looked at her now, confident, handsome, strong, every part of her was filled with a wild longing for this young man who was part of the other world, the very world she longed passionately to see, and to get to know.

Immediately she felt a great sense of inadequacy. A fear overwhelmed her that whatever she did or said would seem foolish to him.

"Can we at least sit here and talk?" he asked, almost pleading.

"What do they call you when they don't call you Basha?" she asked sarcastically, regaining her cool.

He stared at her with raised eyebrows, then smiled, showing teeth that were white, even, beautifully shaped. "Gamal," he said, "or Robert, whichever you prefer." He stared with a look that undressed her and gave her a rising sense of warm excitement. "Well?"

"Gamal," she answered, scorn in her voice. "I prefer Gamal. No true-blooded Arab is called Robert."

He threw back his head with a hearty laugh. "I knew you would, love," he said, then took several more deep swallows from the bottle and wiped his mouth with the back of his hand.

His carefree laughter made her forget her nervous embarrassment. She stared up at him, longing with all her heart to impress him. She realized she was succeeding. His eyes were intent on her fully developed breast.

For several seconds he watched her, steadily, carefully. Half scared, she stared back at him. His eyes met hers. He took hold of her wrist and pulled her gently closer, bending and kissing her, tenderly pulling her hair away from her face and caressing her soft, smooth skin. She dropped to her knees, and he bent down to sit on the grass next to her.

She could smell the heavy liquor on his breath, but just as strong was the masculine sweat which mingled with a light scent of aromatic cologne. The mixture of aromas sent a powerful shivering through her body. His touch intoxicated her as they sat so close, alone in the deserted, quiet countryside by the river.

He bent and kissed her. Instinctively, she tried to pull herself away.

He grabbed her by the waist, while his full, warm lips pressed down on hers. No one had kissed her like this before, she thought as his tongue probed into her mouth. As her arms went around him and her lips met his warm mouth, every part of her wanted him with a passion that was savage, violent, selfish. She opened her eyes and saw his tanned face above her wet with sweat. She raised one arm and mopped his forehead with her sleeve.

"By Allah," he groaned, as if in prayer, forcing her back to the ground.

"Stop it," she screamed.

He froze. Then shifted his weight from her and smoothed her dress. "I'm sorry. I didn't intend to force you," he said mopping the sweat from his face with his sleeve. Please forgive me. You're so beautiful, I couldn't resist the temptation."

To her surprise she remained beside him perfectly still, as if trying to understand what actually had happened and how a man of his position and wealth could have found her tempting and desirable.

"The first time I saw you standing by the river bank, your wet dress clinging to your slim body, shaking your long black mane, I knew how a living, breathing *beshneen* must look."

"*Beshneen*? What's that?" She asked and sat up with a safe distance between them.

He grinned wide, his dark eyes sparkling with amusement, his confidence restored. "Well, it's the Egyptian lotus, love. A flower," he explained. "When the flower is half opened it is one of the most beautiful plants in Egypt, the reason why the natives call the plants, 'the brides of the Nile.' A *beshneen* attains maturity at the time when the Nile reaches its full height." He reflected a moment, then continued, "It dies when the water retires. It is an emblem of life in all its vigor, but it is also an emblem of death as the open flower dies in the ebbing."

Aisha stared at him, completely lost.

"You're so beautiful, my *Beshneen*. Nature splurged on you. So generous. It's almost ironic." He laughed. "The city women spend fortunes on cosmetics and the latest beauty potions from Paris and London, while you're here with nothing. What do you use on your long, shining hair? What is your secret?"

"Camel dung!"

He stared with a half smile on his lips. "And on your long, thick eyelashes?"

"Pink-eye twice a year. When we get over the disease, the lashes grow longer and stronger." The last remark was said with a snort.

He exploded in laughter. "I don't believe it. Oh, *mon Dieu!*"

The accidental slip of the tongue and the influence of his foreign education returned Aisha to her present reality and made her feel inadequate again. She became aware of the gap that existed between people like him and her kind. With a twist of pain, she wondered if she would ever find her way to cross that bridge.

She wanted to scream, *Let me come with you, to the city, to hell, anywhere, away from here, please, please.* But her pride kept her from saying anything. She hated begging, whether for food or favors. Besides, she knew it was impossible. Basha's sons didn't associate with peasants.

"What in Allah's name keeps you here? What a waste," he said.

"But I'm leaving."

He stared at her, surprise all over his face, "Where to?"

"I'm going to the city."

"The city?" His face was suddenly serious. The half smile on his lips was gone. "To do what?"

"To work, eat, live."

"By Allah, it's a jungle, little girl. You'll be devoured alive."

"So be it. But I'll be damned if I stay in this Godforsaken rat-hole. I'm not afraid. I'm damned if I stay, and I'm damned if I go. I hate it here. At least I've got to try." She halted. What could she tell him? How it felt to live in misery without any hope for a better life. To her astonishment, Aisha felt the trace of tears down her cheeks. She looked up to find Gamal staring at her. She thought she saw in his dark eyes a warmth, a tenderness, perhaps, but not understanding. Maybe it's pity, she thought, and became confused, then angry and defiant.

"How would you possibly know what a peasant's life is like in a village?" she said and jumped up quickly, smoothing her dress.

He gave her a glance of admiration, astonishment, or annoyance; she couldn't tell just then. They stood and stared at each other. After a long moment of silence, Gamal straightened up, brushed his pants, then smiled.

"I admire your guts. Why not? If you feel that strongly, it's obvious you're not cut out for this type of life. Good luck, girl. I truly mean it." Then he raised a finger to his lips and frowned. "I hear someone coming," he whispered. "I must leave." He gave her a disarming smile, as if to apologize for leaving her there, and was gone.

She watched him walk for a while, past the palm trees, where he turned, waved, and was out of sight.

Aisha stood there momentarily, staring at the ground as if trying to recapture the all-too-fleeting scene. What would it be like to be loved by a man like Gamal? She tried to imagine it, but she could not. Even the mere thought was insane. That could never happen, she knew. Men like him belonged to another race, proud, rich and powerful. They did not fall in love with peasants, they ruled them. But she wanted to believe that after she moved out of her environment, someday there would be someone who would love her, for the woman she was, as she was. Having cleared her thoughts, she walked to the river and washed herself before she started for home.

When she reached the village square her friend Foula was waiting, her hands on her hips, her bare feet in a puddle of mud.

"I didn't see you at the station," she said.

Aisha started to talk, but the conversation was cut shortly by a piercing scream: "Murder! Murder!"

Men ran out of the coffeehouses, trampling over one another. Women shrieked and dogs howled in the square. The two girls picked up their long skirts and ran.

"What happened?" Aisha asked members of the crowd.

"The usual," said one of the men. "Muhamed made passes at another man's wife and the husband took care of him."

"This time for good, I'm afraid," mumbled someone else.

"The husband had to defend his honor," another man interjected.

In a pool of blood lay Muhamed's torn body, his bowels spattered on the ground. His staring eyes were glazed. His face had the waxen mask of death. The killer squatted by his victim and wept, covering his face with his hands. And then the mourning pandemonium began. Women began to scream, beating their breasts and tearing their hair. A few feet away a young boy applauded hysterically at the performers.

"Spit on the dead man," proposed a woman.

"Why?"

"It's the custom."

"Poor man, he died for love," Aisha said, and spat with disgust at the corpse. "Some things never change here."

Foula shook her head. "Starting tomorrow you'll have plenty of change, but what in Allah's name you'll do if things go wrong, if ..."

Aisha was tempted to reply: *if things go wrong, I'll end up with the beggars, the thieves, and the drug addicts that roam the streets of the big city.* But she said none of these things. They had heard too many chilling stories about villagers who had tried what she was contemplating to do, and were never heard of again. If not for her inexplicable certainty that she could survive, she would have despaired. Surely that feeling was real, she told herself over and over until she truly believed it. But she saw no need to add to Foula's fears and anxieties.

Aisha reached for her friend's hand, and held it to her cheek. "Don't worry ," she said. "Deep in my guts I feel we'll survive. Why don't we go to the station and spend some time together."

"I have to pick up my refreshment box first," Foula said. "I'll meet you there."

"Sure." Then Aisha turned around and ran the length of Main Street.

When she reached the open fields she whirled around, trying to capture the entire vista. The familiar view never ceased to amaze her. Acres and acres of cotton land that looked as if covered by a white, fluffy blanket extending as far as her eyes could see.

Above her was a clear blue sky. Farther north, tall palms and date trees covered with red, yellow and black fruit. Sugar cane reeds kept their heads above the smooth, flowing river. Everything around was restful, colorful, life-giving. A warm, peaceful feeling filled Aisha's heart and made the earlier death scene at the village square seem now like a bad dream.

She ran to the edge of the cultivated field. When she reached the river bank, the sun had begun to gild the tops of the palm trees. She knew it was time for the train with the foreigners to arrive, on its way to Luxor and Aswan. With the consistency of sunset, it roared into the village station, grumbled impatiently, stopped, and then departed as noisily as it had come.

Hardly a day went by that Aisha missed going to watch the

train come and go. It was a sacred daily ritual. The train's foreign cargo left a deep impression on her, and made her aware of a world she yearned to see.

Now from her vantage point by the river bank, she surveyed the village she had known all her life.

Palm trees among the houses afforded welcome shelter from the heat. Pigeon-houses abounded in the form of towers with sloping white-washed mud walls. Numerous hovels were made of sun-dried bricks, plastered with mud and straw. A minaret, where a muezzin chanted the call to prayer five times a day, was isolated along the horizon. An old graveyard with a white-washed dome-building on the highest point of the burial ground was known to be the last resting place of a sheikh. The Nile washed through the lush, cultivated land, adjacent to the mountainous, sandy desert. This was her village, her universe.

She looked at the contradictions of Egypt. The rich, fertile valley and the arid, waterless deserts of shifting sand. As her Uncle Youssef often reminded her, the people, too, were a contradiction. Despite poverty and sickness, they seemed cheerful and contented, but were also very emotional, generally ignorant, and lacking in self-control.

"Our village is a small world of its own," Youssef had explained. "Our fellow *fellahin* are descendants of Arab desert tribes, Negro slaves imported by the Arabs, ancient Egyptians with Caucasian blood, and Nubians. As a result, some of us are black and others, like yourself, much lighter with tawny complexion." And Youssef would usually end with: "We must accept Allah's will, child, and thank Him for His love and generosity." The atmosphere was serene and calm, and yet she could find no peace. Unruly thoughts kept coming unbidden.

Why did nothing ever change in their little universe? Above them, airplanes tore the blue skies, transporting people from place to place, and human voices reached them from far away lands through radio boxes at the turn of a switch, yet neither days nor seasons nor even epochs ever seemed to touch them. Every day dawned and died the same as all the ones before, for all one could tell, all the way back to their ancestors, who had labored on these same fields in the Valley of the Kings and the mighty Pharaohs.

Aisha would sit on the doorstep of her house with her eyes shut and try to imagine herself as part of that other world, the world she witnessed daily in small doses at the station. But when she opened her eyes, she would still see her neighbor's miserable hovel, huge bundles of sticks and dry maize stalks piled high against the wall. On her own side were stacks of cow-and-buffalo-dung cakes used for fuel. She would spread her arms, as though suffocating, trying to smash the frontiers and be free from the barriers that destiny prescribed for the poor women like herself.

"Just like your father," her mother would say. "His blood is in your veins."

Even her wise Uncle Youssef, who could read the Koran, had no satisfying answers.

"When the stomach is concerned, wisdom withdraws," he would say. Or, when he saw that his answers did not impress Aisha, he would recite his favorite lines:

> Poverty's my price! Thy lovers raise
> to heaven their battle-cry,
> Gladly meeting men's derision,
> letting all the world go by.

From a distance came the long drawn out wail of the train as it pulled away from the station. First time she had ever missed the train! She leapt to her feet. The river bank was now deserted except for an old man who sat smoking while his cow cooled itself in the muddy water.

"You're wrong, Uncle Youssef and mama!" she screamed. "I'm not like my father. I don't intend to let the world go by me. Do you hear me?" She heard the echo of her words, then a deafening silence.

The station was half empty when she arrived. She found a bench and sat.

"Dreaming again, princess?" Foula asked as she unloaded her heavy box of refreshments on the floor.

"Why not? It doesn't cost anything!"

"The dream of the cat is all about the mice."

"Sell much today?"

Foula raised her shoulders in a slow, wry shrug. "What's the difference? The situation here is like the ass's tail. It never increases, and it never diminishes."

"No sales."

Foula spat on the ground disgustedly. "Oh, yes! I sold one lousy lemonade to a dirty old man. First he pinched my ass, then he gave me a five-piastre tip, the big spender! But let's face it, most European passengers don't buy from us. They're afraid to catch our germs."

"Then why do you keep trying?"

Her mouth curved in a half-smile. "I guess I keep hoping I'll sell them something." After a pause, "Truth is, I come to take a peek at the passengers. They're so different from us — the clothes they wear, the languages they speak, the way they color their faces. And they all wear shoes! You know, we have nothing in common with these people, except for four things."

"What four things you're talking about?" Aisha asked, intrigued.

Foula held up four of her fingers. "We're born the same way, we die the same way, and we laugh and cry the same."

Aisha looked at her friend and saw the fright in Foula's big eyes pinned on her and burning with anxiety.

"So you're leaving us tomorrow, eh?"

"I guess so."

Foula looked at her. "I'll miss you, princess," she whispered. "I know you'll never come back. No one ever does."

"I'll miss you too," Aisha said, trying hard to hold back her tears.

Foula pulled up her skirt, squatted on the floor, looked at Aisha out of the corner of her eye and smiled. "I've got to hand it to you," she said, "the way you finally convinced your mother."

"It wasn't easy. She was so concerned. But she figured I might run away and end up in the hands of the big city vultures."

Foula smiled. "I've accepted my fate because I believe it's *maktoub,* it's written all in Allah's book. Everything that's coming to us and what's kept from us. It's all written in advance! That's why I can't complain." Then, as an afterthought, "Perhaps I'm too stupid to know any better."

"Stupid, you're not," Aisha said. "Maybe you're lucky to feel that way. Who's to say? I wish I were as happy as you."

"Happy I'm not, but I've accepted my fate."

"Well, I wish I could. But there's something deep inside me, in my guts, something strong that tells me, 'Fight! Fight! Aisha. Change, move, go, or you'll die poor and hungry on a straw mat.' See?"

Foula looked up, her glistening eyes watching her friend. "Have I ever told you my mother's version of Allah's golden book?"

"No. What is it?"

"According to mother, Allah the Compassionate, the Merciful, was busy one day writing each man's fate in His golden book. He was about to get down to us people living in the village when suddenly a wind blew up swirling the desert sand. When Allah got up to see what had brought the sudden windstorm, the *afarit,* the devil, disguised himself as wind and flipped some of the pages. When Allah returned to writing, He didn't realize He had skipped the few empty pages, so He went on with His writing."

"What happened then?"

"Well, now, every time Allah goes through His list of names, offering His blessings and good fortune, He stops at the empty pages, thinking it's the end of the list."

"And he doesn't get to us because we are beyond the empty pages, is that it?"

"Right!" Foula exclaimed and jumped to her feet. "Now you'll understand, Allah be praised."

They stood facing each other awkwardly. Neither knew what to say for a moment. Like Foula, she too believed it was all in God's hands, but in her heart, she knew that nothing would change unless she changed it.

Aisha smiled. "I liked your story about the golden book. I liked it fine."

Foula reached in her pocket and handed Aisha a blue beaded amulet. "I want you to have this. It'll ward off the evil eye, and keep you safe. You'll see."

"Thank you, my friend." It was all Aisha could say trying to hold back her tears. They hugged each other tight. Then Foula left without looking back.

Aisha watched her walk away, swaying her young body with all the affected airs of an older woman. Then she left the station in the opposite direction and made her way up Main Street, for the familiar routines of village life.

She stopped to watch the coppersmith who made bowls and jars, hammering the containers into shape over iron bars fixed in the ground. The top right angle of the bar was flattened out to form a kind of anvil. The old man looked up, saw her, and opened his toothless mouth in a smile. She waved and pressed on.

The central café, as always, was filled with customers. This was a man's world, she decided. No Arab woman was allowed there. Yet men spent hours listening to the radio and playing backgammon while they sipped their tea or coffee. Being an Arab peasant was bad enough, but a poor peasant woman was doubly cursed, she decided.

A scream, a belated warning, and then a deluge brought her sharply back to reality. Overwhelmed, she stood there as if nailed to the ground, staring while water dripped from the edge of her long, cotton dress and formed a pool around her bare, mud-spattered feet. She heard men laugh. Only then did she notice the Arab waiter who stood about a meter from where she was, holding an empty bucket in his hand.

"I was trying to cool the sidewalk," he explained, laughing raucously. "Sorry."

When she realized she had been drenched with the dirty, sudsy water in which the man had washed hundreds of coffee cups, she felt the blood rise to her head.

"Swine! Blind old fool!" she screamed furiously. "Why don't you wear glasses, eh?"

He grinned at her tone, the assurance back on his face. "Glasses?" he asked mockingly. "What do I need glasses for? To read?"

The crowd rocked with laughter. Then he looked down at her bare feet. "Did I mess up your pretty shoes, your highness?" His joke brought new laughs.

"An ass-fool has his answer on the edge of his tongue!" Aisha shouted.

"Give it to him!" cried one of the spectators, who applauded approvingly. "Let him have it, girl!" he roared.

"Ma-a-lesh, ma-a-lesh. Never mind," said an old man, waving her away. "No harm done."

"Ma-a-lesh, eh?" she screamed. "It's always *ma-a-lesh* with all of you. No matter what goes wrong, no matter what happens, it's *ma-a-lesh!*"

She turned to the waiter. "Here!" she said, the palm of her right hand outstretched in a gesture of insult. "Take five and go buy yourself some glasses and a pair of shoes. You need both!" She knew the vulgar gesture never failed to aggravate a man.

His face colored angrily. "You should be ashamed of yourself, you little tramp!"

"We're even," she mumbled to herself as she turned and ran.

Drenched to the skin, but with her humor restored, she reached Ahmed's little store. His specialty was *fuul* beans, which he cooked in two huge earthen pots. His customers were the very poor who could not afford to cook at home.

As she waited her turn, she recalled Ahmed's explanation of how he cooked the brown beans for long hours on a low charcoal fire. From time to time he added some water and red lentils, but he removed the lid of the pot as little as possible, so the beans would not turn black.

"Well, beautiful Aisha. What'll it be for you today?"

"What'll it be?" She repeated with irony. "Like always, it'll be two piastres worth, and give me from the good ones. The beans you sold me yesterday were old."

He looked shocked. "By Allah, girl, I only serve first-class merchandise here. The best!"

She walked around the counter, reached for the container she had left there earlier, and gave it to him.

Ahmed dipped a long spoon into the pot. "Look at these beauties!" he said, measuring the content with his eyes.

"Don't be stingy now. Add some more."

"Oh, women!" he exclaimed, throwing his free hand up in the air in frustration. "Who can refuse a beautiful woman like you? You're as beautiful as the full moon. You're as pretty as a fresh peach!" he chanted as he added more beans to her pot. "Satisfied now?"

"Not yet. Pour me some good oil, not the cheap cotton stuff you've been giving us. I know you've got some olive oil."

"Anything for you, my beautiful flower," and he ran behind a counter for the oil.

"And give me a couple of pickles and some *shatta* red pepper. And half a lemon, too." She smiled broadly, aware that she was asking for more extras than she was entitled to, but she knew Ahmed. For a cute smile, he would sell his soul.

"Oh women! The destruction of man," he said helplessly.

She paid, took her change and with a sugary "Thank you, Ahmed," she went on.

The bakery was not more than a big hole in a brick wall. She watched the old man throw into the oven round patties of dough made from ground husks of corn and bran. Then he fed the furnace with coal, stopping occasionally to wipe his forehead with the end of his sleeve. In minutes the bread was ready, and he started bringing it out with a long wooden spatula. Cooked, the bread looked like a big blown-up balloon — empty inside, dry and crisp on the outside. She bought four pieces and headed home.

She found her mother sitting on the porch with her legs crossed, chatting with a neighbor. Aisha pushed the squeaky door and entered the one-room house of mud-and-wattle walls. She glanced around the room where they ate, slept and lived, noticing spots on the ground where the sun penetrated the flat, thatched reed roof. There was a low, round table where she left the beans and bread.

In one corner, on the floor, was a reed mattress where they slept, a couple of pillows and an old folded blanket. The rest of the dirt floor was covered with an old bamboo mat, a *hassira*. The door screeched again and her mother came in, followed by her father's brother, Youssef.

They sat on the floor around the low table and placed the food in the middle. Youssef tucked the hanging end of his long sleeve, freeing his arm to the elbow. "*Bi-smi-llah*, in the name of God," he said. Then, breaking off a small piece of bread, he dipped it into the dish, doubled it to enclose the beans, and began to eat. The two women followed suit.

They were through eating when the door swung open so fast it had no time to squeak. Foula stood there, a smile on her face, her hands on her hips. "Aren't you ready yet? We'll be late for the *courban*."

"We're as ready as we'll ever be," said Aisha's mother, forcing herself from the floor. She smoothed the creases from her long black robe, picked a shawl that hung from a nail on the wall, and threw it across her shoulders. "Let's go."

They walked past the main square and entered an alley with shacks on both sides. From the open doors and windows, the pale gaslight reached the narrow unpaved street. Occasionally Aisha heard her mother and uncle greet friends as they passed.

"Why are they having the *courban*?" Aisha asked Foula.

"Omou-Ahmed's young son is possessed with the *afarit*, demons," her friend explained, fear and concern in her voice.

"Does anyone know what the *afarit* are?"

"Oh yes! They're made out of fire and live under the earth." Foula rolled her dark eyes fearfully. "They haunt springs and wells in deserted areas, and even the high roads. Sometimes they enter into people of evil intent who wish to harm others. Other times — well, they are quite harmless and will do no injury to a human being unless they are provoked."

Aisha hesitated for a moment. "If one who's possessed gets well, where does the spirit go after it leaves the sick person?"

Foula's arms flung open. "By Allah, I don't know! I guess it either returns to its friends, or goes and possesses someone new."

They had reached the end of the alley. A string of lights dangled over the entrance of Omou-Ahmed's brick house, and little paper flags swayed gently in the night breeze. These were a message to the passersby and the neighborhood that there was entertainment, and anyone who cared to come was welcomed.

More and more guests kept coming until there was no more room inside the house and they had to sit out in the street. The few chairs, which the hostess had rented from a cafe, were taken fast. The rest of the people sat on the floor in rows.

In a corner on the floor there was a copper brazier with burning charcoal. Occasionally perfumed frankincense was thrown in, filling the room with its sweet fragrance.

The minute the musicians started to beat their tambourines, the youngsters darted from here and there and began to jump, dance, and scream. Then Omou-Ahmed dragged her sick ten-year-old son, and with a push, she hurled him among the dancers. Rapt, and with the air of a drunkard, the boy looked about him as if reveling in it all, grunting like a bear.

As the beat of the drums grew wilder, the ritual became an orgiastic frenzy bordering on madness. The dancers jumped, swayed, screamed, howled, all quivering from head to toe. After a while the boy staggered, his head wobbled on his neck, and with the choking cry of a dying animal, he dropped to his knees gasping for air, a whitish foam running from the sides of his mouth.

The boy's mother returned with a knife and a white, screaming rooster in her hands. With a powerful drag of the knife, she slashed the bird's throat. Next she dipped her hands in the animal's warm blood and smeared it over the boy's face and body.

"Allah! Allah!" roared the crowd.

There were sudden bursts of wild wailing and the long belly-thrilling, ear-splitting ululations that burst from every throat, promising a successful ritual.

Trays with morsels of stuffed vine-leaves and bits of cheese and bread were passed around. Coffee was served to the elders. For the young, there was a drink of *sahlab*, made of water, wheat-starch and sugar, boiled with a little cinnamon and ginger sprinkled on it.

The hostess motioned Aisha to come to her. She rose with hesitation and approached the big woman.

"Aisha," she began, and placed a hand on the girl's shoulder. "This is your last night here. You've been dancing since you could stand on your two little feet. Show us everything we've taught you. Dance for us, will you?"

Then the woman turned, and at the top of her powerful lungs, screamed, "Shut up, everyone!"

Surprisingly, the frantic noise subsided at once.

"I want you all to sit down, just anywhere," she bellowed. "Aisha, the future star of Egypt, will dance for us."

Then she tied a scarf around Aisha's hips, and with a slight push, sent her to the middle of the floor.

The first strums of the lute were followed by the clapping of the brass-finger cymbals, the *sagat*, and the beat of the *tar* and the tambourine. Children cheered and everyone clapped together to counter-point the rhythm.

Aisha closed her eyes as if concentrating. Soon, she could only hear the drums beat. She felt her arms move, then her shoulders, then her hips rotated upwards, sideways and downwards in a pleasing, harmonious whole movement, blended with the rhythm, faster and faster until there wasn't a single part of her body that was still.

Intoxicated as if in a trance, she danced and shook every part of her body from her hair to her fingertips. The more she shook, the calmer she felt, as if her body had shattered into a thousand pieces of light cotton flakes, floating from cloud to cloud.

At that moment, Aisha felt totally free, weightless, unencumbered by restraints, needs, or problems. A peaceful feeling of happiness filled her, leaving her warm and contented.

CHAPTER III

Aisha opened her eyes and listened to the voice of the *muezzin* as he chanted the *adan,* calling the faithful to prayer.
"Allahu Akbar!
God is most Great.
I testify that there is no deity but God.
I testify that Mohammed is God's Apostle.
Come to Prayer. Come to Security.
Allahu Akbar!"
"Allah Kerim!" she whispered and slid softly from under the blanket. Then she stood and looked at her sleeping mother. Zakiya's long, disheveled dark hair fell unkempt over the pillow, her pale face looked tired even in sleep. Aisha saw the web of wrinkles around her mother's eyes, the weariness cutting the corners of her mouth. Grief overwhelmed her as she bent and kissed her mother's red, work-worn leathery hand.

Zakiya stirred and opened her eyes. The moment she caught sight of Aisha, she sat up. "We'd better get started if we want to catch that special train," she said, forcing herself from the floor. Changing from one old black robe to another, she walked into the kitchen to start a fire and prepare the morning tea.

After a while, she returned with two tall glasses of steaming tea and some bread. "I only hope we're doing the right thing, Aisha. For your sake." She took a sip from her glass. "I don't give a damn about myself. I've lived my miserable life and don't care no more."

"But you should care, mama. You're still young." Aisha tried to sound cheerful.

Her mother looked at her with her big, jet-black eyes. "Stronger I was once, but young? Never! But we must try to improve ourselves, as you say, and that's what we'll do. We'll go there, for better or worse. She shook her head slowly. "By Allah, we couldn't possibly get any worse — or could we? Your father used to say that there's nothing worse than an illiterate peasant, that we're as low as any creature can get. Your father was a smart man." She fell silent for a moment, then she got on her feet and started to throw their few belongings into an old pillow case.

Aisha wanted to touch her, to calm her fears. Instead, she stood there as if her feet were nailed to the ground.

Her mother looked at her, reflected a moment, then added, "You'd better put this on." She handed her a jacket. "It must have looked pretty when it was new. Now, of course, it's only a faded rag. But this much, it's better than nothing. Thank Allah for his generosity, and remember, there are children in the village who don't even have that much, so be thankful."

"I'm thankful, mama," she whispered. "I am."

She put the jacket on and noticed with relief that it covered the gaping elbow holes of her cotton dress. Then she reached for her shoes. Her very first pair, she thought, and caressed the coarse leather. She rubbed the shoes on her dress and they shone instantly. They were beautiful, even though she didn't think the big brown stitches around the soles matched the red color of the shoe leather.

Just then, Foula's mother arrived holding a saucer with

burning coal, which she placed in the middle of the floor. She threw in some incense and alum. "Hurry, girl, and pass over it seven times. Let's ward the evil eye from you. Last night at the *Courban,* everyone admired you and talked about how beautiful you are. *Ma Sha Allah,*" she repeated three times.

Before Aisha finished the rounds, another neighbor arrived with a basket of bananas and dates for the trip, and a third handed her some bread and cheese. Soon, the house was filled with friends who came to see them off.

Suddenly a woman started sobbing. Her infant, hitched on her right hip, got frightened, dropped the bread he was sucking, and burst into screams. An old man, his eyes closed as if trying to concentrate all his strength on what he wanted to say, choking on his cigarette smoke, strained for words to make his point, while he struggled for breath. "No good will come out of it."

Aisha looked around the room at the human mass which sweated and reeked. They were friends and neighbors. She knew they were all brothers, made from the same mold, still tightly glued to the soil. For thousands of years they had all lived and abided by the customs and laws of the desert and the village. Neither time nor progress had changed them.

To her surprise, she felt her heart swell with love for her people, the same people she usually blamed as complacent and over-passive. How strange, she thought. For as long as she could remember, she dreamed of the time when she could leave the stifling life of the village. Now that it was happening, she could not help but feel the loss of all that had been familiar.

She noticed Foula standing in a corner watching her. She walked over to her.

"We'll never see you again, Aisha," her friend said, unable to control her tears. "No one who goes to the big city ever returns."

Aisha felt a catch at her heart and tears flooded her eyes. "Then I'll be the first. I promise, I won't forget you."

Just then her uncle arrived. "Let's get going," he said, and they all left for the station on foot.

As the little procession advanced through the village, more friends joined them. Children sang and danced, and the village dogs barked all the way to the station. The minute the train arrived, Uncle Youssef, who had traveled before, suggested they rush in and find seats if they did not wish to travel standing all the way to Alexandria.

Pulling Aisha aside, Youssef said, "If things get really tough, remember you can always come back." He cleared his throat and in a softer voice added, "Remember always Aisha, that however long the night may last, there will be a morning."

She reached up and kissed him. "I'll remember, uncle, thank you."

Most of the people who waited to get on had crowded the third-class entrance of the car. Pushing her way through, Aisha managed to be among the first to enter. Leaving her mother behind, she ran down the narrow aisle, darted into an empty seat by the window and sat down, putting her bundle of clothes next to her to hold the seat until her mother came. Uncle Youssef and the rest of their friends gathered on the platform, waving and wishing them health and good luck on their new venture.

Passengers came in with big crates and all sorts of merchandise — fruits, chicken, eggs, bananas. Some of them came in first to secure a seat and then tried to bring their heavy loads through the windows. Finally, the train began to move. Zakiya pulled out of her pocket a colored rag, wiped her tears, and blew her nose loudly.

Overwhelmed with emotion, Aisha stretched her arm as if to catch that tiny part of her heart she was leaving behind, even though she knew there was nothing in the village for her, with its indifference to life and death, its unchangeable social customs, the mockery of life, the waste.

The train moved faster. Soon the village was behind. Still holding tightly to the bundle of clothes on her lap, Aisha tried to clear her head of all thoughts and anxieties. I'll worry later, she promised herself, and started to examine the crowded compartment.

It was filthy and overcrowded, and the wooden benches were uncomfortable. This compartment had little in common with the trains she had seen, carrying mostly Europeans. Somehow their third-class compartment did not seem to belong on the same train.

Across from her was an old man with a dirty *gallabiyeh*, the native long shirt robe that reached to the floor. As soon as he sat, he closed his eyes and went to sleep. Next to him sat a young boy who emptied his pockets and passed his time counting and recounting his coins.

On the same bench sat two women dressed in ankle-length black robes like her mother's. Unlike her mother, the palms of their hands and the soles of their feet were stained by the leaves of the henna-tree, giving a red, deep-orange color. Their heads were covered with the *tarbah*, which was held in position between the eyebrows by a quaint, tube-shaped, copper ornament fastened to the veil. The only features visible were their dark eyes made larger by the rim of *kohl* smeared on the lids. When the women removed their veil, Aisha noticed that one was pretty and young but already beginning to get fat. Both women had tired expressions.

The door of the compartment opened, and the Arab conductor walked in. "Have your tickets ready!" he shouted in order to be heard. "Anyone without a ticket can pay here or jump off. I don't care which!"

"Jump off yourself!" replied someone from the crowd, and the other passengers laughed.

But the conductor was in no mood for humor. He walked down the aisle, punched a hole in each ticket, and then left by the same door he had come through.

"Going far?" asked the older of the two women seated next to them.

Zakiya explained that they, too, were going to Alexandria, and she began to sob quietly.

"My dear," said the woman softly, touching Zakiya's knee. "If we had money for all the tears we shed, we'd be rich!"

"If we had money, I wouldn't be crying," Aisha's mother answered through her sobs.

"I know," said the woman and shook her head. "Money is sweet balm. It heals all wounds."

Zakiya stopped crying as suddenly as she had started. "I shouldn't be crying. I ought to know that we are all afflicted with the same disease, and only God is the physician."

Both women grunted in agreement. "How true," said the older one.

By that time, the compartment was as animated as a chicken coop. The frightened hens in the crates raised hell, babies wailed, men laughed, talked or screamed to be heard, and the entire car reeked like a decaying stable rotting from neglect. The stench was overpowering.

Aisha opened the window and took a deep breath. The train was passing cultivated fields of sugar-cane, maize and corn, and the telephone poles seemed to run along with them, chasing each other. Sometimes the train passed close to the river with its luscious green banks where people washed their clothes and their animals side by side. From time to time they passed an Arab riding his donkey while his wife followed on foot.

As the scenery changed, so did the irrigation system. Farmers tied a mule or water buffalo to a pole and the blind-folded animal went round and round in circles, on the same spot, moving a water wheel with buckets attached. The buckets dipped in the well and filled. As each bucket emerged full, it tilted and emptied into the irrigation ditches which ran the length of the cultivated land.

They passed vast cotton fields where crowds of workers, mostly women, picked the cotton by hand. Here and there, Aisha could see the shabby mud-houses in which the farmers, their families, and animals lived.

It was around noon when the train entered the big station of Tanta and stopped. She remembered her Uncle Youssef, who had often made the trip. Three times a year, on the great festival of the Saint el Bedowy, thousands came from all parts of Egypt on a pilgrimage resembling that of Mecca.

Some of the passengers got off there. Others rushed in to take their seats. Arab vendors pulled carts loaded with newspapers and candies and shouted their wares. Ragged boys ran around selling lemonade, beggars asked for *baksheesh.* Then the train moved again.

She couldn't help noticing a new passenger. He was in his early thirties, tall and handsome, with big dark eyes and a strong, stern face. He looked smart in European brown pants and a striped white shirt. He even had a necktie. In spite of the noise and the shouting, he seemed entirely absorbed in reading a newspaper.

"Hey, what has the paper to say?" asked a young peasant, edging closer.

The man with the paper raised his eyes and looked at him. "The devil is blood-thirsty again. That's what the paper says."

Suddenly everyone was quiet and all eyes focused on the stranger. The young peasant scratched his head with embarrassment and rubbed his face. "What do you mean?"

"I mean the whole world has gone mad," said the man with the paper. "I mean war, friend. War that destroys and demolishes man, beast, peasants and non-peasants alike."

There was a moment's silence. "Tell us more," said the young peasant as he squatted on the floor.

The man began to read. Although it was in Arabic, Aisha had the feeling that no one understood what he was talking about. They all listened, but they kept looking at the man waiting for an explanation.

The reader sensed their anticipation, cleared his throat, and started to interpret the text in plain spoken dialect. "The Germans are fighting like lions. They advance so fast that no power can stop them. They kill people."

"Allah have mercy on us!" whispered a listener.

"They throw bombs from airplanes and set fires everywhere. Their army marches fast. They gain territory every day. England may be next to fall into the German hands. The German radio says they'll stop at nothing until they conquer all of Europe!"

"They may come here then," said a man with a broad, happy smile.

"They may," answered the man with the paper.

"What of it? Let them come," added another. "They might kick the British out of here. Let them come!"

Some men laughed and others applauded the remark.

"And what do we know about the damn Germans?" asked an elderly man. "Hell, what if they're worse than the *Englisi*?"

"We may try and see," added another passenger. "Unless we try, we won't know." A few men shook their heads in agreement. Many rocked with laughter.

The man with the paper spoke again. "I can't see much difference," he cried in a hoarse shout. "If we don't have the

Germans, we'll have the British. If not the British, we had the French before, and the Turks. We've had all of them, foreign bastards taking advantage of us and sucking our blood."

"Right!" everyone agreed. "The professor is right and knows what he's talking!"

Aisha laughed. Her mother looked at her concerned. "What's so funny?"

"The man didn't say he is a professor."

"He can read the paper, no?"

The discussion about the war went on and on while the train was rocketing along. Aisha tried to listen, even though she understood little and cared less. It was clear that her people, the natives, did not care much for the *Englisi,* even though she couldn't tell why, just then.

Maybe they did not know the answer themselves, she reasoned. Maybe Egyptians bear a grudge against all Europeans, and being discontented with their miserable lot, they had to blame someone. In the old days, it was the devil or fate.

It was late afternoon when the train slowed down to enter the big station of Alexandria which, strangely, was called *Mohatat-El Masr,* or Cairo station.

There were many platforms. As she looked from the window at the rows of tracks, shining under the bright sun, she was reminded of a snake-pit she had seen once in the field, with crawling, silvery reptiles. The train entered the covered platform, whistled and rattled, and with a thunderous poof, came to a stop.

As they stepped off the train, they were instantly swept by a massive human wave that filled the vast station. It was as if suddenly the earth had cracked open and begun to heave up people of every shape, color, and dialect.

Ragged porters ran to help passengers with their luggage, taxi drivers fought to secure a fare, uniformed representatives of big hotels called names of passengers of the first and second class, while Aisha and her mother stood in the middle of the crowd holding on to each other, unable to move a step.

She felt her mother's hand holding hers and followed her to the exit. They stood and looked about. Her mother pulled a rag out of her pocket and wiped the sweat from her forehead. Then the familiar sight of horse-drawn buggies gave her some confidence, and she smiled.

"Allah, bless them," said Zakiya with relief. "If it weren't for them, I wouldn't believe I'm still in Egypt. I've never in my life thought there were so few of us and so many of the others."

They walked to the first buggy on the waiting line and she gave the coachman her aunt's address. As usual, she bargained for the fare, then they mounted the carriage and rolled along the busy street. When they arrived at their destination, they climbed to the roof of a three-story building and knocked at the door of the small room.

Three barefooted children appeared, followed by a middle-aged woman dressed in a long black robe. She had a fine, Caucasian oval face, prominent forehead, large black brilliant eyes, straight Semitic nose, and a mouth well-formed with full lips. Looking at her father's sister, Aisha knew how her father must have looked.

The woman's eyes sparkled with recognition. Before either of them could utter a word, she ran to them and threw her arms about them so the three of them formed a huddle. Still clinging to Aisha, she called to her eldest son, a boy of fifteen. "Don't stand there! Go and fetch your father."

"He isn't here," answered the boy. "The tenant on the first floor sent him to the grocery store for potatoes."

Her aunt Fatma slapped her thighs in despair and sighed deeply. "My poor Sabry! He goes through hell every day," she said and sat down on the floor-mat with her legs crossed, motioning the others to do likewise. More calmly now, she explained that her husband, who worked as a *boab*, was hardly ever given a chance to remain by the door and attend to the duties of a doorman, for which he was hired.

"'Sabry, go to the bakery,' commands one of the tenants; 'Sabry, go to the butcher,' begs the next, and 'Sabry, go and buy me a lemon,' demands a third," Fatma explained with mockery in her voice. "It's disgraceful! These people don't need a doorman here. What they need is a slave to do their errands." She turned to face the newcomers. "But what else can we do?"

"A clever spinner spins with an ass's foot," Zakiya said. "We must manage as best we can."

Fatma shook her head. "There aren't many jobs open to people like us. You're right. At least here we have a free room to live in."

Three children and a puppy had gathered around, examining the visitors curiously. Aisha took some dates from their bag and passed them around.

"Look at my Aisha!" her aunt said, as if not daring to believe what she saw. *"Ma sha Allah!"* she added so that her praise would not be taken as casting the evil eye. *"Ma sha Allah!* She was hardly two years old when I left the village."

"Welcome! Welcome to our poor home," shouted Sabry from the door, dressed in a long, striped *gallabiyeh*. "Did you come for a visit?"

Zakiya explained that they intended to stay, provided they could find work and a room in which to live. "We'll manage with bread and salt until Allah sends us something to eat with it."

Sabry shrugged. "Why not? The good thing about living in the city is that no one starves alone. Either we all go hungry or somehow we manage to eat." He laughed raucously as he rubbed his huge hands together. Then he spoke of an empty room on the roof of a nearby building, which was for rent. "I know the doorman in charge. I'll be glad to take you."

When the time came for them to leave, the aunt took Aisha in her arms. "My home is your home," she said. "You're welcome to stay with us as long as you wish!"

Zakiya pulled the rag from her pocket and wiped her eyes. "*Allah Ye Sallemak!* May Allah preserve you and repay you for your kindness. I don't know what we would've done without you — two women alone, no man at our side, and in a big city like this."

Fatma tried to calm her. "Don't cry. Allah is by your side. He'll help."

Zakiya wept louder.

"Why do you cry?" asked Fatma.

"The words of an enemy make one laugh, but the words of a friend make one cry," Zakiya said quietly. Then they kissed and left with Sabry.

The rental was a tiny room on the terrace of a tall building, shown to them by an old man. It had two windows that gave the place a warm feeling and was furnished with an old sofa, an iron bed, and a small round table with two chairs.

Not far from there was another cubicle of a room that housed a European toilet with running water, which they were allowed to use. Compared to the village, this was luxury. There was also a laundry room, which the old man explained they could use for cooking whenever it was not being used as a laundry. Everything considered, Aisha felt Allah was trying to help them.

She ran to turn the lights on, but there was no switch.

"You mean to tell me that a building this size doesn't have electricity?"

The old man shrugged. "The building does. It's just the roof that's left without. I guess the he-goat, the owner, figures this way he'll have one less electrical bill each month. He pays the utilities."

"It doesn't really matter," Aisha said with disappointment. "We've been using gas lamps all our lives. I had just hoped."

The two men turned and looked at her.

"Do you think you'd be happy living here, young girl?" inquired the old man, removing his turban to scratch his bald head.

Aisha cast a sideways glance at her mother and saw with fright that the woman's eyes were pinned on her, burning with anxiety. "I'm sure I'll love it, provided it's not too expensive, of course," she said.

The old man explained he wanted to help Sabry's poor relatives and was willing to let the room go for one pound a month. "Rents have gone up lately," he reminded them, and both men agreed it was a rare bargain. "That old donkey, the owner, has more money than he'll ever need, even if he lives to be a hundred. If he knows the room is vacant, he'll want to raise the rent. His eye is not full. The dust alone will fill his eyes."

"We'll take it," Zakiya said. Thrusting her wrinkled hand into her bosom, she drew out the knotted cloth where she kept the money.

Aisha left the three of them in the room and went to the open terrace. The view was spellbinding. The evening breeze was heavy with the scent of blooming jasmine. The setting sun had dressed everything in a golden-purple transparent color, and the fading light fell like a spray of silver dust over the tops of the flat-roofed buildings. Below, the street light and the thousands of lighted open windows shone like scattered trembling candles that burned in a million colors.

Would this beautiful city of lights be friendly to her? Would her dreams ever come true? She wondered as she stood there, close to Heaven, it seemed, and prayed to the almighty God for help. The cold feeling of anxiety that had weighed on her heart since they had left the village now disappeared. In its place was a sense of bewilderment, an anticipation of things to come.

From the end of the street came the song of a passing vendor. *"Lebaanersh!"* chanted the milk seller. Cars sped up and down the streets and the small cafe across the corner echoed with the voices of Arabs who sipped hot tea or puffed at their monstrous bubble pipes.

That night, after they had supper at her aunt's house, Sabry walked with them to the little neighborhood store where they bought a lamp, fuel, and a few groceries. Then Aisha and her mother returned to their little room to spend their first night in Alexandria.

The roar of thousands of voices and the rush of the cars, their horns blaring, kept Aisha awake most of the night, until the soft music of the radio from the nearby cafe finally put her to sleep.

CHAPTER IV

That night after they dined, Aisha went for a walk. They needed money to pay off the grocer's debt, but where? How? She tried to think as she walked listlessly onto a street that was wide with elegant stores and restaurants.

The strong smell of barbecued meat made her stop for a moment to peer into the well-lit restaurant. The flower-decked tables were filled with people, and the place was buzzing. At irregular intervals, patrons arrived or left. It was late, and the few pedestrians hurried through the dark street.

Suddenly, the restaurant door burst open and an Arab staggered out. He was short, burly and very drunk. She went close enough to smell his sour wine breath.

"Can you spare a shilling?" she asked feebly.

"Why, you pretty little thing ..."

"Can you spare a damn shilling?"

He laughed. "I'll give you a pound," he said and grabbed her hand.

"Money first."

He pulled out his wallet. Her breath caught. Instinctively, she reached out and grabbed the wallet.

The man's hands grasped her shoulder, but she pushed him away. He sprawled on his back, his eyes open wide looking up at her. For a moment, she stood there staring back, amazed at what she had done. She heard footsteps. As realization dawned on her, panic set in.

"Sorry, friend. But at least you've had a decent meal tonight," she said, surprised at the coldness she could muster.

There was a burst of crude cursing, but she didn't stick around. As she ran, she went through the wallet. It contained eight pounds. Pulling up her dress, she shoved the money into her panties for protection and threw away the wallet.

At home, her mother swallowed the story Aisha told her and thanked Allah for planting money on park benches. Their credit with the grocer was extended for a few more days.

Two days later, she chose a different street and a bigger restaurant. She didn't know what time it was, but it was still daylight. One of these days, she promised herself, she would learn how to tell time, and when she had enough money, she would buy herself a watch. Few people in the village owned watches. They could tell time by the position of the sun, the muezzin who called the faithful to prayer and, of course, the radio cafe.

A stout middle-aged man with his belly bulging ogled her for a second or two, then came closer.

"Waiting for someone?"

"No."

"Pretty girls like you should be inside."

"Got no money."

His eyes shone. "No problem," he said as his dark eyes appraised her. "Come and eat. I'll pay."

She had never been inside a restaurant. Why not, she thought. He seemed a kind man.

"I said I'll pay. Come."

Taking her by the hand, he led her through the crowded restaurant, his heavy cheeks jouncing with each step. He found a corner table, and they sat. When the waiter came, he ordered for both of them.

"Eat. Eat, little one," he said when the food was served.

He ate in big scoops, devouring his meal as if he hadn't seen food in ages. His gaze never left the low-cut opening of her bodice. He looked at her with lust.

"You're an exquisite little thing," he gabbled, his mouth full. "A real peach!"

She nodded.

"You're as beautiful as the bursting lotus bud."

She laughed it off, and tried to enjoy her free meal.

"How about a little ride? I have the car right here," he said after they left the restaurant. "Then I'll drop you at your place."

She got in and the car lurched forward. At the first stop light, he leaned to her side, gripping her by her chin and forcing her face upward so he could look at her. "By Allah, you're a lovely little thing."

Her full stomach rebelled at the odor of his unwashed flesh, and she began having second thoughts about riding with him. He drove across the city. Streets and buildings passed them in a blur.

Suddenly, she realized the car had stopped.

"Why do you stop here?"

"This is Nousha, known as the rose garden," he said, removing his jacket.

"But it's late ..."

"Just for a minute, to stretch my legs," he said, peering at her. "Come, I'll show you the park. It's fabulous. There are statues and fountains, and all kinds of flowers."

He came around and flung open the door.

She stepped out, and he pulled her, leading her dazed and shoeless toward the hedge that fenced off the park grounds.

She turned to leave, but he grabbed her upper arm roughly and pushed her behind the bushes. He began to pant, grasping her breasts, her buttocks. She struggled and twisted. He panted, his flesh forcing against her. She shoved harder and pulled away, but she stumbled and fell.

He jerked her to her feet and his arms went around her. She kicked. He bit a kiss on her mouth. She raised her hand to hit him, but he grabbed it and pinned it behind her, forcing her further back until she thought her spine would crack.

She froze as he exposed himself. Her knees buckled, and she could feel the blood drain from her head. Filled with rage, anguish and revulsion, she bit her lip. She could hear herself screaming inside her head, but she didn't make a sound. Instead, she turned her head and puked. He pulled away from her. Still in shock she got up and in a daze, she started to walk back to the car.

"I'll be there in a minute," said the fat, bald-headed man. "I've got to pee."

Her fear changed to blind anger, and she began to shudder. Then she saw it. On top of his jacket, which he had left on the car seat, lay his stuffed wallet. She reached over and grabbed it.

"Hey, where you going?" he shouted, pulling on his pants.

She stopped and whirled around. There was a safe distance with the car between them. "I hope not where you'll go."

"Where?"

"To hell, old bastard. You dare chase me, you fat son-of-a-bitching bastard, and I'll strangle you. You hear?" She spat and fled toward the park, knowing he couldn't drive the car through there.

Tears stung her eyes as she raced through the dark, narrow, winding, sweet-scented paths of the park. *That'll never happen again,* she swore to herself, knowing that streetwalking was definitely out.

Three weeks went by and her mother had no calls for work. She tried her best to hide her anxiety, but Aisha knew the woman was as scared as she was.

Their money was dwindling fast. They economized on fuel and spent the summer nights in the dark. They sustained themselves on beans and bread, just as they had in the village. They both knew they could not continue for long, even with such measures.

It was not only fear of dying of hunger that panicked and angered her, but the thought of being dragged back into the henna-stinking, squalid world of failure from which they had so recently escaped.

Since there was no place to turn for employment or help, her mother trudged off every morning to look for work. She made the rounds from neighborhood to neighborhood, and talked to the native doormen who seemed to know their tenants' needs.

Aisha felt the stirring of panic at the thought of what might happen to them when they ran out of money. In the village, there was always somebody to offer help in sickness or when times were bad — a relative, a friend, or a neighbor to fall back on if worse came to worse, but in the strange city, everyone was deeply involved in his own problems of survival.

She even began to feel guilty for having left the village. She regretted the times she had cried, begged, and urged her mother to leave the hopeless, cold poverty of the village for the city where there would be plenty of work and money.

She recalled her mother's words: "What chance has any of us to break away from the pattern to which we were born?

What God wills, what God desires, that will be!" But Aisha refused to accept that. Deep in her heart, a strange certainty filled her. "No, no, I won't give in. I'll fight to my last breath," she vowed. Somehow she would conquer this city around her.

One afternoon, her cousins came by to take her for a walk. Her mother insisted that she go. "No use both of us sitting here waiting for something to happen. Go out, see a bit of the city and have fun."

They walked through the narrow streets of the neighborhood until they reached the wider streets where the buildings became taller, cleaner, and better looking. Most of the apartments had balconies with potted flowers that filled the air with their heavy aromatic scent.

She noticed that most of the well-dressed pedestrians were Europeans, while the natives were as shabbily clad as her fellow villagers. There was as much poverty in the city among the natives as there was in the village. But here the contrast was more striking, more humiliating, more painful.

Cars sped in all directions, and buggy drivers waving their horse whips in the air, shouted at pedestrians, *"Halibalak reglak!* Mind your feet." The children walked near a group of Europeans who talked loudly and made all kinds of gestures. Aisha decided to eavesdrop and was shocked. It was obvious that these people did not even speak her country's language.

"Aisha?" The voice of her cousin interrupted her thoughts. "We'll try to cross the street, so we better stick close together," he warned, taking her by the hand. "These drivers will run us down and they won't even slow up!"

With the two younger children between them, they dashed across the four-lane highway of the Cornich, which separated a row of tall buildings from the blue Mediterranean shore.

They reached the parapet, and she leaned against the wall. In the calm, pale-green waters, she saw the perfect reflection of the buildings from across the street. The beauty of the sea was spellbinding.

They walked for a while until they reached a stretch of land that advanced into the sea, forming a mole. The jetty had been transformed into a recreation area where children ran and played, filling the air with their laughter. From a vendor, they bought two corncobs and split between the four of them.

Below the parapet, there was a huge pile of rocks which formed an impressive breakwater. Aisha stood and watched the sea and the rocks as they confronted each other. The sea came at times smoothly caressing, as if trying to kiss the ancient rocks, then dashed back with anguish against the ramparts which tried to curtail its freedom, shooting up a spray that mounted the wall and splattered them.

She was reminded of the river. With the regularity of the seasons, the Nile waters would rise, inundating the fields which border it, and allowing the peasants to make their arrangements in planting their fields with the utmost precision. But the sea seemed unpredictable, with an energy and vitality such as the river never had.

Aisha was deeply touched by the beauty and strength of the sea. As she inhaled the salty air, she felt her lungs being filled not only with air, but with a certain power.

Like the sea, she felt the world was setting barriers for her. Like the sea, the hungry wild beast from the depths of her being was fighting for freedom — freedom to move, to grow, to follow the natural rhythm and bear fruit.

Four weeks later, her mother received word from the neighborhood grocer that a wealthy Syrian lady needed a woman to do her wash, and Aisha's sagging spirits took a leap.

Early the following morning, they arrived at the address. An Arab servant answered the door, and they stepped into a large entrance hall where tropical-leafed plants reached the ceiling, giving the impression of a well-kept garden in a third story building. They followed the servant into the kitchen where another Arab girl, dressed in European clothes, washed the dishes while she talked and laughed with the tall, handsome native cook.

After a few minutes of waiting, the cook placed two tall steaming glasses in front of them. "Have some hot tea while you're waiting," he said with kindness.

Zakiya thanked him and took a few hurried sips. "That's good quality tea," she remarked, smacking her lips approvingly.

The kitchen was big and well lighted, with electrical devices that were strange to both women. From the oven came the sweet smell of baking lamb. Life had to be easy and good in a home like this, Aisha thought.

The door opened and in came the woman of the house, dressed in a long silvery-blue house robe. She looked in her 40s, was slim, had long dark hair that reached her shoulders, and had big, black expressive eyes that were properly made up. Aisha noticed her soft hands with long polished nails.

"I want you to be extremely careful with my linen" she said in good Arabic without even looking up at them. "They're imported and cost a lot of money."

"I can see that, madame," said Zakiya. She fearfully picked up a tablecloth from the woman's hands. "I'll be extra careful, rest assured."

"I hope so," said the woman, then lighted a cigarette and drew a deep puff. With a glance, she inspected the kitchen, asked the cook a casual question about the food, and left the room.

"You take your time and do a good job," said the maid as she dropped two huge bundles of clothes on the kitchen floor.

"Aren't you gonna count them?" Zakiya asked.

"I've done that already," the maid assured her and left.

"Why count them?" Aisha asked.

"Because no Arab worker is trusted, that's why," her mother said, anguish in her voice.

The maid returned with two bars of green soap, a small gas furnace, a bottle of fuel, matches, and a big cauldron. "I'll help you carry some," she volunteered and picked up one of the bundles. The two gathered the rest of the things and started to leave with as much load as they could carry when the maid stopped them.

"This way," she said urgently. "The lady doesn't approve of servants using the main entrance," and she pointed to a service door. "And when you come the next time remember to come through here."

When they reached the terrace, having climbed the narrow utility stairs of the five-story building, Zakiya stopped, panting for air. More than ever before, Aisha realized, perhaps for the first time, the hardships her mother had endured through the years for that piece of bread she brought home to feed her.

Zakiya looked at her sadly, her cheeks pale. "Are you tired, Aisha?" she asked and stroked the girl's hair with affection.

"No, mama. Don't you worry about me," she said, holding back her tears.

"She's fortunate," the maid said. "She hasn't started earning a living as yet — I can tell. When I was placed in the first house, I was half your daughter's size. Don't worry, she'll get used to it. We all do."

"I'd rather die!" Aisha shouted, more sharply than she had intended.

The maid stared at her in surprise. "What's the matter with you?"

"Nerves. Just nerves," said Zakiya. She tried to smile, but

her eyes were anxious and her hand was trembling. "Don't mind her."

The girl shrugged, showed them the laundry room and left.

Zakiya filled the furnace with gas, put a small piece of scrap paper at the top of the machine, and struck a match. As the paper burned, she pumped the machine hard and soon there was a red-green blaze. Then she filled the cauldron with water from the tub and threw in some of the white clothes to boil.

When Zakiya started sorting the clothes, Aisha left her and went out on the terrace. From up there she could see the beautiful quarters where the wealthy Europeans lived. Large balconies with flowers, lounge chairs and tables, rolling awnings to protect them from the strong sun. A tall minaret, springing up from the jungle of the houses, silhouetted in the blue sky and made a vivid contrast with the modern European dwellings.

She heard the cry of a passing vendor who carried an empty sack across his shoulder. *"Robabekiya...salah el koursi!"* chanted the junk buyer who canvassed the better parts of the city, buying dilapidated, discarded items, which he then sold to the natives at the neighborhood bazaars.

Bazaars were fun, Aisha thought, as she leaned over the warm parapet. She recalled vividly the last time her mother took her to the village bazaar to buy her first pair of shoes, so that she would not go to the city barefooted.

The bazaar was situated behind the main cafe and consisted of a narrow alley bordered by primitive stalls. There, the local vendors displayed bundles of clothes that hung loosely, shoes, jewelry, even vegetables and fruit.

They had reached the stall with the shoes. Two by two

hung the shoes from a string that passed through a hole at the back of each shoe and was tied to a nail on a big wooden board. Zakiya had unhooked two pairs of bright red ones and asked Aisha to try them on for size. The merchant saw them and approached, rubbing his hands together.

"Here, the best shoemaker in the whole country! The best shoes for the smartest feet, and at the best prices!" he chanted. "Even the king buys his shoes from me!"

"Hey!" called a passerby. "What color shoes does His Royalty prefer?"

"Why, red, my friend! Red, like the rubies. Red to match the Cadillacs he drives!"

Everyone within hearing distance burst out laughing.

Meanwhile, Aisha struggled to fit her swollen feet into the narrow shoes. "Why don't you stop cracking jokes and bring us a couple of bigger shoes for her," her mother cut him angrily. "Can't you see her feet look like stuffed tomatoes in those?"

"At your service, woman! Bigger shoes for the beautiful girl." After trying three different pairs, she finally managed to get a pair in which her feet felt comfortable.

"By Allah! Just look at these shoes!" cried the vendor, taking a step backward to admire his merchandise.

"How about telling us how much they cost?" Zakiya asked.

"For you," said the man, "I'll make a sacrifice. Give me twenty piastres, and the shoes are yours with my best wishes."

"Keep the wishes to yourself. Twenty piastres is robbery," said Zakiya. "What do you take us for, *Englisi?*"

He had looked at them feigning sadness. "What does the wolf care if the sheep-fold is destroyed. By Allah, you try to ruin me! But pay me ten piastres and the shoes are yours. I want you both to be happy."

They paid him six.

"*Mabrouk!*" he said. "Wear them in good health."

Hunger brought Aisha back to the demanding present. She left the parapet and returned to the laundry.

The room was hot and stuffy. Her mother was bent over the steaming cauldron, sweat pouring down her face. Aisha sat in a corner and waited. From time to time she rubbed her stomach lightly to suppress the aching feeling of hunger.

Sometime later, the Arab servant returned and brought them a dish of fried rice with tomato sauce and a couple of slices of brown bread. She inquired if they needed anything more, and when they said they did not, she left.

"Come on, child. Let's have a bite," Zakiya said, drying her swollen red hands on the sides of her black robe, her face dripping with sweat, and her wet robe clinging to her body like skin.

They sat on the floor in a dry corner and placed the dish between them. They had not had a bite all morning, and they ate ravenously.

"Coming to the big city hasn't changed life much for us," Aisha said.

Her mother was silent for a moment. "It looks as if we took the hair off the beard and put it into the moustache!"

The proverb struck Aisha as funny and she laughed.

Zakiya smiled warmly at her daughter. "If you know how happy I feel when I hear you laugh ..."

"Ma, wouldn't you say these people here are rich?"

The woman nodded. "Yes, I would."

"Then why is it they eat that cheap village bread?"

"They buy this kind of bread for the servants, not for themselves. Maybe it's just as well. Poor people like us shouldn't acquire expensive taste."

When she had finished the day's work and all the clothes hung in long rows on the terrace lines, the sun was in the west. They returned to the kitchen through the service door and had another glass of tea. Then the maid paid them twelve piastres left by her mistress.

"They pay better in the city," remarked the mother on their way home. "You only get half that much at the village."

"Yes, but it takes more to live here," Aisha reminded her.

"If I could only find enough work."

And the calls started coming for washing and house cleaning. Zakiya worked hard at anything and everything that came along.

Soon they were able to buy food staples and cook at home. And when the evenings cooled and they could not sit on the terrace for long, they were able to spare some fuel and used the gas lamp.

Early one morning they heard a great commotion from the street below, and they ran to the terrace. They saw a convoy of heavy trucks carrying foreigners, all dressed alike, while hordes of people stood on both sides of the street watching the long procession. Dogs barked and children chased after the trucks calling the men *askari,* and begging for *baksheesh.* Some of the soldiers smiled. Others waved at the spectators. A few threw coins, and the children shrieked with joy.

"What are these foreign soldiers doing in our city?" Zakiya asked.

"It must be the war they talked about on the train." Aisha reminded her.

As the days went by, the tension rose. More and more army

lorries and trucks with foreigners were seen all over the city. The neighbors did not seem to know what was going on either, and they did not even seem to be much concerned.

They heard of monstrous ships that had arrived in the port of Alexandria and more and more uniformed men were seen everywhere. Airplanes flew constantly above their heads, but as long as nobody bothered them, nobody seemed to care.

"These fools, the Europeans, must be in some kind of trouble again," said the grocery man to the two women. "Let them cut each other's throats. What do we care? We Egyptians have nothing to do with whatever is the trouble, and besides, what do we have to lose? Let them do the worrying!"

One afternoon, Aisha's cousins came over to take her back to the jetty where she had first fallen in love with the sea. When they arrived, they found the entrance to the recreation area had been barricaded with barbed wire, and there were guards at the gate. Behind the fences were men in uniform building barracks, while others set up anti-aircraft guns.

"By Allah, these foreigners are going to kill us all," Aisha said.

"To the contrary, young lady. These soldiers are Englishmen, and they are here to protect us against the enemy," explained a bystander.

But no one knew who the enemy was, and from where he would be coming. Each day was a wracking struggle to eat and stay alive. Beyond that, nobody seemed to care.

CHAPTER V

In the quiet of the early autumn dawn, while dense dew dampened the city, Aisha heard the high voice of the *muezzin* from the nearby mosque, penetrating the palm-cooled air and the sleepy consciousness of the inhabitants.

Perched on the terrace parapet, she watched the awakening of the city. On the street below, a white-robed Arab prayed on his knees facing east. He was totally unconcerned about life around him.

The air was heavy with morning blooming jasmine, honeysuckle, and burning incense. The food peddler arrived on the scene rolling his portable barbecue kitchen, and the aroma changed to that of frying fish and lamb-kebab.

Farther down the street, the singing outdoor barber was shaving an Arab who sat in a chair on the sidewalk, holding a mirror in his hands. Once in a while, the barber stopped to sharpen his razor on a strap of leather, which he held between his teeth. Then he resumed the shaving and his singing as if he did not have a worry in the world.

At the end of the street, the vegetable vendor who marched alongside his donkey chanted praises for his goods: "Tomato-o-oes, rubies of the East. Oh, onions, sweet as honey! Grapes, black pearls of Heaven!"

Then his voice was drowned out by festive cymbals, rattled by the carob-juice seller, carrying a two-fauceted bronze jug on his back. From one faucet he poured and served the juice and from the other came water with which he rinsed his glasses before he served his next customer.

By now, Aisha was familiar with the scenery and the street noises. The laughter of young children who roamed the streets, the clip-clop of the horse-drawn buggies, the horns of the cars, the clang-clang of the trams, the blasting radio from the neighborhood cafe, the chirping of the birds intoxicated by the morning light, the cooing of strutting pigeons on the roofs — all noises of the awakening city.

"I think we ought to move," Aisha's mother said from the door, "or we won't have enough daylight to finish the wash."

For weeks now, her mother had stopped taking Aisha with her when she went for a day's work, because whenever they saw the two of them, they would double the workload and still pay wages for only one. But that day, she had decided to take Aisha along.

"She's such a generous woman, that one," her mother explained as they left their room. "She feeds me well and always gives me a few extra piastres. I like her. She has a heart. The last time I worked for her, she told me she had some old clothes she'll let me have. Come on, I'd like you to meet her. Her name is Maria."

A middle-aged European woman greeted them at the door, a broad, kind smile on her lips. "For a moment I thought you wouldn't show up today" the woman said to Zakiya. "I wouldn't blame you, of course. You looked so tired when you stopped by yesterday."

"I know some working women are not reliable and don't keep their word, but I always do." There was pride in Zakiya's voice.

The woman looked at Aisha. "This must be your daughter you've been telling me about?"

Aisha's mother nodded. "I hope you don't object to her coming."

"Not at all. I'm happy she came along. She's young and ambitious, I hear. Do you go to school, Aisha?"

Aisha stared at her with amusement. Then she laughed. At first it was a nervous laugh, but she was afraid it sounded loud and ugly. "School? Me?"

The woman's expression did not change. She looked at the girl wearily, her hazel eyes worried. In the tense silence, there was the faint sound of a door closing.

"Schools aren't for poor people like us," Aisha's mother said quietly. "Although she had hoped she would go to school, if life were different."

"Let's go in the kitchen," the woman said and motioned them to follow her. "We'll have some tea and talk before you start working."

They followed her into a small, well-lighted kitchen. In the middle of the room was a round marble-top table. A vase with flowers stood in the center. They sat at the table.

"You know," said the woman as she poured the tea, "when I first came to this country, I was just a little girl, much younger than Aisha." There was a packet of cigarettes lying on the table near her. She took one out and lit it.

"I was an orphan and a refugee. I couldn't speak a word of Arabic. My parents had been well off back in Smyrna, and they had big plans for me."

She drew deeply on her cigarette. "But they were both slaughtered with thousands of others, by the Turks in the revolution of 1922."

She paused, poured some more tea, and tried to control her emotions. "It was only a miracle I was saved. I escaped with a few others in a fishing boat. When we saw land we thought it was Greece. But we found out we were in Egypt! None of us knew a word of the language. We didn't have a cracked piastre in our pockets, but we had guts. No Greek takes it sitting down. We fight for what we want."

She stopped, seeming to regret her words, as if she had let out a secret. She laid her cigarette carefully down in the ashtray. "I was placed as a maid in a home. Life is hard, Aisha, and not just for the likes of you. It's hard for most of us." She spoke Arabic with a strong foreign accent, but with anguish in her voice.

"But there's a difference!" Aisha cried impatiently.

The woman grinned. "What's the difference?"

"People like you fight," said Aisha passionately. My people are too submissive. We bow our heads and take what's thrown to us because it's written that way, because we believe that this is Allah's will, our destiny. That's the difference!" Aisha found herself shouting, unable to contain herself.

The woman stared at her, surprise all over her face. Then she laughed. She turned to Zakiya. "She's all right. You should stop worrying about her. She'll do fine. The girl's got what it takes."

Then she reached across the table toward Aisha and took her hand. "Just remember, girl, you mustn't let yourself turn sour or get mad at the world. You can't whip it — it's too big. If you're going to fight the system, use your brain. It's got a lot more power than your fists."

She paused for a moment, then continued. "Times are changing. A girl must be educated to be able to earn a living and be a better partner to the man she'll mary one day. Believe me, this is in agreement with God's will."

"In shallah." Zakiya's voice was almost a whisper.

"Let me ask you girl, do you really want to go to school?"

"Yes!" Aisha responded fervently. "I want to learn things and be somebody, but how in hell can I? We have no money. There isn't much people like us can do, or is there?"

"Why, of course there is! I can arrange for you to go to school, if you want me to. French is the business language here. To be able to compete and earn a living you must know French, at least. You'll face competitors who are polished in five or more languages."

"But why would you do that for me?"

The woman stared at Aisha in surprise. "Because somebody did exactly the same thing for me years ago, and it changed the course of my life, and because I feel a great sense of gratitude toward my adopted land and its kind people. It's really simple."

Then she went on to explain she could arrange for Aisha to go to the Catholic school for girls. "I'll have a letter of introduction ready for you before you leave tonight. You'll take it to Sister Annette. You can't miss the big school, it's at Rue des Soeurs. Ask and people will show it to you."

Impulsively, Aisha went down on her knees and kissed the woman's feet.

"Please don't do that, child," said the woman seemingly embarrassed, and tried to help Aisha to her feet. "Allah is most Great."

Overcome by emotion, Zakiya took the woman's hand. "May God prolong the years of your life. May God give you happiness and prosperity for your kindness," she said as she wiped her eyes with the end of her long sleeve. "We thank you, Madame Maria."

"Please don't."

"Who gives not thanks to men, gives not thanks to God!"

"Everything is going to be all right," said the woman with assurance. "You'll see."

Aisha felt utterly confused. Up to this day, she had believed that no one was concerned with anyone else's troubles. Was she wrong? That woman wanted to help, out of the goodness of her soul. Could school be the answer? The city seemed so huge, so cold, so chaotic, and both she and her mother were utterly unprepared for survival. Now the woman's kindness touched her deeply and filled her with new hope, as they climbed the steep stairs to the laundry room at the roof.

Her mother's humming reached her from the laundry room, as she sat by the terrace wall, which was warm against her back. Memories of another time, another place flooded her mind. The scene was vivid. She was back at the village and she could see their little house clearly and one particular evening returned to haunt her.

Her mother and Uncle Youssef sat on the floor with their legs crossed. Uncle Youssef took from his pocket a small tin box with tobacco and started to roll a cigarette. "Time goes fast, and we'll soon have to find a nice man to marry Aisha," her uncle was saying, reminding them of the promise he had given his departed brother and Aisha's father, Ahmed, on his death bed, that he would take care of the two women.

"I remember," Zakiya replied. "I never liked him working at the factory, but Ahmed, rest his soul, wouldn't listen. He insisted that foreigners were nice people and paid good wages. His dream was to save enough money to take Aisha and me to the city, where we would have a better chance. My poor Ahmed! He was so good. He never so much as raised a hand on me, never. Why did he have to die so young?"

"It was written," Youssef mumbled.

Zakiya's face flushed crimson. "Nice people, indeed! When

I went to see them after the accident, they told me they were sorry because Ahmed was a good worker. They didn't have to tell me that. I knew he was good! They told me that they never thought the big frame of the cotton machine could come off its hinges and kill a man. When it did, all I got from them was ten pounds, and I was left in the streets with a baby in my arms.

The scene was vivid in Aisha's mind. She recalled wanting to know why her mother had not demanded for more money at that time and had asked her.

"Of course I did. But nobody cares for us! What does heaven care for the cries of the dogs? There's no justice in this lousy dog's world we live in. We're poor beggars. We're trash, and that's all we are."

"But we have courts, haven't we?" Aisha persisted.

"Courts we have, yes, it's justice we don't have! The law says we can only take Europeans to their own courts to be judged, not in ours. So, even if we had the money for an Egyptian lawyer, what could he do? Anyone could buy the best of our lawyers with only a couple of miserable pounds and have our case thrown out. Tell her, Youssef. Am I wrong?"

"No, Zakiya, you're not wrong. It's just as you say. But my dear, why get upset? Remember, it's the will of Allah. Everything is *maktoub* to be that way."

"The will of Allah?" Aisha's mother had shouted furiously. "Which Allah? The one you men go and pray to in the mosque while we women don't even have the right to enter? And why would Allah want things to be that way?"

Aisha brought herself back to the present. The village seemed so far removed, so long ago. Yet her mother's words still echoed in her ears,*"No one cares for us."*

But somebody did care, Aisha thought and perhaps Allah meant for her to go to school and get an education. Her brain struggled in vain to separate reality from imagination. There was a new life ahead, she wanted to believe. That woman could be her lifeline, a new beginning.

When they returned home that evening, Aisha washed the only cotton dress she had and borrowed the iron from the doorman's wife to press it. She waxed and cleaned her red shoes, washed her hair, and bathed. Late at night, exhausted but full of hopes and dreams for the future, she went to sleep.

Aisha arrived early at school the following morning. She stood outside and watched the uniformed girls as they came and entered the big gate of the school yard.

A man walked by, and she asked him the time. It was eight o'clock, and she decided to go in. Two girls stood in a corner talking.

"Which is the way to Sister Annette's office, please?" Aisha asked.

She walked to the door where they pointed and knocked.

"Entrez," said a voice from inside. She did not know what that meant. When she heard the word again, she opened the door hesitantly.

It was a large sunny room with book shelves all along the walls. Two bright dark eyes smiled at her from underneath a white veil. The woman sat behind a huge desk. Right above her on the wall, Aisha noticed a tiny imitation of a man without clothes, except for a small piece of cloth covering the lower part of his body. He hung upon a crosspiece of wood and appeared to be dead or in terrible pain. His head drooped on his shoulders, and there was a red bright spot that looked like blood on one of his sides. It was a painful sight.

"Oui, mademoiselle?" the woman asked and Aisha panicked at the sound of the strange language. The veiled woman nodded and smiled.

"I'm looking for Sister Annette," Aisha whispered in Arabic, and waited anxiously for a few seconds, wondering whether the other understood her.

"I am Sister Annette, child," she replied in the same dialect. She had a strong accent, but a kind smile, which was very encouraging. "What can I do for you?"

She handed her the envelope which the woman had given her the night before. The nun pointed to a chair for her to sit, opened the letter and read.

"So, you want to come to school and learn," she said softly.

Aisha simply nodded her head.

"I can see you are determined. The fact that you realize the value of learning and want to improve yourself convinces me you are intelligent, and I'm sure you'll do well. It's fortunate the school year has only begun, so you haven't lost much. Your name is Aisha, if I read correctly, no?"

Aisha nodded again.

"You won't have to worry about the tuition money. Your benefactress will pay as long as you stay with us."

This came as a surprise, so she just nodded.

"How old are you, Aisha?"

"Well, you see, my mother is not educated, and we don't really know. I was born in a small village in Upper Egypt, and my uncle thinks I was born during the Christian year of 1926, or thereabout."

The sister seemed impressed. "That makes you thirteen years old. Right?"

"I guess I am, if you say so."

The nun smiled. "In my culture, you would be considered a child, but I know in yours, girls often marry at nine, so you're regarded as a woman."

Aisha thought she was talking nonsense, but she smiled and nodded.

The nun wrote a bit more. Then she said that a regular

class with children her age would be too hard for her to follow.

"You mean I can't go to school?"

"I didn't mean that," the sister answered with a smile. Then she went on to explain that children who didn't know French entered first a special preparatory class for a year, and then they were placed in regular classes according to their progress.

"Some learn fast," she said, "others don't try as hard. Girls like you are often eager to learn so they can get out in the business world and make a living. Others don't feel the need."

"Oh, I'll try very hard. Please do let me try," Aisha begged, almost in tears.

The nun looked at her for a second. "I'm sure you will, child. "It won't be easy, but I know you'll try. You'll need a uniform. Perhaps Sister Marie can help us."

She pressed a buzzer, and a few moments later another white-gowned sister entered the room. She had a big rosary and an immense coif starched stiff. Around her waist was a chain with many clinking keys.

The newcomer bowed her head slightly, and both women began to talk in French. Then the nun asked her in Arabic to go with her to the school wardrobe. Before she left the office, Aisha glanced once more at the man on the wall and was sure the older sister noticed it.

Half an hour later, they returned to the office with a uniform. Sister Annette gave her a book to take home, wished her good luck, and instructed her to return the following morning at eight and report to class three.

"I just can't believe it — my own daughter going to school," her mother said that night. "If only some of our village friends could see you!"

Aisha must have gone through the book hundreds of times

looking at pictures of dogs, cats, and houses. "Wouldn't it be wonderful to be able to read what these books have to say?"

Tearfully, her mother bent over, rubbed her shoulder, and patted her on the head.

Aisha threw herself into her mother's open arms.

"Do you think I can learn, mama?"

"I'm sure you can, child. Have no fear. The only thing that worries me — "

"Worries you? What?"

"One day you may feel shame for your peasant mother."

"Never!" she cried and threw her arms around her mother.

"Allah's blessings upon you, daughter," she said softly, wiping her eyes, "and my blessings, too."

Aisha woke at dawn, scrubbed herself till her skin turned the color of an over-ripe tomato and tied her long, dark hair behind her neck with a string. She glanced at the piece of a mirror on the wall, and all she could see looking back at her were two large, black eyes the shape of almonds, crowned with long, thick lashes that reached the ridge of her thin brows and a beauty spot above the corner of her upper lip.

She smiled happily and threw a kiss in the air. "You'll do," she said to her other self.

At 7:30 she was ready, so she kissed her mother and left the house for school. "Be careful," her mother reminded her. "And don't speak to anyone in the street, just walk straight."

"You don't have to worry about me," Aisha assured her, trying hard to control the crazy beating of her heart.

As she walked through the streets of their neighborhood in her clean uniform, she felt pride for her upright carriage and gait, which she owed to the habit of carrying heavy water-jugs and other burdens on her head.

Soon she became aware of the nauseating filth that covered the streets of their quarters. For the first time, too, she noticed the ragged Arab children who grovelled in the piles of garbage, a sight she had never seen before. She hastened her step until she reached the wider and cleaner streets of the city.

The school yard was filled with uniformed girls. She heard a bell and saw the girls disperse in different directions. The classrooms were numbered but she could not read the European figures so she stopped one of the girls and asked.

"Can't you read? It's right in front of you," the girl replied impatiently.

Aisha entered the room to which she had pointed. The students had already taken their seats behind benches and sat in pairs. Fearful, she remained standing by the door while the beating of her heart deafened her. Two girls looked at her, laughed, and said something in a foreign language. Although Aisha could not understand, she could tell they were talking about her.

After a few seconds of being stared at and whispered about, she became aware of a pain at the pit of her stomach and a nervous contraction in her throat. She turned around for some help but all she could see were rows and rows of hot, penetrating eyes fixed upon her.

Her first impulse was to flee from the room and vanish. She turned for the door, but before she could reach for the handle, the door opened and a tall, emaciated nun with spectacles walked in. The girls stood up, and Aisha knew it was too late. She remained planted there while her heart pounded.

"Bonjour, mes filles," said the nun with a soft, warm voice.

"Bonjour, Soeur Louise." The answer came in a discordant chorus.

The sister motioned with her hand for them to sit and then

turned to Aisha. "You must be the new girl," she said in Arabic. "What's your name?" She smiled kindly.

"Aisha," came the feeble whisper.

"Girls," the sister continued in Arabic, "I want you to meet Aisha. She'll be in our class. Now, is there anyone here who would like to share a bench with Aisha and help out with what we've covered so far?"

There was silence in the room.

The sister looked about, still smiling, and cleared her throat. "How about you, Claudette?"

"This is Clara's seat, *ma Soeur*," replied the girl, pointing to the empty seat beside her.

"Ah, yes. I forgot," mumbled the nun. "Perhaps Aisha could sit with Mary, no?"

The girl hesitated momentarily. "But I was going to ask you to move me closer to the blackboard. I can't see from here."

Aisha felt a disturbing undercurrent. She heard the girls titter. When she looked up, the set smile had left the nun's face. She seemed annoyed. She raised her head, her voice sharp, her throat constricted.

"Well," she said, "I want Tereza to sit with Aisha and try to help her."

"But *ma Soeur*, she's got lice — all Egyptians do!"

For a second, the words hung in the air. Aisha could hear nothing but the blood throbbing in her ears. There was a chuckle or two and then a dead, hideous silence.

"That's not true!" Aisha shouted. "That's not true! I'm clean. Just because I'm an Egyptian doesn't mean I'm filthy."

After her outburst only her sobs could be heard in the silent room. She wished she were dead.

As she stood there, sobbing helplessly, she saw a blond girl approaching. Aisha's mind was made up fast — she'd beat the devil out of her if she tried anything.

The girl walked straight to her, smiled, and extended her small hand. "My name is Soula. Please, come and sit with me," and without waiting for an answer, Soula took Aisha's hand and guided her to her bench.

The sister stood up, her pale face changed now to the purplish color of a plum.

"I'm ashamed of you!" she said forcefully. "Cleanse your heart and lips, my children, and pray for forgiveness. Pray God to deliver you from haughtiness in the heart." Suddenly, she turned and left the classroom.

Hurt and embarrassed, Aisha did not dare look up. She heard girls talk in low whispers, but their language was unintelligible to her.

"Don't cry, Aisha," pleaded her new companion. "That girl is a stupid snob. Please don't cry."

Her sympathy brought a new torrent of tears. "I know her kind," Aisha said in disgust. "They treat us like dogs and they hurt our feelings. They forget we have feelings, too."

Aisha felt her new friend's hand holding hers firmly, yet gently. She looked up at her but could not see her too well through the tears. However, for the first time since arriving in the classroom, she had a feeling she had found in Soula a friend who would be willing to help her get started in school.

CHAPTER VI

Till then, two primitive passions had governed Aisha: fear of hunger and a yearning for freedom. Now, a new passion burned inside her, the thirst for learning. She became consumed with a drunken desire to learn and make progress, to improve herself.

At first, her ignorance proved a blessing. Whenever classmates taunted her, it was in a language she did not know. And by the time she was able to understand their insults, she had gained confidence in herself, and she had Soula, a friend who was always there to help her.

Aisha realized that Western people believed Arabs were all lazy, dirty, primitive, superstitious, devoid of self-control, and unable to learn. She knew she couldn't fight this battle alone, and change peoples' mind. Besides, she wanted to spend her time and energy learning. She had a strong memory, and her ears, trained to rhythm and music, could pick up with ease any and all sounds, including the guttural Gallic way of speech.

In no time her mind began to open, and she learned so fast and so much that at times she felt as if her head would explode, oozing topsy-turvy French grammar, vocabulary, idioms, history, and French culture. To her astonishment she also discovered that once she tackled the second language, a third, English, was easier yet to learn than the one before.

After supper one evening, she was studying while her mother was ironing.

"How is school?" Zakiya asked her.

"Just fine. I'm a genius, Mama!"

Her mother smiled and shook her head slowly. "For all I know, you may be!"

"I'm learning. It's not easy, but I can learn. I'll show them how wrong they are."

Her mother looked up from her ironing. "With patience you can do anything. A poor man without patience is like a lamp without oil."

"I have patience."

"I know you have, daughter. You are a true Arab, noble and tolerant."

"Mother! One minute we admit we're ignorant and the next we talk of how great and noble we are!"

"Don't be too hasty," said Zakiya, a rare flare of temper in her voice. "Nobility is not measured by the degree of one's learning, child. The first step to knowledge is to know that we are ignorant."

She waited, her glistening black eyes watching Aisha. "A truly noble person learns to endure bad fortune. And because we are noble, we have managed to survive." Her words faltered on the edge of a moan. A pained sigh came from deep in her body.

"The greatness of a man," she continued quietly, "is the degree of his tolerance, of how much pain one can withstand with dignity."

For an illiterate, her mother never failed to amaze Aisha. But she could not fully agree with her. Deep in her heart, she felt that the true man is one who resists. She knew the very word Muslim meant, one who submits. When they were slapped on one cheek they were supposed to turn the other. But she believed that turning the other cheek was not always the ideal solution.

And while Aisha fought her individual struggle, trying to put some order and sanity into her life, she saw the world around her being demolished.

At school, Sister Louise often read the news to the class and discussed the countries involved. One morning, in May of 1940, she told them that Holland had been invaded. Then Brussels fell, and just before the closing of school for the summer vacation in June, they learned of the fall of Paris. That day, the Sister's pale eyes were red. The students knew that Paris was the city where she was born and where her relatives lived.

Soon, warplanes filled the skies and warships filled the harbor of Alexandria. The streets were crowded with many uniforms: British, Australian, Canadian, Indian, South African, French and Greek sailors.

On a sunny morning in July, the seaport of Alexandria shook with cannon fire. The citizens heard that a battle took place between the enemy and the British fleet. Blackout regulations followed, and every shade had to be pasted with black paper. Aisha witnessed the transformation of the city. More and more Arab beggars filled the streets. *Hashish* and opium peddlers operated in the open. Prostitution seemed to prosper.

From one day to the next on her daily walks, she saw shops changing into bars. Cheap show-places and cabarets sprang up everywhere and everybody seemed to have money and money changed hands fast.

Maids and washer-women became hard to find as factories paid more, so Zakiya was up to her neck with offers for work. It was only a matter of having the physical strength to keep up with the demand for her services.

Not a day went by that Aisha missed going to the general store where the latest news concerning war and general gossip were exchanged and interpreted.

"What's new today?" she would ask.

"The Italians advanced to Sidi-Barrani, 60 miles inside Egypt."

Another day: "Who are the bastards who drop their bombs everywhere?"

"Germans."

Following the fall of Greece and the Island of Crete, the Germans started visiting Alexandria nightly. Their planes came low and dropped their bombs, while the anti-aircraft guns of the allies boomed and pounded, igniting the dark skies like a fireworks display.

After the panic that followed the first air-raid attacks, the people became bolder and more accustomed to the sound of the howling sirens. Aisha and her mother, like most people, stopped running to air-raid shelters and stayed in their flats. The attitude was that a man should die with dignity in his bed, not underground like a rat.

Aisha also noticed another drastic change. While before it was always Europeans against natives, a new antagonistic mood surfaced among the multinational residents of the city, and pitted neighbor against neighbor. And while the European feelings were at fever heat, the Egyptians prayed for anybody's army to march in and kick the British Imperialists out of Egypt!

By the middle of December, the sound of falling bombs and

the sight of the blasted buildings were parts of a normal scene. Then the Allies started making progress. They pursued the Italians beyond the Egyptian border into Libya and Bengazi, and all seemed quiet again.

The days became slow-moving and monotonous. Nothing happened. Aisha and her mother remained in their closed world. Then summer came again and the days grew hot, and Aisha's restlessness returned. After school recessed for the second summer, her anxiety grew.

It was during one of those uneasy afternoons that she met Anna.

Aisha was sitting on the terrace reading a book about the French Revolution. Absorbed in her reading, she didn't see the woman approach. Aisha turned around and saw her remove her clothes in slow, graceful movements. Underneath, she wore a brief bathing suit which partly covered her loins and her full breasts. She was the first European tenant who had ever bothered to climb to the roof.

Aisha gazed at the woman intently, noting her defiant black eyes, intemperate mouth, and youthful, olive skin. The woman gave Aisha a warm smile, kicked off her slippers, and started applying sun lotion over her body.

"You must be Aisha," she said casually in French. "I've seen you in uniform and found out from the doorman's wife who you are."

"Don't tell me you're one of the school nuns."

She looked surprised, then shrugged and burst into laughter. "A nun! I must say, you have a sense of humor, young lady," she said as she took a cigarette out of a pack and lit it. Then spreading her towel on the floor she stretched on it.

"Anna Trovini is my name," she said and extended a hand. "I live on the first. My parents lived here, too. That is, until recently."

"What happened?"

"They are Italians ... I wish to hell they weren't."

It was Aisha's turn now to laugh. "Are you sorry they are what they are?"

"Right now I'd be a fool to say that I'm not. You're darn right I'm sorry." Anna said and sat straight up.

"Isn't it funny?"

"What do you mean?" Anna asked bluntly. "Where's the joke?"

"A minute ago, I was just about ready to apologize for being an Arab. Now you — no one seems to be happy with whatever one calls himself these days, Italian, German, Egyptian —"

She looked at her for a moment, then laughed. "It doesn't seem fair, does it?"

"No."

"It's that stupid war. My father was born and raised here, but because of the war, thousands of Italians like my father have lost their jobs, their properties are confiscated, and now they are rotting in concentration camps." She took another puff and watched the grey smoke rise. "I only had a couple of semesters to get my degree. Instead I quit my studies and went to work. Well — some people might not call it work, but that's beside the point. I make a good living."

"I wish I could say the same," Aisha said. After a brief pause, "would you like some coffee?"

"No, stay put," Anna said. "I want to get to know you better. Tell me about the school and the nuns. Hearing you speak the language, I must admit, they've done an excellent job."

"Well, I feel as if I'm split down the middle. I feel I'm becoming two different people in one body."

Anna showed no surprise. "Go ahead, tell me."

"For instance, from nine to five in the afternoon, I must

think, speak, dream of French sounds, manners, and culture. Then I come home and I become an Arab again. I speak the only language mother and I know well. We still sit on the floor, like we've always done, place the tray with the food between us, praise God, and we still eat with our fingers, just as we've always done, no forks, no spoons, no nothing."

Anna reached out and touched her hand. "I'm extremely interested in what you're saying. Go on."

"But it's so confusing. I love and admire these people, but at the same time I hate them for trying to make me something else."

There was an uncomfortable silence. Aisha stood up and started pacing. Then she turned around. "Miss Anna, you must've read hundreds of books. Could you tell me something?"

"What is it?"

"Am I going crazy?"

"No, no, dear." She laughed gently. "Your problems are not unusual."

"They're not?"

"Not really," Anna said and shook her head. "Many people who must live in a bilingual world go through this. I know how you feel. On the one hand there's the attachment to the traditional Arab culture and values, and on the other, the attraction and admiration for the Western culture. Cultural dichotomy has been the destiny of the Westernized Arab in all North Africa countries since the introduction of French."

"And yet," said Aisha, "for one to be able to work and earn a living in this country, one must learn French and English, Arabic is not enough. Not only is it not enough, it's not even useful. What is a native to do?"

"I know," Anna responded. "An Arab wants or needs to acquire the Western culture, but at the same time, he distrusts it."

"It doesn't make any sense, does it?"

"Well, in a way it does. In a funny way it explains the attitude of your educated class with their ambivalent love-hate relationship with their own Arab country, and the Western powers, too."

It was as if a sudden strong breeze blew out of nowhere, clearing the misty fog in her head. For the first time, Aisha could find reasons for so many aspects of her life that seemed cruel and senseless before.

"I was thinking about this same thing one day and asked the nun at school. You know what her answer was?"

"What? I'd like to hear it."

"She said that we've always had a great difference between rich and poor people."

Anna nodded but did not seem convinced. "True, there was always a distance between the upper and lower classes in Arab lands. In the old days it was between the rich and the poor, the educated and the ignorant. But at least they still shared the same culture! Today it's different. Today's Western-educated Arab feels like an outsider, and other Arabs resent him."

Aisha was impressed. *"Ma sha Allah, ma sha Allah! Salla 'a' n-Nebi.* Bless the Prophet. How smart you are!"

Anna laughed and inspected the tan on her legs. "I wonder what time it is."

Aisha leaped to her feet, "I'll find out," she said and ran.

"Sulleiman!" Aisha yelled from the top of the stairs.

"What?" Came the bellowing voice of the doorman all the way from the ground floor.

"What time is it?"

A brief pause. "Almost four, and I was taking my nap before you woke me up!" shouted the old man.

"I must be getting ready," Anna said and rose. She stood

erect and stretched her arms like a swimmer about to plunge off a spring board.

Aisha hesitated. "There's one thing I'd like to ask you."

"What is it?" Anna began to dress.

"If what you say is true, then how is it that none of you Europeans living in Egypt seem to feel this ... what do you call it," she paused, feelling uncomfortable, "this ambivalent feeling?"

"Well, I guess we're sure of who we are and we're proud of our heritage." Anna looked up and scanned the sky. "You see, we choose the best each culture has to offer us, and we reject the rest. No strong attraction, and no resentment."

She placed her arm on Aisha's shoulder. "Don't ever cut your gorgeous hair. As for your eyes, they're the most bewitching eyes I've ever seen. You're a truly beautiful young woman."

"The eyes are of little use if the mind is blind."

"How wise!" she chuckled.

"Miss Anna," Aisha hesitated, "if ever I — if I need a job, could you help me?"

Anna seemed to be turning the question over in her mind as she examined her more carefully now. After a brief silence, she smiled and patted her on the shoulder. "Why, of course! when you're ready for work, come and see me. I believe I have a job in mind that'll fit you like a glove. In fact, you were born for it."

"Bless you," Aisha whispered. "I think I'll come and see you soon."

CHAPTER VII

Aisha waited three days and then went to see Anna. She explained to Anna that she could not expect her mother to feed her any longer and had to find a job and earn some money.

"Mother's constant pain in her legs is killing her. She groans even in her sleep. There's money around, and I want to earn my share of it. I'm ready to do anything ... anything to earn a living."

"What about your schooling?" Anna asked.

"I've thought about that. Even if I prolonged my education, I couldn't get more than a sales job. Besides, I intend to continue learning. I could take lessons in French and English, but I have to have money first."

Anna seemed to be taken aback by the determination of Aisha's voice. "Give me two days to talk to my boss," she finally said. After a thoughtful pause, she added, "Entertainers are hard to find these days, with European imports cut off because of the war. You're a natural, Aisha. You have an exotic beauty that is very appealing, so let me see what I can do, and I'll let you know."

Two days later, the doorman handed Aisha a note from Anna. "Come by the apartment Tuesday at three. We'll go together to meet my boss."

An hour later, Aisha was knocking at her neighbor's door.
"I can't go anywhere," she said helplessly.
Anna stared at her. "And why not?"
"I have no clothes to wear, nothing but my school uniform."
"We can take care of that."
Anna walked out of the room, and returned holding two summer dresses and a pair of silver sandals. "I can't get into these any more since I've gained weight. Why don't you see if you can use them?"
Aisha thanked her and hesitated.
"What now?" Anna asked.
"I was wondering — could we go another day instead of Tuesday?"
"What is it with Tuesday?"
"Well, Tuesday is thought to be unfortunate, some people call it *the day of blood.*"
Anna blew out a small cloud of cigarette smoke and looked at Aisha. "I see. What would be a good day then?"
"Oh, Thursday is considered fortunate. It's called *el-mubarak,* and Friday, of course. Friday is blessed above all other days. It's the sabbath of Muslims. It's called *el fadeeleh,* the excellent!"
"Very well," said Anna. "Thursday the fortunate, at three." She opened the door for her.
Aisha picked up the dresses and the shoes and looked back at her. "You're most kind, thank you, and God bless you!"
"God bless you, too."
At three o'clock Thursday, she went to Anna's apartment.
Anxiety had had kept her up all night, but she felt miraculously refreshed in her low-cut yellow print dress that fit her snugly revealing the outlines of her body.
"*Mama mia!*" Anna exclaimed when she saw her. "You're

gorgeous. You make Leonardo's Mona Lisa look like a scarecrow!"

"Oh, come off it!" Aisha said, unable to accept the compliment. But deep in her heart, it made her feel good and gave her the reassurance she needed.

The two women left the building and walked a short distance to the main street, where they waited at the corner. Five minutes later, a taxi pulled up. The driver greeted Anna, complimented her on her appearance, and opened the door of the car for her.

"No matter what part of the town that man happens to be, he'll break his neck to come on time for me," Anna explained and smiled at the Arab driver. "He's worth his weight in gold."

On the way to what Anna called her "workplace" she tried briefly to fill her in, but Aisha had no idea what was expected of her. She was going to be dancing her native dance and getting paid for it. There was no problem there. She knew she was good. She was told that she was the best at the village, and was determined to succeed.

"I know you'll impress the old goat," Anna said gravely. "She won't believe her luck. Her name is Madame Minoushe, and she's the boss. Her husband is a weakling but you'll be dealing with her. Use your brains, and don't let her sweet-talk you. Insist that she hires you as a dancer, the best dancer ever born under the desert sun, you tell her, and insist that she pay you a weekly salary, plus commission on every drink you get."

Anna lit a cigarette, watched the gray smoke, then turned and faced Aisha. "Whatever amount she offers you, ask for a bit more. Remember, Madame cares for Madame and she'll take from the sore-footed his sandal, as your proverb goes."

Aisha dared not ask for more details, afraid she might not have the courage to go through with it. They said no more until they arrived at *Les Etoiles.*

The place was empty, except for a few Arabs cleaning up. They were greeted politely and were told that madame was in her office. The two women passed among chairs and tables and went into a small room located near the bar.

"*Bonsoir*, Madame Minouche," Anna called from the door.

The plump little woman with the bleached blond hair and false eyelashes that made her small eyes look like button holes, looked up from behind a desk. "*Bonsoir, cherie,*" she said, and motioned them to enter.

"This is Aisha," Anna said, her eyes fixed on her boss.

The woman stared, half-closed her eyes to see more clearly, then her face lit up.

"Hm! Delighted to meet you," she said, without taking her eyes off Aisha. Then to Anna, in a soft, casual voice, she said, "Thank you, *cherie*, for bringing her over."

"Why I'm happy to be of help, madame," said Anna. She added, "Just be fair with her."

The woman laughed. "I am more just than a balance! Relax Anna, and please, be seated."

"I'd rather not, if you don't mind. I want to go ahead and change clothes and put on my makeup." Then Anna bent over as if to kiss Aisha, and whispered in her ear. "Remember, she has a mouth that prays and a hand that kills!" Then louder, "Good luck, girl!" And with a friendly pat and a light squeeze on Aisha's arm, she left the room.

"Sit down Aisha," said the woman, having appraised her carefully.

Aisha pulled up a chair and sat, her heart pounding.

"I must say, you're stunning for an Arab!"

"Arabs come in every shape, madame."

"Are you a virgin?" she asked bluntly.

Aisha hesitated momentarily. *It's none of her darn business.* "I'm clean as the day I was born. Why?"

The woman smiled, a little uncertainly. "Well, I wonder how much you know about life — "

"You mean sex?"

She nodded mutely.

"Women in our village discuss sexual matters, even the most private, in the presence of children. We grow up knowing all there is to know about sex."

"I was just curious. Why you want to do this kind of work?"

Why not? she thought. *What else is there for me to do?*

"It's not easy or pleasant work," madame went on. "A cabaret is not the Garden of Eden, as you'll soon find out."

"Funny that you should mention that," Aisha said for lack of a better answer.

"Why?"

"Because I found out recently that the story of the Garden of Eden in the Koran is about the same as the one in Genesis, even though I think our version is better." She had a lump in her throat as she looked at Madame Minouche, unable to concentrate her thoughts or make sense of what they were talking.

Their eyes met and held.

"You can talk to me frankly, Aisha. Why do you want the job?"

"Why?" she asked mockingly. "By Allah, what else would you have me do? Become the president of a bank, or wash clothes for ten piastres a day? I want a comfortable place to call home, and I want my mother to stop washing everyone's shitty clothes for the price of a loaf of bread." She spoke more sharply than she had intended.

Madame lit a cigarette with slow, unhurried movements, then looked at her desk. "I'm sure you'll have no trouble getting the things you want. You have beauty, determination, and some education, and you also have a figure to kill for. I only hope you've got a brain in your head. I'm sure you'll make it. This is the right place, child, and the right time, too, if we survive the animals, our customers, and the enemy bombs, *bien sur! Tu comprends, ma chère?*"

Aisha had no idea what she was talking about, but she heard herself saying, "I leave that part in Allah's hands. He'll take care of me. Man thinks, God guides!"

"*Inshallah!* God willing. Yes, this is the right time," the woman said urgently. "We don't know how long this dreadful war will last, but if you're smart and fast — "

"Fast? Why fast?"

"*Ma chère*, let's be realistic. Everything comes to an end, even wars. As the Arab proverb goes, 'A wise man makes a trench before the floods.'" She stood up, struggling to push her corset in place.

When the woman stood, Aisha realized that she was not as short as she had thought, but she was fat and so tightly corseted that she must have felt the need to stand and stretch for an occasional breath. Next, she tried to maneuver her overflowing bosom into her bra, which was positioned high, pointed, bursting.

The scene was comical, but Aisha curtailed her laughter.

"I must warn you on a few elementary things you should know," madame went on. "For instance, the law does not allow us to serve alcohol to women. Men don't realize that, or if they do, they don't obey. Because they pay for regular drinks, some object when we substitute women's drinks with tea or soda, and when they do object, they give us trouble. Men are such funny beasts." She lit another cigarette and took a few hurried puffs.

"Another thing worth mentioning is the Egyptian police. They're very strict with girls who go to bed with soldiers, but of course, most girls do it anyway. That's none of my business.

Once the working women leave my establishment, they're on their own, and I don't give a damn what they do. Besides, I don't run a convent here. But girls have to be careful because if they're caught, they can lose their working permit."

She walked to the door and yelled, "Ahmed! Bring us two lemonades."

Two minutes later, an Arab waiter came in with two tall glasses. She motioned for Aisha to help herself. Aisha thanked the woman and reached for one. Madame took the other and hurriedly took a sip.

"I have another Arab girl working for me here," she began, her eyes fixed on Aisha. "Zania makes a fortune and she's not half as pretty as you are. She learned to talk English right here from the soldiers. She's a real devil, if I ever saw one in the flesh!"

After a brief pause, "I'm sure she'll be delighted to pass on to you her great wisdom. When it comes to men, she's a professional, but she has neither class nor heart. I can't stand Zania's presence, but she gets a lot of drinks, which means she makes me money and that's the reason I keep her. She's good business and adds a little native color."

She took another sip from her lemonade, then shook her head ruefully. "You're different and I can see you have class. Anna spoke to me about you. I know your village which is renowned for its beautiful women, and a few belly dancers from there have risen to the very top. Anna said that when you dance you can bring tears into peoples' eyes. True?"

"Well," Aisha said, taken by surprise, "I can make people cry, and I can make them laugh. When I dance I express life. Yes, life and death, love and anger. A good dancer must express something. I don't just shake."

"I'll offer you top price. Ten pounds a week," Madame said.

Aisha asked for fifteen. They settled for twelve. In her mind, Aisha ran a fast calculation. Her mother would have to wash clothes every day for six months to make that much, while she could get paid more doing what she loved and had done all her youthful life for free.

"We try to offer service and superb entertainment," madame was saying, affecting modesty.

Aisha smiled confidently. "I'll give you the best you ever had."

Madame opened the drawer of the desk and pulled out some money. "I'll advance you money to get a costume, and I'll also give you the address of a seamstress. She's good, reasonable, and knows her job. You tell her I sent you."

"What type of costume?"

"When you dance at your local celebrations and feasts, a dancer ties a scarf around her hips to accentuate her movements and dances in her ordinary ankle-length dress. In a cabaret, we need to offer our customers more. You'll get a traditional costume, a bra and floor-length skirt, slit on both sides for freedom of movement. I'll talk to the seamstress about it. I want sheer, filmy gauze material to enhance your figure without concealing it and I want it rich, with lots and lots of sequins, beads, tassels, glittering charms, the works! I want you to be sexy, but not vulgar."

"I know what you mean," Aisha lied.

"Good! When do you want to start?"

"Tomorrow."

"Tomorrow is fine."

A fat hand with a ring on each finger was held out toward her. They shook hands. Then Aisha took the address of the seamstress and the envelope with the money.

"Thank you, madame."

"*Allahu Akbar!*" said Madame Minouche.

With a feeling that things were happening too fast, Aisha turned and went out.

Before Aisha realized it, she was a natural, normal part of the nightly scene.

The room was crowded and full of smoke. There were glasses and bottles on all the tables. Uniformed men of many nations mingled with the working women in heavy makeup, low-cut dresses with bare arms and backs. Most of the men shouted to be heard, but others were singing while a five-piece band played loudly. They all had one thing in common: they all drank excessively to drown their sorrows.

For an entire week since she started working, she had managed to be left alone, seated at the back of the room, observing the operation and listening to the women's gossip, while she waited for her costume to get ready. But when payday came she was as broke as the day she had started. Whenever a man would venture to her table, she found an excuse to leave him and ran to the dressing room to hide. By the end of the week she had not enticed anyone for drinks and therefore had not earned any commission.

From her observation post she saw the old siren approach. Bejewelled and in her tight, low-cut dress, she thought Madame Minouche's breasts looked like two over-blown balloons ready to pop. She greeted customers warmly and rested her hand with maternal benevolence on their shoulders.

"Are you enjoying yourselves?" The hostess was asking right and left with a fixed smile. She saw Aisha and came over.

"Aisha," she sighed. "Unless you get them to offer you drinks, you won't make a piastre, dear."

"I need some time, I'll do good, I promise you."

"I know you will. Take your time dear. Take all the time you need, if you can afford it."

From her vantage point, Aisha watched the working girls in action. There was Emile, a beautiful young woman with a sweet personality. Aisha was told Emile's husband had brought her to the cabaret himself and got her the job. Every night he waited faithfully at the exit, presented himself as her brother, and saw that Emile and her money returned home safely. No matter how much money she made, she always needed more. Rumor had it that her faithful husband spent it at the race track as fast as she earned it.

There was Ketty, the "virgin," as the girls called her. She was tall with honey-colored hair and the figure of a statue. Ketty won her title because she never went to bed with men. Gossip had it that Ketty worked there to support her three small children and pay the medical debts her husband left her before he died. She saved every piece of candy or chocolate the soldiers gave her and took it home to her little ones. Aisha liked Ketty from the first day they met.

Elvira was a bleached platinum German with the strength of a bullock and the muscles of a man. She wasn't young, but she was well-preserved and was an excellent acrobatic dancer. She looked as if she had seen better days and better places. No one knew much about her because she kept pretty much to herself.

And there was Anna, her neighbor. Anna Trovini attracted men like a queen bee attracted workers in a hive. Soldiers loved to talk and joke with her in their own language, and Anna spoke six. As Aisha observed her neighbor's every step, she realized that Anna's greatest advantage over the other girls was her natural poise and the fact that she was a splendid linguist and an extremely beautiful woman. The women at the club gave her the title of "Her Majesty." With a joke and a smile, Her Majesty would put the most difficult man in his place, avoiding trouble or misunderstanding. But Anna, like the rest of them, was there to earn a living. And even though it was obvious that she did offer her services beyond the cabaret boundaries, she was selective and discreet. She operated with class.

Zania's loud and vulgar laughter made Aisha turn in her direction. Though she was aware Zania was some years older than forty, she still had a youthful figure. She was tall and slim, but clumsy. When she moved she waddled along on her skinny legs and used her big hands like oars. For her age, and for unexplainable reasons, Zania was an attractive woman. She had a disarming smile, and her black eyes had a somber, mystical fascination which attracted men, especially men in uniform.

It was obvious that Zania had no formal education, nor talent for anything artistic, but a hard life had endowed her with an animal's sense. She could smell danger and money before anyone else around. Working in the cabaret was strictly a business for her, in fact, she had great contempt for the British, the elite Egyptians, and all foreigners, and she took no pains to conceal her feelings. It was during Aisha's third night at work that Zania found her alone in the dressing room and offered a free sampling of her ruthlessness.

"These suckers are loaded with money. All you got to do is help yourself."

"That's stealing," Aisha said. "I'm not a thief."

"You don't have to be a thief. You just get them to drink. Most of them can't hold their liquor anyway, and when they're drunk they'll hand you their money, easily. Besides, be reasonable, my dear. What do they need money for out there in the desert, eh? It's a waste, a sin. Especially when people like you and me can put it to better use."

"Waste?" Aisha asked incredulously for lack of a better question. "It's their money."

"Sure, it's theirs, but most of them don't come back to use it, anyway. In my language I call it waste, which by the way, is your language, too, remember — even though the Frenchies twisted your brains a little, just enough to confuse you."

Aisha had tried to ignore the older woman's sarcasm. "But if I get men to spend money on me, well, they'll want to sleep with me. Won't they?"

Zania shrugged and grinned. "So what? They want to sleep with me, too, but am I stupid? Do I look the stupid kind?"

"Hardly. Even so, last night when Ketty got ten drinks from a soldier and then refused to go with him, the son of a dog almost tore the place down. If I ever go with someone, I want it to be because I desire him, not because of his money or because I have to."

Zania merely smiled unpleasantly, arching her penciled eyebrows. "How very romantic. But let me tell you something, dear friend. In order to survive, you must learn how to handle men."

"How?"

"Well — like I let them believe that I'll go with them."

Aisha nodded and waited.

"As soon as we step outside, I have my friends that take care of the bastards."

"What do you mean?"

Her black eyes flared. "What do I mean?" she repeated with mock sternness. Then she motioned for Aisha to come closer. "My boyfriend is a taxi driver and he waits for me to take me home every night. When I leave with someone who's been persistent, and he won't let go of me, my man knows exactly how to take care of the bastard."

"He kills him?" Aisha whispered hoping she was wrong.

"If he has to. Why not?"

Aisha shrank in fright. "By Allah, that's terrible! It's wicked, killing them? We're all brothers under the skin —"

"Brothers?" Zania exploded, swung around and looked Aisha incredulity on her face. "*Walad el Kalb*," she hissed, and spat in scorn. "Feeling sorry for them? Our masters, the British? These are the people you feel sorry for? Our imperialist masters? How dare you call them our brothers," and with a vulgar gesture, she stormed out of the room.

Now, from where Aisha sat, she kept a watchful eye on Zania. She was surrounded by uniformed men and seemed to be enjoying herself. After the initial shock, she had to admit that what Zania had said was true. Aisha was aware of the great wave of anti-British feeling that was swelling up, a public outcry against the British. She also knew how the British expected the natives to behave as loyal allies, while being treated as conquered subjects. Foreign soldiers treated the Arabs like dirt and made filthy jokes, using obscene language about their king, a man few of them admired, but who was as much a national symbol as their flag.

"Penny for your thoughts." She heard a man's voice and turned to face the uniformed man who stood beside her chair, a glass in his hand.

Blond, baby-face, and eyes the bluest Aisha had ever seen. For an imperialist master, he looked so young and so handsome, she thought, and smiled.

"Mind if I join you?" he asked earnestly.

"Please do," she said, and all her fears and apprehensions were instantly dispelled. *Surely no one with such blue, blue eyes could be as bad as Zania let her to believe.*

"My name's Bob, Bob Armstrong."

"I'm Aisha," she said quietly.

"What a lovely name! Ah-EE-sha," he repeated, and

blushed. "Could I offer you a drink, Aisha?" And before she could answer, he called for the waiter.

The Arab waiter came running, smiling. "*Mabrouk!*" he said to Aisha happily, and took the order for her first commission.

CHAPTER VIII

After a restless night full of apprehension, Aisha prepared herself for work. Before she left, her mother brought out an old rag, the size of a handkerchief, and opened it. There lay a glittering bracelet representing a serpent with two heads, one on each end.

"My mother gave it to me the day I married your father," she said. "I want you to have it. It'll bring you luck."

Aisha flung her arms about her mother's neck and kissed her. "Oh, Mama," she whispered, deeply moved. "I know it will," and tried the bracelet on her wrist.

"No," her mother said. "It goes up high on the arm."

At the entrance of *Les Etoiles*, a huge poster showed a blown-up picture of a half-smiling, half-naked girl with huge black eyes, glossy, dark waist-length hair, in a blur of sequined veils with the caption: "Aisha the Star of Egypt, in her Oriental dance."

As Aisha stepped in, she met madame's husband. He was an old man with spectacles, tall, thin, and slightly stooped. He looked at her with gleaming goat-eyes and smiled. "Tonight's the night, Aisha. Are you ready?"

"As ready as I'll ever be, *monsieur*."

Ketty and Anna came in the dressing room to help her change.

She put on the costume which fit her like a glove. It was a dazzling outfit that glittered and sent out a shower of sparks. She pushed her hair back and fastened her earrings. They consisted of gleaming clusters of crescent moons and reached the top of her shoulders. Then she added six thin gold tinkling bracelets on each ankle, and she was ready.

Both girls stood and stared for a moment.

"My dear," said Anna, taking Aisha's arm in hers. "You'll tear their hearts out. You're smashing!"

"I'm scared," she confessed.

"Nonsense," Ketty said. "They'll love you." She shook her by the shoulder as if to make sure Aisha heard her. "You'll be good. I know you will."

Zania walked in and after a brief examination she bent over and kissed Aisha on the cheek. "Good luck, girl. Make me proud of you," she said, a rare tone of sincerity in her voice.

The regular band had stopped playing, and the lights dimmed. As the European musicians left, the Arab orchestra settled in their seats.

"Showtime," announced the band leader with a microphone in his hand.

The packed room rocked with shouts, whistling, and howling. From the back of the room came the clatter of breaking glass as the musicians played a bright introduction.

"Go on!" Anna said, and gave her a light shove.

Aisha held back, unable to move, as if her feet were glued to the floor.

"Go out, girl! Go and tame the wild beasts!" Anna gave her another push.

Aisha took a deep breath, swallowed hard, and leapt forward into the glare of the spotlight.

The noisy room hushed, and she felt the hundreds of eyes

scorching her flesh. All she could see was a blur of faces, grinning, smiling, sneering. Her cheeks began to burn and sweat formed on her forehead and armpits. She felt as if she were hovering in a vacuum, until she became conscious of the music and the beating of the drum which grew louder and louder, until she could hear nothing else.

This is my chance, perhaps my only chance! Pour your heart out, Aisha. Show them what you can do, she thought and took a deep breath.

For thirty minutes she swayed, twirled, and gyrated to the rhythm of the drum, sometimes in a fast tempo, other times in slow, seductive steps. Her braceleted arms and legs quivered and felt as if the tendons would burst through the skin, but her heart was in every step and every movement. In those thirty minutes, she danced for her audience the story of her life. When she finished, she was bathed in sweat.

There was a sudden explosion of wild applause. Cheers broke out, drowning the music, and money started flying from every direction, coming to land to her feet and for the first time she felt the exhilarating feeling of stepping over good money. She left the stage in tears.

Madame ran after her in the dressing room. She hugged her. "You were superb, Aisha! You're star quality, my dear! You have it made."

She handed her twenty pounds which the waiters had gathered from the stage floor. "I've never seen such a manifestation before, and I've seen a lot of life to know what I'm talking about and this is a bonus from me," she said and handed her another ten-pound bill.

Aisha looked at her. "Do you know what it means, madame? Do you know how it feels to be loved, to be successful?"

She nodded. "I know."

"I'm so happy I want to cry. I feel as if I've lost a little devil I've had inside me. He's been with me for a while now, but after tonight, I won't need him. I love the whole wide world! I love you, too," and Aisha planted a kiss on the old woman's cheek.

"You're a little witch!" madame whispered quite shaken.

Aisha laughed as the tears streaked down her cheeks.

The money rolled in, but the threat was always present, too. Everyone there lived under the shadow of death. She knew she might meet death in the form of the falling bombs sent from the Heavens above, or she could face it in the hands of angry, desperate men who, under the influence of alcohol and dope, were no better than wild beasts who had been trained to kill and destroy if they were to survive themselves.

From the first day, Bob Armstrong had become her constant companion. He called at work whenever he was in town, always bringing a small gift, a box of chocolates, a cologne. Aisha came to like Bob. He was young, somewhere in his twenties, and always looked as if everything was a surprise to him. He had an abounding enthusiasm and a refreshing innocence. He was handsome, polite, and shy, and she felt wholly at ease with him.

One night she was with Bob at the cabaret, just after the Allies had won a battle in the desert. Everyone was in a festive mood. Most of the men were drunk. People kissed each other. Some laughed for no reason, others cried, and some prayed for God to safeguard them.

Suddenly, an Australian soldier threw a bottle. It hit an African sailor on the head and bounced into a mirror, which came down in hundreds of pieces. The sailor's eyes flickered in surprise. Calmly he lifted a vase with flowers from the table and brought it smashing down, vase and all, upon the head of an Indian soldier who sat at the table next to him.

In seconds, the cabaret became a battlefield.

Women began to scream as bottles and chairs hurled in every direction. For a minute, Aisha stood petrified, too stunned to move, and she watched the fight as more and more men with an urge to exercise their fists joined in the scuffle.

"Stop it," madame bellowed. "Do something, some of you!"

Meanwhile, the waiters stood, looking on in stupefied amazement, each waiting for someone else to decide what should be done. Then they scurried away.

Aisha started to laugh. "Someone's doing something," she reflected as she looked at the shambles about the room.

Bob sprang to his feet in white-faced fury. "Get out of here, Aisha. Hear me?" And he ran to try to separate or join the fighters.

She looked about the room and realized the main exit was blocked by the fighting men. Then the whole thing struck her as so unreal and so funny that she started to laugh.

From behind, an arm reached out and touched her body. Startled, she twirled. A soldier's purple eyes narrowed and his teeth closed savagely.

"Hullo, babe," he hissed.

"Why — you impertinent dog!" she said with disgust and spat on him.

Her rudeness didn't ruffle him, and she saw his hands stretching out for more of her. She flicked her arm out, held it the smallest fraction of a second, then brought it down sideways as hard as she could on the man's face.

His hand flashed up instinctively and his eyes blinked with shock. Then she heard a gasping snarl. "Damn you!"

She flung herself to the floor, crawling on her hands and knees until she reached a corner where she stopped and took shelter under a table.

"*Les salauds*!" She heard Madame's volley of curses and pleadings. "*Mon Dieu*! Please, gentlemen! Somebody call the police! Antoine! Stop them before they ruin the place."

From underneath the table Aisha stared at madame's husband Antoine, and she shuddered at the thought. The poor man was dabbing at his neck with a handkerchief. He looked back at his wife beseechingly, a tired, pudgy man. "God's blood!" he muttered. "How the devil do you stop that?" he shouted in disgust, shrugged, and whirled out of the room and into the kitchen.

Aisha became aware that she was the only woman still there. None of the working girls were to be seen anywhere. A shot was fired, then a second. She felt terror-stricken and started to leap like a cricket all the way to the dressing room. There was no one in there. How did the girls leave, she wondered, and started to search behind the portable wardrobes with the garments and the formal dresses that filled the room.

Then she saw a small utility door. She tried the handle and the door opened into a dark tunnel. She stood for a minute straining her ears. No sound came from the direction of the tunnel. From behind, she could still hear the wailing of the fighting men. Fresh air hit her nostrils. In the near-darkness, she started to walk until she reached the other end of the passage. A blue street light dimmed through the half-opened door and she leaped to the back alley.

"As soon as you smell smoke, clear out," Anna explained as she saw her approach, a cigarette in her hand. "Life is violent here, and these men are desperate and armed. No need dying with the war heroes in that trap. Soldiers often get medals for having died in a foreign land, but unfortunately, no one gives war medals to whores."

Still, Aisha was making money. By the end of six months, not only was she able to repay Madame's loan, but she had saved two hundred pounds. This was more money than she had ever seen in her life. With her mother, she hoarded it in a box underneath the mattress. Every so often her mother would pull it out and count their savings. For the first time, they felt secure and alive.

"That's what we need, mother," Aisha said one morning. "With lots of money I wouldn't hesitate to face the devil himself."

"Money isn't everything, child."

"Oh, no? Well, I wouldn't want to live a day without it again. I want to have all I can, and what I can't."

Zakiya stared at her daughter. "The thirst after gold is worse than the thirst after water." She sighed. Then she looked down at her clasped hands. "And another thing, since I've stopped working, I feel sluggish and lazy. A woman was made to work. Idleness is a vice. My father used to say, 'A well is not to be filled with dew.'"

Aisha burst out laughing. "Dew or no dew, I bet your legs feel better since you've stopped climbing from terrace to terrace to wash. I don't hear you complain any more."

She nodded. "True, I feel better." Lifting up her skirt she inspected her swollen legs, with thick varicose veins that looked like strands of protruding wire. She gave a light slap to her right cheek, shook her head and sighed. "And people say the lazy person has no legs!" She laughed until she had tears in her eyes.

"I have a little job for you."

"What is it?"

"I want you to spend time looking for a decent apartment for us to move in. I'm sick and tired of this stinking hole at the top of the roof, constantly climbing stairs. What's money good for if we can't use it to live well?"

"We might have to go back to where we started," Zakiya reminded her cautiously. "What then?"

"That'll never happen. We'll never go hungry again," Aisha said with determination.

"I wonder — just how far would you go Aisha to get what you want?"

"I've often wondered that myself. I guess I'll go as far as I can."

Her mother pursed her lips. "Well ... there is an apartment for rent —"

Aisha leaped to her feet. "Where?"

"Right on Saad Zaghloul Square, near the big hotel overlooking the ocean."

"Mama!" Aisha cried excitedly. "That's the part of town where I'd like to live. How did you guess it?"

Zakiya's eyes glittered. "I brought you into this world, didn't I? I've raised you, and I still know what's in your heart, at least I think I do."

Aisha went up to her and kissed her. "You don't have to worry. I promise you no matter what, my heart won't change. Ever!"

"I hope so, child, for your sake."

"Well, what about the apartment?"

"It's furnished. The rent, I'm sure, will be so high we can't touch it. They're all high in these European buildings."

"But it's not a question of money. It's more, much more than that."

Zakiya's dark brows shot up. "I don't follow you."
"Did you talk to the people in charge?"
She shook her head. "No, child. I did not."
"Why not? You know it's hard to find rentals these days."
"I know. I guess I didn't have the courage. I just didn't dare, Aisha. I've only talked to the doorman who mistook me for a servant. Anyway, he wasn't very interested in discussing rentals with me."

Aisha stared at her in astonishment. For the first time in a while, she took a good look at her own mother, and with a queer jerk of the heart, she saw her as she really was. The sight of the old, ragged, tattered woman left her stunned. It wasn't shame that she felt, but sorrow and guilt, which tore her heart to pieces.

Her heart wrung with distress and unable to contain herself, she leaped up and threw herself in her mother's open arms.

"Is that what he took you for? The blind fool!" She tried to laugh as she fought back her tears. "He can't even guess the beauty that's hidden beneath these rags. But we'll show him, won't we? Oh Mama. Mama!" She sobbed.

"Why, you're crazy. You're talking all nonsense."

"Crazy, I am, yes. And an asshead," she mumbled. Then, "We're going shopping right now. If we start early, we'll be back in time for me to go to work. And tomorrow I'll stop by the apartment and talk to the man myself."

They were silent for a while, each with her own thoughts. Zakiya sat regarding her clasped hands, then she looked up. "Why that sad look on your face?"

"I find it so hard not to blame myself —"

"Blame yourself!" But why, dear? You've always turned your money over to me. I should have spent some, I suppose, I never thought —"

"If I hadn't been so stupid, so preoccupied in my own affairs —"

"Stop the nonsense, child. You know I never cared much for clothes. As long as there's food on the table, I'm happy." A smile flickered over her tired features. "All right. If we're going out, go get ready. It won't take me long to change."

They dressed in a twinkling and left.

Her mother had never been inside a big department store. She could hardly conceal her excitement. They visited some of the biggest stores in town: Hannaux, Rivoli, Salons Vert, Shalon, and for the first time in her life, she tried on a dress cut the European way.

Zakiya took a look at herself in the mirror and frowned. "By Allah, I can't go out in the street wearing this. It's too short. It's a disgrace!"

The sales girl gave her a look of exasperated impatience and ignored her last remark. "But it looks so elegant, so chic, madame."

"Yes, but look at my legs. They're exposed!"

"Women all over the world wear these types of garments, and they're not ashamed to let their legs be seen that much, I assure you," said the salesgirl, bemused. "You'll get used to wearing Western clothes, and you'll love them. Most Arab women do."

"I know," Zakiya admitted with a sudden sense of guilt. Then she looked at herself in the mirror again and blushed. "Under the fine apparel, a she-goat is hidden!" she said, using another proverb from her vast collection. Her face wistful as a child's, she looked around and gave the mirror a smile. "I like this dress."

They bought three.

In the shoe department, they bought two pairs with low heels, silk stockings, and a purse, the first she ever had. The modern purse fascinated her. As soon as they walked out of the store, Zakiya thrust her hand in her bosom, pulled out the knotted rag in which she carried her money, and spilled the contents in her new purse.

"I'll have to remember to keep the money in here from now on," she said in sheer delight, and laughed.

Their next stop was the beauty salon. After the hairdresser finished working on her, Aisha could not recognize her own mother. She looked years younger and fresher. As the excitement had put some color in her pale cheeks, she appeared a different person.

"If the women in the village saw me like this!" Zakiya said. "Why, they'd think I went out of my mind!"

On the way home and under the pretext of looking for her handkerchief, Aisha caught her mother taking hurried glances in the small mirror that came with the purse. She appeared unable to believe the wondrous transformation.

As Zakiya walked proud and straight, she seemed unrecognizable. Her face gleamed as if the afternoon sun had embraced it and drenched it in warm colors. Her eyes glittered with a strong light, her nostrils flared. Her lips quivering, she laughed as if she were young, a woman reborn.

Aisha slept little that night. Fear of losing out on the apartment tormented her. When the early sun crept through the dense autumn dew that hung over the city like a silk net, she rose and started to get ready.

Before she left, her mother stopped her by the door.

"Feed the mouth and the eye will be bashful!" She held out her hand, rubbing her thumb and first two fingers suggestively. "With the right amount of money, they'll give you anything. And another thing, play big and important or the doorman won't even let you in. They have no use for underdogs."

As Aisha had expected, the Arab doorman studied her face carefully, appraised her clothes, and looked at the glittering rows of bracelets on her arms. She was sure he took them for real.

She met his look as steadily as she could and smiled sweetly. Then she fished some money out of her bag, folded it, and extended her arm with the expert air of one accustomed to tipping. "Life is so expensive nowadays," she said.

He agreed, scratched his head, and took the money with a smile that curled the corners of his mouth.

"Thank you very much," he said, placing his palm to his breast, then his lips and forehead. "Allah bless you!" and bowed respectfully. "Your servant, madame."

On the way to the first floor, she mentioned casually that her father was a rich landowner with acres of land and a big house in Cairo. "But father spends a lot of time traveling all over the country on business trips. We have many relatives here, and since I have enrolled in the local university, my father is anxious for us to get suitable lodgings in town." She was amazed at the ease and speed with which the lies sprang fourth.

"Very considerate man, your father," said the doorman. "We'll be honored to have you in our building."

Then the old man pulled a key out of his *gallabiyeh* and opened the door of the apartment.

Aisha was overwhelmed. Her heart kept pounding crazily. Like a robot she walked through the reception hall, the bedrooms, the kitchen and bathroom, glancing at furniture without seeing anything. Details made no difference. Everything was more than they ever had. She paid the man twenty pounds for two months rent. He promised to have a receipt the next day and handed her two sets of keys.

"*Mabrouk!*" he wished her. "With good health."

She felt so happy just then she could have kissed the old man. But she restrained herself. *Rich people did not demonstrate their emotions so eagerly, so freely. It wasn't proper, nor civilized.*

"Thank you," she said, calmly. "We'll see you tomorrow."

She had not walked far from the building's entrance when she heard hurried steps. She froze. *If he's changed his mind, I'll kill him!*

She whirled to face an elderly woman in rags, holding an infant in one arm and an empty can in the other. The face of the child was covered with dirt and flies.

"Is anything wrong?" Aisha asked unnecessarily, for anyone could see the woman was a beggar.

"*Baksheesh* kind lady! In the name of God, the Compassionate, the Merciful. A tiny help to feed my starving sick child. He's dying from hunger. Please, lady."

This was the first time anyone had begged Aisha for alms! She dropped some money in the can and hurried home.

The following day she returned with her mother. As soon as they entered the apartment, they closed the door and started the grand tour of the place. Everywhere about were evidences of comfort and taste. Beautiful mosaic floors, carved oak furniture and a velvet sofa in the entrance hall. Modest but comfortable bedrooms, carved chests, full-length mirrored closets, electricity at the touch of a switch, running water. It was obvious the previous owners were well-bred.

When the inspection was over, her mother gasped and turned paste-white. "By the Mighty Allah! I've never, never as much as dared dream of so much," she stammered, shaking her head slowly, genuinely stunned. "I'm afraid it's all a dream!"

Aisha laughed. "Then we both have the same dream, and at the same time."

Her mother looked around the living room for something to sit on but changed her mind. "Not in here — not just yet," she said. "I'd rather go to the kitchen and use the wooden chairs until I get used to the idea that the furniture is ours."

Aisha followed her. Zakiya sat slumped low, as though every muscle in her body were tired. "I've never realized how little we had before," she whispered as tears ran down her cheeks freely.

Aisha felt nearly as shaken as her mother appeared to be, but a strange sense of well-being deluged her heart and body.

CHAPTER IX

In the dressing room, she painted her lips with deep red lipstick and put some silver glow on her eyelids. Bob was in town on leave and she wanted to look her best. He was waiting at the bar.

During the last two years at the cabaret, she had met a lot of men. Some were interesting and kind. Others were ugly beasts; a few she liked more than others. For her, these foreigners were like passengers riding a train, and she thought of them as tourists, like the ones she used to see in the train that came through her village. She knew and accepted this. Then why was it that she felt different with Bob? Why was she so happy to see him again, after months of absence?

Earlier that evening, Bob had said he loved her. He even said he wanted to marry her! Of course, she said it was impossible. It was crazy even to think of her mother and herself living in England, among foreigners who considered them uncivilized.

She reminded him of their Arabic proverb which said, 'Every lion is roaring in his own forest.' Yet she couldn't help the way she felt.

Bob respected her and treated her with the utmost courtesy and kindness. In fact, he seemed to regard her as an equal, with dignity and genuine affection, and this threw her into confusion more than anything else. Confidence swept through her heart, knowing such a man was attracted to her gave her a gratifying feeling, a feeling she liked, she realized, as she gave a last stroke on her hair and left the dressing room.

When Bob saw her, he stood up and held the chair. "Did you become that beautiful for me?" he asked with admiration. "I know exactly how Anthony must have felt about Cleopatra."

"Who are they?"

Bob smiled. "Oh, two of the greatest lovers who lived, loved and died in this very city. Let's drink to their memory." He raised his glass.

"Was Anthony like you? Did he come from far away?"

"Yes, in a way he was. Anthony was a soldier, too, and came from far, fell in love with the city and a beautiful woman, just like you, I'm sure, and surrendered forever. In fact, I believe, Anthony never returned to his homeland."

Aisha laughed. "Oh, I don't like that story. It's so sad."

He remained serious. "Darling, I've only got a few more days in town and then I'll be going back. Back to the empty, hot desert, living from day to day and hoping to return all in one piece to marry you. Why can't we take advantage of the short time we have together?" His hands reached out and held hers. "Tell me why, Aisha."

"Bob, you don't understand," she said as she fingered the stem of her glass.

"Is it because it's customary for an Arab girl to be a virgin when she marries?"

His frank remark startled her. "No," she whispered as she tried to understand her own feelings. Was it love she felt for Bob or only a strong physical attraction, she asked herself utterly confused? What would be like to be loved by a man like Bob — Aisha tried to imagine it and could not.

"Aisha, I love you. I love you more than I ever loved anyone before. Please don't put me off." His voice was becoming hoarse with desire.

She felt a sudden, strange leap of sympathy for him, a leap that made her lose her balance.

He spoke again. "When you look at me with your big velvety eyes, I have a feeling you look beyond me, far beyond, into my soul. Can't you see what's in my heart?"

They remained silent for a while, eyes shining with love and bodies taut with desire. Then he took her hand into his. She felt his warmth and strength flooding her.

"I want to make you happy, Aisha. Life is so short, so absurd — couldn't we try, at least?" he asked, fixing his eyes on her with almost hypnotic power and sending shivers out that seemed to stir in her womb.

She looked up at him and nodded her head.

"Is that yes or no?"

"Give me some time Bob, and I'll let you know."

But time was a luxury no one could afford or plan on it. To her sorrow Bob Armstrong never came back. He was killed just before the Afrika Korps laid down their arms in Tunisia.

From then on, the remaining years of the war had no special meaning for Aisha. They came and went like clouds in the sky, chasing one another, except for two major events which remained etched in her memory to haunt her. One was the untimely loss of her kind friend Bob, her English gentleman as she called him, and the other, the memory of the incident in the taxi the night she almost died in the hands of the abusive soldier.

People slowly became aware that the war had begun to ebb. Prisoners were released. The refugees and the exiled troops that had gathered in the Middle East started returning to their native lands. Uniforms in Alexandria became less abundant. Only the British seemed to have taken roots. Life for most citizens began to return to normal. It was as if Alexandria were recovering its past pleasures.

Once again, social life was flowering. The beautiful city turned in full swing to her prewar glamorous night life. Dancers and diners thronged the elegant nightclubs. Under the starry skies, San Stefano, The Ship, Auberge Bleu, and Romance echoed with soft, languorous music, warmly lit by candlelight, while beggars outside the main doors sold jasmine wreaths to the elegant ladies.

The military clubs closed as fast as they had opened. But Aisha had more offers for work than she could ever fulfill. By then, her reputation as a dancer had soared. There were nights that she made three routine performances in three different nightclubs. And for appearing at private parties, she could demand as much as five hundred pounds and receive it.

Nightclub patrons, she observed, all had one thing in common: money. Elegant men and women wore fashionable clothes, laughed, and drank champagne and Metaxa brandy. They talked about the good old days, the native unrest, the government scandals. They laughed and compared ways of smuggling or investing their money overseas. They lined up carefree vacations in foreign lands, and schemed in pursuit of a beautiful, peaceful tomorrow with the certainty of the past.

And there were the nouveau riche who invaded the old established circle and were uncertain of themselves, so they spent more money, doubly anxious to appear refined and show they had what it took. They, too, seemed annoyed, and talked about the inconvenient changes in the natives' ways. As anyone could see, there had been a noticeable change in the attitudes of the natives.

"It's no longer a functional disorder but a semantic maladjustment, increasingly dissociating things from signs and action from reality," as an eminent Egyptian Pasha explained to Aisha one night, clinking the ice in his tall glass. "These natives can become a serious nuisance, if not controlled," he had remarked and his elegant entourage wholeheartedly agreed, as if they had nothing in common with the *natives* they were talking about.

Eventually Aisha came to realize that, lurking underneath the glittering facade of the gay night life of wealth and beauty, there was still the wretchedness of the masses that seethed.

No sooner did the war end than the Egyptian people began to revolt, each class motivated by its own aspirations against the central symbol of all its ills and grievances — British domination. For most Egyptians, the British army was the embodiment of their own weakness.

As part of the hangover from the war, the natives now remembered and talked of their oppression. The British had held down all their Egyptian aspirations since 1882, and now, at the end of the war, Egypt was still occupied. As a result, there were violent clashes between demonstrators and the police, sometimes between the British army and the students who formed a common front with the workers. There were mass arrests and more violence.

In the university and in the streets, there were frequent clashes between Wafdists and their political adversaries. The Muslim Brothers, in their hatred of Marxists and unbelievers, provoked brawls. Parties formed alliances and played a secret part in the violence, and every politician and the Palace dreamed of leading the crowd.

But the aristocrats looked to the past and their semifeudal privileges. Their sole response to the people's grievances was brutal repression, and they could not imagine Egypt without British protection. The staunchest supporters were the big landowners of Turkish origin, the Palace and its entourage, who were often unfamiliar with the Arab language. But they controlled important business interests in the cities and the plantations in the countryside.

There were also the Egyptian landed proprietors who opposed the Palace aristocracy of Turkish origin, but resisted any measures that might undermine their status as big landowners. And there was another class of aristocrats committed to urban investment, with close ties to the Misr Bank and the Federation of Egyptian Industry controlled by foreign capital. Meantime, two-thirds of the peasants were unemployed and victimized by the most brutal pressures.

The peasants' miserable existence had driven many, like Aisha and her mother, to the cities. But most of them never found work. In general, their situation was somewhat better than it had been in the countryside. The city offered more opportunities for untrained workers in the lowliest jobs. But they still faced essentially the same conditions of insecurity that drove them from the countryside. They were no longer country people, but were not able to become a part of urban life either.

Most Egyptians never knew what was happening in their own country. But after the victory of El Alamein, the British censorship was somewhat relaxed. Radio was available to almost everybody and more natives could read a newspaper so the news traveled fast. The influence on the people was greater than ever before. Young Arabs came to regard the British uniform with increasingly undisguised revulsion.

They all came to read in the *Akhbar al-Yawm* in 1945 about a three-year-old incident which only then the paper was able to bring to light. The impact was profound, and in view of the events which followed, it emerged as one of the crucial incidents in contemporary Egyptian history.

It seems that on February 1, 1942, a few days after Bengazi had been retaken by the Germans, students in Cairo had demonstrated in favor of Ali Maher, a leading anti-British politician. The cry went up: "Rommel! Rommel!"

The next day, King Farouk dismissed the pro-British government, which had broken diplomatic relations with Vichy France at the request of the British Embassy, without even bothering to consult the king.

On February 3, before King Farouk had time to consult with anyone on the formation of a new government, Sir Miles Lampson, the British Ambassador, decided to call on Farouk at Abdin Palace. Lampson arrived, followed by General Stone, with a squadron of tanks and armored cars, and surrounded the Royal Palace. The Ambassador stormed into the palace with several South African officers carrying pistols.

When a court official approached them and asked them to wait until they were announced, Lampson brushed the man aside saying, "I know my way," and walked straight into the king's study to present him with an ultimatum: Farouk could either appoint a man the British then trusted as Prime Minister within twenty-four hours, or lose his throne.

Lampson gave the Egyptian King the choice of signing either of the two documents that he handed him. One proclaimed King Farouk's abdication, the other the appointment of a new prime minister. Virtually a prisoner in his own palace, the king played an obscure role for the rest of the war.

When the story broke in the press three years later, the impression of the whole sinister affair on the peoples' minds was all the more damaging for being retroactive. In a strange way, and for the first time, all the natives agreed: the country was sick.

Aisha saw and heard it all and lived with it day by day, until she began to dread what might happen next. She felt the earth beneath their feet was uneasy. This was a haunted, suffering land, she realized, and she felt lost and angry.

By Allah, she thought despairingly. For years and years they lived and survived, and now, just as she was getting ahead and was finally in a position to earn a living, it seemed that everyone around her plotted and contrived and took steps to change things. *Couldn't they wait at least until she had stashed enough money and bought some property or land so that she could feel more secure?*

But patience was not the prevailing mood. Riots, clashes, and demonstrations became frequent in the capital, in Alexandria, and in the larger provincial towns. Then on Thursday, February 21, 1946, a demonstration broke out in Cairo and the popular slogan in favor of evacuation, *gala*, was heard everywhere.

"No more partisanship. All parties must unite."

That day, the crowd attacked a British armored car which in retaliation opened fire indiscriminately. A pitched battle took place on the Gizeh Bridge, where twenty students were mowed down by machine guns and a hundred were injured. The victims were given martyrs' funeral, and collective resentment was roused to the breaking point. Then on the morning of March 4, the terrified citizens of Alexandria witnessed the native fury as they had never seen it before.

It was a beautiful day without a flaw. The brilliant sunshine, the light breeze, the fluttering sails on the horizon, the radio from the corner café blared — everything was breathtaking and normal.

Aisha was leaning on the balcony rail when a clatter and a faint volley of shouts from somewhere around the square startled her. At the end of the street appeared a procession of hundreds and hundreds of people shouting, *"Gala!"*

"What on earth's that?" Zakiya asked from the door.

"They're out screaming again."

Immediately the streets below and the park became deserted. Everyone ran for cover. Slowly but steadily, the huge mob of demonstrators advanced armed with stones, knives, and clubs, waving their weapons in the air, yelling *"Gala."* They weaved their way through the square and came to a halt in front of the police kiosk with the Union Jack floating.

"Down with England!" cheered the hysterical mob. "Revenge for our brothers!"

"The fools," Aisha said disgustedly. "What can they do? Before they know it, there'll be an armored car, and they'll scatter like flies."

Her mother shook her head. "The camel has his projects, and the camel driver has his projects, too."

"What do you mean?"

"I mean that the interests of the government and the governed are never alike. These are angry men."

"Out, out!" they bellowed, rushing forward.

Shots were fired. Instantly the mob surged onto the kiosk.

More shots, screams, panic, chaos and then smoke. The scent of gasoline, burning wood, and charred flesh, pierced the air. A sudden darkness fell. Then, like a ball of lightning, the flames went licking up the wooden frame of the kiosk.

For a split second, the rioters stood and gazed at the bonfire, then they cheered and burst into peals of laughter. "Bravo!" came the cries of approval and relief.

"The police!" roared the crowd.

Zakiya gave a gasp of dismay. "Oh God!" she cried, "Oh, no!"

"Kill them!" shouted the thousands thronging the square.

Aisha saw the woman in the next flat cross herself, then dry her eyes.

"Why?" she asked, beating her fist against the wall. "Why?"

Her mother shook her head. "These are hard questions, my dear. There aren't easy answers."

In the distance, they heard the sirens of ambulances and more police cars. The swarm of ravens started to disperse, leaving behind the dead and injured, sprawled around the gutted kiosk. Fear gave a nightmarish cast to the whole scene. It couldn't be real, Aisha thought. Or if it were, then her people had gone mad.

She felt sick and weak. The world began to whirl and rock dizzily. A buzzing sound in her ears drowned out every other sound, and abruptly it was dark. She felt her mother's strong hands holding her, keeping her from falling.

"I'll be all right," she reassured her mother, and she sat on a chair.

She remained for a while longer observing the scene. Eventually the wounded and the dead were picked up and loaded into the ambulances. Left on the ground was a heap of rubble, twisted iron, brick debris, puddles of blood and dirt, and ruins which continued to smoke.

"Lunch is ready," Zakiya said from the door.

Later in the news, they learned that the demonstration ended with thirty dead, including two Englishmen, and 350 injured. That night at the Casino San Stefano, Aisha was having a cup of coffee in her dressing room before the show. Her door was partly opened when a man thrust his head, "Hi, Aisha."

She recognized him as a member of the European orchestra that played there. "Hi!" she said, and waved.

He cleared his throat. "How did you like today's messy affair?" he asked.

She realized he was talking about the bloody demonstration. "Lots of fun, eh?" she said with sarcasm.

He stared down at her in wonderment. Then he dismissed

the matter with a shrug. "Things will get worse before they get any better. But I didn't come to talk about that." He hesitated.

"What's on your mind?"

"Well, I was asked to find out if you're interested in making some money — on the side, that is."

"Isn't everybody?" She felt amused.

He glanced around evasively with a curious look of anxiety. She laughed. "By sleeping with a Pasha —"

He shook his head.

"I know," she said, keeping up with the guessing game. "Smuggling drugs."

"Oh, no!" He seemed horrified at the thought.

She looked up at him rather numbly. "No?"

He shook his head again. "Nothing dangerous," he said. "It's information they want," and with an abrupt movement of his hand, he wiped the sweat off his brow.

"Who? What information are you talking about?"

He caught her look and grinned, unabashed. "You have powerful connections. In your profession, you get to meet and talk with the big and the influential. You hear all kinds of information. Just information . . ." A mocking smile curled the corners of his mouth.

"Who wants this . . . information?"

A gleam of surprise in his eyes showed that he had expected her to react differently. He took courage. "The British Intelligence. The Secret Service."

She swallowed hard and tried to drown her anguish. "Is that what you're doing on the side?"

"Not me! I have no contacts. Hell, I don't know the kind of people you do. I wish I did, though. They pay well. The whole country is crawling with spies these days. Every party has its own — the British, the palace, the politicians," he said, amused satisfaction on his face.

She looked at him. He was old and skinny and looked emaciated. Anger on him was a waste, she thought.

"Get out of here, friend," she said calmly at first. Then her heart began to swell with anger that she could not control. "Scram! Get the hell out or I'll claw your eyes from their sockets. Get out!"

He leapt backwards. Fright was written all over his face. He drew in his breath, "Sorry I've mentioned it." He looked at her beseechingly, a tired, pudgy man with a wrinkled brow and worried eyes.

"You're not a man," she said. "You're a worm!" and she spat at his face, missing him by an inch.

He swung, incredulity and anger on his face, and left, slamming the door violently behind him. She heard his hurried steps move away.

In the suspended silence, she recalled the dead Arabs in their white *gallabiyeh* as they lay lifeless on the street near the smoking ruins of the kiosk and the wounded policemen and others who wailed from pain and shuddered. She was frightened. Was there any hope left? If so, where?

There was a rap at the door. "Miss Aisha, your number comes up in ten minutes," said a man's voice.

"I'll be ready," she said, and began to undress.

CHAPTER X

The first autumn breeze brought an end to the long summer. Everyone who was able began to relocate to winter quarters in Cairo.

The king moved to his winter palace. The government officials and the civil servants followed suit, so did the foreign embassies and the throngs of tourists who came from the four corners of the earth. They were all drawn to the winter capital, and with them went the swinging elite crowd of the champagne parties and the night life of Alexandria.

Aisha had been offered two contracts for work. One was for occasional appearances at the Badi'a Casino, which presented every sort of show, from the Parisian Can-Can dancers to the *danse du ventre,* her specialty. The other offer was from the famous Semiramis night club, which fed and entertained the cream of society of the capital.

After she discussed things with her mother, they decided it made no sense to let the apartment in Alexandria go when they would be moving back and forth. More than that, they liked the idea of knowing they had a place of their own, a home to return to any time they wanted. Besides, they could afford it now.

When all the packing was done and she looked around at

the empty, gaping drawers and cupboards, she felt sad. They had been happy there. This had been their first decent home. Here, for the first time, they had discovered so many simple pleasures of life, like the luxury of a real bed, the comfort of an ordinary table and chairs, and the indescribable pleasure of having running water at the tips of one's fingers.

Aisha lit a cigarette and went out on the balcony. Nothing had changed much through the years. The park was animated as always with the playful children who screamed, the café radio that blared, the old men who dozed off on the benches. Except for the military kiosk, everything else remained the same.

The remembrance of that dreadful day of destruction and death returned in vivid colors. Momentarily she had a nauseated feeling. Then the nausea passed and the scene faded.

"We're all set," called her mother, showing their brand new luggage that stood ready in the hallway. There was a knock at the door.

"It must be the taxi driver," Zakiya said.

Waiting was Hassan who faithfully drove Aisha home safely since the night of their close brush with death.

Aisha handed him an envelope. "There is enough money in here to buy your own taxi and gain your independence," she said and hugged the young man. And she thought, the only reason she was still alive was because of him.

"Allah bless you," he whispered chocked with emotion. "You're most generous." After he placed the envelope in his pocket, he picked up the suitcases and they were on their way.

By one o'clock that September day of 1947, they left Alexandria aboard an air-conditioned sleeper bus. Seven years had gone by since the day they had arrived like beggars with bundles in their hands, Aisha reflected, as the express devoured the miles.

She smoothed the skirt of her new tweed suit. Completing her chic attire were grey high-heel shoes, a grey beret slightly tilted to the left, and a belt with three thousand pounds hidden in the frame of the buckle.

Her mother saw her and instinctively brought her hand up to her belt. Her eyes smiled reassuringly, then she winked happily.

The story behind the buckles made her smile. It started when they began preparations for the move to Cairo and found themselves suddenly faced with the predicament of how to carry and transfer their savings which, to their surprise, amounted to five thousand pounds, and which, up to that day, had been hoarded all over the house, here and there.

Since they trusted neither banks nor men, they found themselves in a rather tight spot. As the days passed, they became frantic and began to stay up all hours of the night, trying to find a solution. Aisha realized that, once again, like so many times in the past, they were faced with a serious monetary problem, the difference being that this time their difficulty was having more money than they could carry, a pleasant kind of problem but nevertheless a serious one.

One night, in desperation, Aisha asked a wealthy Syrian who frequented the club for smuggling pointers. She had been told he was an expert.

The man laughed when he heard her troubles. "First thing," he said, "you must change your money into big bills, like fifties, hundreds, or thousand-pound bills. The bigger the note, the better it is, and you can do that at the bank. I assure you it's all right. Then, it's a matter of choice and where you want to sew your treasure — your lapels, inside the collar or the hem of a dress, or you can stuff your shoulder pads! The way they pad the shoulders of womens' suits today, the more padding the more fashionable they are. What you need is an expert who'll do it while you watch, and the job is done."

Aisha's first instinct was for the shoulder pads, but Zakiya rejected the idea for fear they might take off the jackets somewhere. After a brainstorm session which lasted till the early morning hours, they finally settled to go with the buckles. It took five slim papers to fill both frames, and they had no worry of having their purses snatched from their hands or forgetting their jackets somewhere.

The city now was behind them, and they were traveling fast on the narrow asphalt road that was surrounded by sand. Slender palms stood out against the intense blue of the sky and the plain sandy land stretched away, mile after mile of yellow and purple nothingness. From time to time they could see a group of native dwellings made of sunbaked clay, small square buildings in the middle of the wilderness and yet so close to civilization.

She remembered their village, and she realized with sadness that no other people on earth endured the hardships their people did. Never enough to eat, never enough to cover their naked bodies, exposed to the heat in the summer and cold in the winter.

Her mother looked at her, guessed her thoughts, and smiled as Aisha slipped her hand around her buckle, caressing it smoothly, then leaning back and closing her eyes.

The memories of poverty and struggle had faded with time. Their previous life seemed so remote now that it was almost like a nightmare Aisha wanted to forget. Comfortably settled in the soft seat, she felt safe and warm. Poverty and danger didn't exist. Life was beautiful, and it was fine just to feel safe, comfortable, and happy.

It was just before sundown when they reached the city.

The glare of the desert day was gone and the soft red sunlight changed from purple to grey and yellow. Then it changed again to silvery blue, painting everything in the aquamarine twilight of Egypt.

As soon as the bus entered the capital, she was struck by the overwhelming size of the city, but immense as it was, it did not seem large enough to accommodate the terrifying jostling masses that overflowed its natural bounds and buildings.

Cairo had about four million inhabitants at that time and was the most densely populated city in Africa. The newspapers claimed that people were actually lost in it — some 2,000 men, women, and children each year.

Immediately they noticed another difference. Alexandria was really part of Europe, where Greek, French and Italian dominated the scene. Even the native hawkers advertised their wares in Greek: *"Patates, kala kolokythia!"* they chanted. But Cairo was Egypt. There were more Arabs who acted and lived like Arabs, and the majority spoke the native tongue. This was the place where East met West in the most striking way. It contained the ancient and the modern, the primitive and sophisticated, the social inequality alongside the modernistic and the backward.

It was late when they finally arrived at the depot, which was swarming with elegant incoming travelers and local beggars dressed in soiled white robes.

Cairo had a dry climate. They could feel the early winter air crisp and fresh. The natives now covered their necks with shawls, worn around the head like a turban, so that only their eyes and noses were visible. The porter found them a taxi and gave the driver the name of the hotel where Aisha had made reservations.

"The Shepherd's hotel is a grand and very expensive place,"

said the young Arab with sarcasm. "The millionaire foreigners go there." He grimaced as if he strongly disapproved of their extravagance.

They left the hotel half an hour later and took another taxi. "Drive us all over," Aisha said to the driver. "We want to see your beautiful city."

The old man smiled happily, pride on his face. "With pleasure, young lady." They leaned back on their seats, more confident now.

They passed by the Badi'a Casino where she was to perform on special occasions, the Hotel Continental, the Opera House, as the driver gave lengthy explanations.

They saw open cafés packed with backgammon players, huge squares, and business streets with large and small shops. They also noticed beautiful avenues with big, fashionable stores, elegant window displays, open-air ice-cream parlors, tea rooms, and art galleries.

From Abdin Square and the Palace, they reached the Citadel, known as the City of the Dead. Their expert guide pointed at the flag. "Finally the British evacuated the Citadel," he said.

"I guess to ease the pressure somewhat. The king himself came in state to hoist our flag. It was such a beautiful ceremony. It brought tears to my eyes."

They wandered over the Qasr el Nil bridge, from which he pointed out the dilapidated barracks that had housed foreign troops, recently evacuated. Close by were the government buildings and the Parliament House.

"How about stopping at a good restaurant?" Aisha asked. "We're starving."

"I know just the right place. It's not far from here and specializes in pigeons cooked on a charcoal open fire. The food is delicious!"

"That sounds just right," she said, and felt a sudden stab of hunger.

They reached the native restaurant. "Shall I wait for you in the cab?" asked the old man.

"Certainly no," Aisha said. "We want you to go in and have a complete dinner on us and send us the bill with the waiter. Then you'll take us back to the hotel."

The old man smiled. "God bless you. Thank you. You're most generous," he said.

She felt her mother's hand squeeze her arm. "I'm glad you thought of that," she said. "I'll enjoy more my food now, knowing he's not waiting hungry."

The place was fairly crowded. They saw the old driver choose a table by the door, as they entered and sat. The waiter came and took their order.

From the open charcoal grill, where the cook roasted the birds seasoned with herbs, came a cloud of smoke and the sweet aroma of oregano, thyme, garlic, and sesame. Soon, the food arrived — grilled pigeons split in half served on a mound of pilaf, a small dish with a *Hummus bi Tahina* sauce, cold beer, and a plate of sweetmeats.

Aisha cut a piece of bread and dipped it in the thin sauce. It was delicious. "You know they serve the *Tahina* dip as an hors d'oeuvre in the best restaurants," she said. "Most Europeans like it after they try it. How do we fix it? I should learn to prepare it."

"It's easy," her mother replied, her mouth full. "It's made of chick peas that have been cooked slowly in water until they're very soft. You strain them and either pound them or you put them through the food mill with a couple of cloves of garlic. Then you stir into the puree a cupful of *Tahina*, olive oil, lemon juice, some water, salt and pepper."

Zakiya stopped and returned to gnaw the pigeon's wing

stubbornly, as if determined not to leave a scrap of meat around it. Then with the back of her hand she wiped the juice that dripped from her mouth.

"When the dip is thick as mayonnaise," she continued, "you'll stir in about two tablespoons of dried or fresh mint. This is an Arab traditional dish and you should learn how to prepare it, Aisha," she said, as she rammed the last great lump of meat into her mouth.

The waiter brought them some coffee, and they attacked the sweetmeats.

On the way back through the bustling streets and squares of the Capital, the driver turned the radio on. The voice of Umm Kulssum, who was considered a national symbol and the golden voice of the Orient, filled their ears and made their hearts beat faster.

The driver's face relaxed. "Enjoying this?" he asked, with pride in his voice.

They nodded.

When they arrived back at the hotel, the man bade them goodnight and wished them happiness and good fortune at their path.

"We'll need that," Zakiya said. "May your days be long and happy, too."

In the lobby of the hotel, there was continual coming and going. Streams of foreign guests moved about, talked, laughed, rushed, or lounged in the comfortable chairs of the entrance hall.

It had been a long, exciting day for them, and they felt tired. Aisha bought a newspaper, and they headed for their room. She began to undress and her mother started to unpack, humming Umm Kulssum's tune.

Aisha slid into her robe, settled on the lounge chair beside the lamp, and opened the paper. Egypt's defeat at the

San Francisco meeting of the United National assembly and the partition of Palestine were displayed prominently. The article said that since Egypt was treated as a minor and semi-colonized country, the defeat was unavoidable. It went on to express a sense of injustice which was enough to whip up the Egyptians' anger.

She yawned and turned to the front page. She froze. The entire page, complete with photographs and big headlines, dealt with the story of cholera which had broken out in Egypt. According to the article, the rampant epidemic was ravaging the provinces, some close to Cairo. By a symbolic coincidence, the epidemic was similar to that of 1883, which followed the British Occupation.

She decided not to think about it just then and folded the paper carefully.

CHAPTER XI

Before the week was out, Aisha had started working at the Semiramis nightclub and had moved into a new home.

The house was a charming old villa with a small yard. It stood on the Gizah bank, not far from the university, in a quiet district tinged with Europeanism.

Meanwhile, the dead in the stricken villages mounted in the hundreds. The epidemic was taking its course.

Aisha did not have to tell her mother about the cholera. The radio did a good job informing them that the natives in the provinces and the small villages died like flies for lack of hygiene and medical facilities.

And her mother started to bring home preventive measures, all she could put her hands on. In fact, she brought so much that Aisha began to feel she lived in a fortress, equipped to protect them not only from the cholera, but evil eye, envy, moral and social evil, witchcraft, the plague itself.

Strings of blue beads, protective charms against this and other evils, red tassels, amulets made of camel's hair, water from the Nile that was believed to possess healing power and could remove all ill effects from the suffering, alum and wild herbs burned on and off, all these for personal protection.

To safeguard their new house, Zakiya hung the horns of a sheep over the doorway. An ear of corn went up, too, and various decorative plates of old carvings were plastered into the main entrance wall.

"And now that we've taken all the necessary precautions, let's go and get a shot," Aisha urged her. She had heard at work about the inoculation centers which were set about the city. Most Europeans took advantage of them, but her mother would not even consider going.

"Not me!" she refused firmly. "If it's *maktub,* I'll get the disease no matter what. If it's not, what business do I have to get the virus into my system?"

Aisha knew that once her mother's mind was made up, nothing could make her change, and since she was not sold on the idea herself, she gave in at the end. She only prayed and hoped her mother's charms did not fail to fulfill their expectations.

From the first night at work, Aisha noticed the elite class of privileged minority that frequented the nightclub. In contrast with Alexandria, where the affluent native clientele was very limited, Cairo had as many rich Egyptians as Europeans.

Judging from the prices the club charged on everything, the place was meant only for the ones who could afford such luxuries, keeping out the have-nots and unwanted. It was obvious that if life for the rich and fortunate was pleasant in Alexandria, with their summer villas where they entertained the mighty and the powerful, life in Cairo was just as pleasant.

It was her third night at work, and she was in her dressing room getting ready for the show. By this time she had accumulated a fabulous wardrobe of various outfits in which she performed. She was having a hard time making up her mind which one to use when she heard a timid knock at the door, almost like a light scratch.

"Come in," she said, wondering who it could be.

"It's me, Ali," said a young boy smiling from the door.

She recognized the young fellow. He was about fifteen and she was told he shined shoes, ran errands, and lived on the generosity and tips of those who used his services.

"I don't think I'm due on the floor yet, Ali," she said. "I can still hear the French canary singing."

He laughed. "Oh, no. It's early for you, Miss Aisha. I just came to tell you how nice you are, and how kindly you treat all of us servants, and also ... well, to remind you that I'm available for all kinds of errands. I do a good job, and I'm fast." As he spoke, he twisted a ring back and forth on his finger.

"Thank you, Ali," she said, sensing that he had not come just to tell her that. "I'm touched to know of your feelings towards me." She tried to guess what the young man had in mind, but could not. From the mirror she saw him rub his hands in embarrassment as he stood in the middle of the dressing room. She waited for a second, then asked.

"What's in your mind, young man?"

"I was just thinking, you're new in town, and well, I was wondering if you need a servant to help around the house."

"Not you?"

"No, *Yia sitt,*" he said, avoiding looking at her. "It's my cousin, my aunt's younger child. When her mother died a year ago, my aunt that is, the four girls were placed in homes to work. But this little one —"

"The little one is giving trouble?"

"I'll be darned if I know. She was working in a good, wealthy home, but she ran away, and she doesn't want to stay with them. We're five children at home and my mother is sick, so

I thought I'd ask you." His voice had suddenly become deep, his eyes somber.

"I never thought of having a servant, Ali, but mother is getting old." And suddenly she realized that perhaps a girl could be good company for her mother. As for herself, she would feel less guilty for leaving Zakiya so much by herself. "Why don't you bring your cousin around the house, say around noon tomorrow? Let me look at the girl, and I'll think of something."

The boy's eyes opened. "Oh, I'm so grateful! I'll be there at eleven." His face beamed with happiness as he placed his palm to breast, mouth and forehead. "Thank you, Miss Aisha."

As she finished explaining how he could get to the house, she heard the band play the last part of the French song and she rushed to finish her makeup.

After the performance, Ali returned to the dressing room.

"Miss Aisha, Mr. Robert is out waiting to see you," he said with as much excitement as if he were announcing that the king of Egypt was there.

She turned to face Ali. "Who is Mr. Robert?"

Ali's eyes flared. "Oh, he's a big newspaperman. Very rich, very handsome. Everybody knows Mr. Robert Fawzi!"

Everybody but she apparently, she thought as she hurried out to meet him.

"Oh, hello," he said, bowing slightly, a glass in his hand. "You were *magnifique!* Even the women enjoyed your dancing, which tells a lot." Robert Fawzi's eyes ran up and down Aisha's figure in such a way that she felt unclothed.

"Please, allow me." He led her to a table, stopping on the way to shake a hand, exchange greetings, and pat a friend on the back. Like Ali said, everybody knew Mr. Robert. She could see right away he was good-looking, and conceited.

After they were seated, he ordered two drinks and introduced himself. Then they exchanged the meaningless pleasantries suitable to the time and place.

As she looked at him, she figured he was somewhere in his forties. His black hair was striated by a few strands of grey. His eyes were bold, with an air of insolence, and he looked at women as if he owned them. Yet, when he smiled, he had the most indisputable charm any man possessed.

Robert was a dashing figure, the type that people, especially women, turned to look at. On top of that, he appeared wealthy and spent his money freely. His clothes were the best that Western style and tailoring had to offer, and he wore them with a natural, elegant air, as if he had done so all his life.

He talked with ease as if his life was an open book, and before long she found out that he was a journalist, and he had everything going for him. Born of a Syrian father and Egyptian mother, he was reared in Egypt and was educated in the best private schools. He knew everyone worth knowing and covered the social scene of the capital, which was a natural job that required no great effort on his part. Married and divorced, he appeared now to have neither illusions nor faith in matrimonial ties. "I'm a man free of bonds and ties," he explained.

She decided he was impossible. She knew she should have nothing more to do with him. Yet, there was something very exciting about him, something different from any man she had known.

"You of all people, as a journalist, must really know what's going on these days? Do tell me what's happening? Cholera, riots, fights ..."

His face lit up. "Does anyone really know? Egypt is sick. I don't mean the epidemic, but a more deep-seated illness — the decay of hope, the wastage of action. No one seems to know what direction to take, no clear-cut objectives."

"But they seem to know what they want. People scream for evacuation, no?"

There was a look of incredulity in his eyes. He quaffed the glass of champagne and gave a smack of his lips.

"Yes, orators and insurgents scream, and the rest of the idiots rise up in arms. They kill themselves, and they don't even know the reason why. I'm telling you, we're heading in so many directions at the same time, it's pitiful. One party wants Evacuation and Unity of the Nile Valley, while the king is fighting to get rid of the Wafd party and the anti-Wafdists. The students have formed a common front with the workers, striving for a revolutionary replacement of bourgeois legality. The prime minister's target is to fight communism, and suddenly every intellectual in the country has become a strong suspect."

He paused, took a sip and continued. "Before long, the minister is murdered. Others — let me tell you more — strong party leader, Nahhas, keeps reminding everyone that his British friends would deal with no other party than his own. But you're not really interested in this mess, are you?" he asked with bland mockery in his dark eyes that challenged her to get to know him better.

"And why not?"

"Ah, women!" he said with scorn. "Besides, you seem to have had an easy life. Aren't your parents filthy rich?"

"Why, no — " and she was just about to start her sad story when she noticed the cynical smile on the corner of his eyes, and she pulled herself together. "Not exactly. We've had enough to allow me to get a good education, you know."

He nodded. "I know, I know. So you left the soft cushions of home life and you want to try on your own, the hard way. You want to find out how it feels to be working, earning a living." He was so suave, so mocking, so sure of himself.

"Doesn't everyone?" She laughed. *Oh, my God. If you only knew the hell I've been through.*

He stared at her. "Yes, we're all swimming with the current. It's sad, though." He seemed preoccupied.

"What's sad?"

"I try to see things with objectivity, with a sense of logic or order, but it's not possible anymore."

He offered her a cigarette. She noticed it was imported and expensive. She took it. She felt she needed one.

Then, with her attention half on what he said, she asked, "Who's guilty for the whole damn situation?"

He gave her a charming, shrewd smile. "Who's guilty?"

She nodded. "Yes, who?"

"If you mean guilty for the urban violence, I'd like to know myself. The terrorists, the politicians, or the victims? Right here in the capital, bombs explode right and left. This past May, a bomb went off in the Metro cinema, killing five innocent spectators and injuring others. The courts can't even function anymore when they're having riots and demonstrations inside the courtroom!"

"I gather you disapprove of rioting?"

He gave a gasp of dismay. "Hell! I believe in non-violence, and I strongly decry such outrages." In a softer tone, he said, "Most men my age do, even though we believe in the true spirit of the 1919 Revolution."

"But the new young people don't trust their teachers any more, after a whole generation of failures." She had heard that comment at a Basha's party and threw it in now to impress him.

He gave her a narrow look through the curling smoke. "True. But even so, today's militant young lack the sense of order that distinguished their ancestors. Moreover, they don't have the necessary sense of direction for the success of any national movement."

He paused. "The waste of all this dynamic fighting is that there are no goals, no proper perspectives. It's sad because there are honest patriotic men who are sincere and try to help, but there are more scoundrels who, for selfish reasons and personal gain, exploit and aggravate the masses, bringing about anarchy and chaos." His expression became somber and a cynical half-smile touched one side of his mouth.

Then he stood up and frowned. "The truth is, you don't give a damn my dear, and I don't either. I really wonder if there's anyone in the whole country who does." And without asking if she cared to dance, he came around and helped her to her feet. "I like that tune. Let's try it."

Taking her by the arm, he guided her through the flower-decked tables to the crowded ballroom. The band played softly in the corner of the dimly lit room. They joined the thronging dancers, moving to the slow rhythm of the music. Robert's grip around her waist was firm, his steps sure and steady.

"You have a gorgeous figure, by Allah!" he said, and she felt his grip tightening. His eyes met hers and held there. A smile flickered over his lips. She met his look as steadily as she could.

"God's blood," he whispered. "Where were you hiding, girl?" He looked amused. His eyes shone.

In spite of her determination to keep cool and her vows to avoid him in the future, she felt excitement prickling up her spine.

CHAPTER XII

The next day, Ali arrived promptly at eleven, pulling his cousin by the hand. "Here she is," he announced happily, shoving the girl forward. "This is Fatma."

Dressed in a short soiled cotton dress, Fatma, who could not have been a day over six, came and stood in front of Aisha, taut with anxiety. Her round black eyes, which appeared enormous from fear, regarded her with uncertainty.

Stunned, Aisha turned to the boy. "You don't mean — she's the one who was working as a servant?"

"Why, yes," Ali said, perplexed.

Just then, Zakiya joined them from the kitchen. She opened her mouth as if to say something, but shut it again and sat on a chair. She just looked at the two children, nodding her head.

"Come here, child," Aisha said.

Fatma hesitated.

"Nobody's going to hurt you."

The young girl approached reluctantly and stood erect, keeping her distance.

She kept staring at the two women. Her curly dark hair was uncombed, her cheeks were pale, and her inflated abdomen made her spare limbs look like stumps. Her miniature hands and feet were painted in henna dye as high as the first joint of fingers and toes and the inside of her hands and soles.

Aisha raised her arm. Her intention was to touch Fatma's shoulder reassuringly to ease her fear.

Instinctively, the child's hands flashed up to her head and her eyes blinked with shock, as if she had received a blow. She remained covered a few seconds. When she realized no one was going to hit her, she peeked through her outstretched palms.

"I won't beat you," Aisha said softly. "I want to hold you closer."

The girl stared suspiciously but did not move.

"Did the others strike you on the head?"

She nodded. "All the time, until my nose bled. Sometimes it kept bleeding for long."

Aisha could not hold back her tears.

The girl saw her and her eyes flooded. She smiled. "You cry," she said and pointed her tiny finger at Aisha. Then, with a smile, she said, "Can I cry too?" The tears were already streaming from her eyes.

Aisha heard her mother sob, beating her cheeks. "Allah, have mercy on us," she mumbled. "Allah preserve us!"

Ali kept staring from one to the other, a sheepish grin on his face.

Aisha picked up the little girl and made her sit on her knees. "Why did they beat you, Fatma? Didn't you do your work well?"

For a minute the girl remained silent, just looking at her. "Well?"

"I did. I scrubbed the floors, I washed the dishes, and sometimes I helped with the clothes and did the shopping, too. I even learned how to bargain and save them money!"

"That's interesting. How did you do that?" Aisha asked, intrigued.

The girl spoke more confidently. "The lady I worked for always complained that people overcharged me at the market and I was stupid. So, I told the merchants the stuff I bought was for my family and we had no money and I'd cry a little. Many times they believed me and didn't charge me the full price."

"Why did you run away?"

The girl remained silent, her big eyes fixed on Aisha. She waited.

Ali spoke. "She stole a couple of things, the woman said." He talked as if he wished to bring the matter to an end without any further delay.

"I did not steal!" shouted the girl emphatically. "I was hungry."

Aisha's mother jumped to her feet. "Hungry?" she asked in dismay. "Didn't they feed you, child?"

Anger wiped out the fear from the girl's face. "Every time they had fish for supper they only gave me *fuul* to eat," she said sternly. "Nothing but beans. The fish smelled so good and I like fish, so I took a tiny one and ate it! And a couple of times I took some white bread and I ate it. That's not stealing, is it?"

The women remained silent, just looking at each other.

"I ate it," she continued in self-defense, "but the woman who counted the fishes beat me hard and kicked me out, screaming I was a thief. I'm not a thief! I never took anything, only food when I was hungry. A few times, maybe. Please, believe me." Her sobs echoed in the silent room.

It took a tremendous effort on Aisha's part to hold back her anger, rage, and fury, which at that moment had reached explosive proportions. Then realization, shock, and agitation settled in and left her tired. *If I could get my hands on that woman I could kill her without the slightest remorse.*

"We believe you, child," she said, holding Fatma's emaciated body. "Don't fret any more."

In her arms, the girl's tiny thin body seemed like that of a sparrow's. She felt the child's muscles tighten up like vibrating wires and her body stiffen. She stroked her hair and patted her back. The girl began to relax.

"How would you like to stay here, to live with mother and me?" Aisha asked.

For a second, the girl remained quite still, rigid. Then she leaped to her feet.

"You mean you want me?" she asked, her eyes as big as saucers, her chin quivering.

"We want you very much."

"Oh, yes!" she shouted. "I'll do anything ... I'll work hard, I'll scrub the floor! Please, don't let me go back to the others." Then she saw Zakiya's outstretched arms and ran to her.

"Poor child," she said with a tremor in her voice, hugging Fatma. "I know how hard they treat little slaves like you. I know too well." Her mother took a handkerchief out of her pocket and blew her nose loudly.

"Were they Europeans, the people she worked for?" Aisha asked Ali.

He shook his head. "They were Muslims. I guess that settles everything, no?" The boy exhaled with relief. "She sure was a burden on my hands."

Aisha assured him that he did not have to worry for Fatma any more and that he could come and visit her whenever he liked. She offered him some money to pay for their car fares. "Give the rest to your mother, to buy something for your little brothers," Aisha explained.

"No, *Yia Sitt.* Never! I'm your servant."

But she insisted. He thought it over for a second. "I'll never forget your kindness," he said and brought the money to his lips and his forehead as a sign of appreciation. "Allah bless you." Then he excused himself and left.

"I'll give her a good scrubbing," her mother said, and shook her head slowly, frowning. Then she raised her arms. "And may Allah see that those who treat little orphans unjustly swallow fire into their bellies and burn in the flames of Hell. Yes, burn in Hell!"

"I'm all for it, Aisha said. "Meantime, I'll go and get her some decent clothes and shoes. Come here, baby," Aisha called to Fatma. "Let's measure your feet."

She made her stand on a piece of paper, and with a pencil she marked the size of her foot.

"Don't buy her entire dowry today," her mother reminded her, as Aisha was going out the door.

In the evening, as Aisha was leaving for work, Fatma ran to kiss her. Dressed in a red-on-white cotton print dress with red ruffle trim, white shoes, and a satin red ribbon in her clean hair, she looked like a porcelain doll.

"How do I look?" she asked Aisha her eyes glittering like blazing coal.

Aisha opened her arms, and the girl threw herself in. "You're the most beautiful girl in the whole wide world."

She felt the girl's tiny arms tighten around her neck. She laughed openly now. Her fragile, weightless body quivered with excitement. As Aisha held her in her arms, she became aware of a strange wretchedness. *I'll kill anyone who tries to harm her again,* she vowed.

"Another one!" Ali said, smiling, as he poked his head through the dressing room door. His extended hand held a long-stemmed red rose. "This is the third, no?"

"Right. But if the man continues to send me roses and

then departs, I'll never get to meet him. Who is he, anyway? Are you sure it's not Mr. Robert?"

"But of course I'm sure it's not Mr. Robert!" He grinned. "This time the man has not left. He's still out there drinking. He's with a friend. Hurry."

Intrigued to meet her secret admirer who kept sending her a single red rose at a time, Aisha hurried out of the room. "Point him out to me," she said, hiding with Ali behind a curtain. "I'll be following close behind you."

"Oh, you can't miss him. He's an officer — "

"Police?" she asked, and stopped in her tracks.

"No! Army."

Both men rose when she reached the table where the two uniformed men sat. She noticed the one was younger and his tall, lean figure looked handsome in his officer's uniform. "Would you honor us for a drink?" asked the older of the two, of medium height, solid build. "I'm Ghalil," he said. "And this is Ibrahim."

They shook hands.

"Thank you for the lovely roses," she said, and looked at Ibrahim, hoping he was the sender.

"It's him all right," said Ghalil, shaking his head. "I used to send flowers to pretty girls myself. When I was single, that is. Now, with a wife and two grown sons, it's not the same, I guess."

Ibrahim made some polite remark to cover up his embarrassment. Ghalil was lighting a cigarette. Then he called the waiter and gave the order.

"Which army are you in?" Aisha asked casually.

The two men exchanged a bemused look. "Why, ours of course!" Ghalil said, eyes widened, watching her intently.

Ibrahim straightened his back and smiled grimly.

"Please, forgive my ignorance, but I didn't even think we had an army. I grew up at a small village near Assiut."

Ibrahim looked surprised. He explained that he, too, was a *fellah* and came from a small village in Upper Egypt. Later, he had gone to the Military College and now he was serving as a junior officer in the Frontier Corps.

Aisha watched him closely as he spoke. He had a pleasant voice and was remarkably good-looking. He had a fine oval face, black eyes deeply sunk, a straight nose that was rather thick, and beautiful teeth. Then she noticed a familiar habit that most men in her village had. As he spoke, he depressed his eyebrows, half-shutting his eyes, as if to protect them from too much sun. He's clever, she thought, those eyes don't go with stupidity. And stubborn, and wary. She wondered what problem he was keeping in his heart.

"What are you thinking?" asked Ghalil, who was trying to weigh her, just as she'd been measuring his friend.

"Well, I was just wondering — I mean, where was our army during the war?"

The two men exchanged glances of understanding and smiled. Then, unable to contain themselves, they burst out laughing.

She felt annoyed at first. Then she decided she wouldn't let herself get angry. "Well, I'm so happy to see you appreciate a good joke. No one seems to be laughing any more. We're all getting to be so darn serious these days."

Ghalil regained his composure. "We're not laughing at you," he said in a low voice. "But we laugh so we won't cry."

"Cry? Why?" she asked.

"Because it's truly sad. You touched a sensitive spot. But if you're interested, I'll be happy to tell you. Are you?"

"Sure, I'm curious. I live here, don't I?"

Ibrahim fidgeted on his chair. He twisted the stem of his glass, but he seemed content to let Ghalil, who was his senior, lead the discussion.

Ghalil carefully extinguished his cigarette. "When Churchill succeeded Chamberlain as Prime Minister of Great Britain, Churchill decided that Egypt should be completely subordinated to the British war machine. So, he began by neutralizing the Egyptian army."

"How?"

"Churchill ordered the Egyptian High Command to disarm and withdraw all Egyptian forces from Mersa Matruh in the Western Desert. At the time, Mersa Matruh was divided into three sectors, one held by the British and two held by two Egyptian divisions." Ghalil took a sip and lit another cigarette.

"On November 20th, 1940," he went on, "the Egyptian army was notified of the British demand, and we were ordered not only to evacuate our positions but to hand over our arms to the British. Our humiliation was shattering and complete. So, for the rest of the war, we sat on our arses and waited."

Ghalil called the waiter and ordered another round of drinks. He seemed cool and detached, but she sensed he had plenty of hidden emotion behind his quiet face.

Aisha turned to Ibrahim in dismay. "I didn't know — "

"Most people don't. Up to now, we avoided discussing our grievances and politics in general. But we believe now that it is our duty to inform the people."

As Ghalil looked from Ibrahim to her, he seemed to be making up his mind about something. "I'm sure you know of the famous incident of February 4th of 1942, of how the British ordered King Farouk to either appoint the Wafd leader Nahhas as prime minister or abdicate the throne. Don't you?"

She nodded. "I've read about it in the papers."

"Well, what you don't know is that this is the old British routine. Their formula always was to divide the people so they could rule. And I must say they've managed beautifully. By imposing upon Egypt two years of dictatorship with the Wafd party, they've helped the party bring in nepotism, bribery, abuses, and incompetence."

Ghalil seemed worried. His fingers played nervously with the glass. He was choosing his next words with care.

"We'll never forget the humiliation," he said, and held out both his hands. "And when the Axis was defeated and the British had no further use for Nahhas, they permitted the King to dismiss him in 1944. Meanwhile, careerists, traitors, and imperialists were and still are grabbing all they can."

"It's like trusting the key of the pigeon-house to the cat!" Aisha said.

Ibrahim smiled. "Funny that you should mention one of my father's favored proverbs. He used it a lot." He avoided looking at her.

"And my Uncle Youssef," she said.

She had a feeling that Ghalil was weighing his words very carefully, as if he wanted to tell her enough without telling too much.

He met her eyes and smiled. "I'm sorry I gave you a lecture, but I wanted you to have all the facts straight. I do want to add, however, that it does no good to blame everything on the British or the other people of the West. Neither does it do any good to blame such conditions on the character of the Egyptian people. The only relevant facts are that such conditions exist, and that we, the Egyptians, with or without foreign assistance, are the only people who can improve them."

She shrugged. "I really don't give a damn. I used to get so upset, I wanted to fight the whole wide world."

"What brought the change in you?" asked Ghalil.

Ibrahim spoke. "As soon as our bellies are full, we forget poverty and injustice —"

"Devil take me, it's not that. I simply believe that we're in such a deep mess that we'll never get out of it. It's chaos. Who do you fight? And for what?"

They were silent.

She glanced round the dimly lighted room. The nightclub was crowded now, cheerful and bustling. "There's only one thing that keeps me going, that gives me strength."

"What's that?" Ghalil asked. His eyebrows went up.

"I want enough security to feel safe. Money, land — land that no matter what will stay mine. I'll be safe then. Meantime, I tell myself, if the monkey reigns, dance before him." When she finished, she saw Robert sitting with another man at the bar. Their eyes met. She threw up her arm and smiled. He waved back.

Ibrahim looked startled. His face showed the shadow of embarrassment. His smile was still there, but it was less amused. She had the feeling he was annoyed. Or, could it be jealousy, she wondered?

His composure regained, he asked, "Friend of yours?"

She nodded.

Ibrahim bent to light her cigarette. In the yellow-orange flame, she noticed his eyes were sad. "So you don't care." His voice sounded hurt.

She did a desperate mental recap. "Why should I? What difference does it make who leads or who wears the crown of glory? No one gives a darn for the likes of me, the peasant, the *fellah* who goes hungry and dies for lack of food and medicine. The poor in this country are worse than animals. I've come too far to lose it all by asking for a stray bullet in my back."

Ghalil looked up in surprise. There was a sudden gleam in his eyes. "It all depends on what you die for!" He raised his glass. "Let's drink to our friendship and our country's welfare and prosperity."

She noticed both men became suddenly serious as their eyes met. She laughed. "That's something I'd like to see."

"The tree falls not at a single stroke!" said Ibrahim, and explained this was another of his father's favored proverb. "It takes patience."

Ghalil sighed and leaned back, finishing his drink. He glanced at his watch. "I must get going," he said, and rose.

Ibrahim offered to give him a ride, but Ghalil refused.

Then the two men exchanged a few hurried words that she could not hear. They shook hands. "I'll see you soon, I hope," Ghalil said. He smoothed down his trousers, pulled at his coat and was gone.

It was late, and most patrons had left. Aisha felt tired. She yawned and leaned her head on Ibrahim's shoulder closing her eyes.

"Can I drive you home? I have a friend's car," Ibrahim explained. "In fact, it'll be a pleasure."

They drove in silence. At the door of her house, he asked if she would like sometime to go for a ride with him. "You're new here, and you haven't seen much of our city. If you like, I could pick you up on your day off."

"I'd love that. I'll be off Monday."

"Bring your mother along too," he said.

"I will."

Later in bed, it struck her as odd that he knew she was new in town and that she lived with her mother, facts she was sure she had not mentioned during their conversation. It also occurred to her that when she gave him her home address, he had simply nodded and asked for no more details. He knew.

CHAPTER XIII

She glanced around the living room. Yes, she thought with satisfaction. It was a gracious room with elegant furniture and large windows that overlooked the front garden. Ibrahim would be impressed, she knew. She handed her mother a bunch of red roses and some yellow marigolds she had just cut. "Put these in a vase."

"A vase? We don't have one," she said with a start.

Aisha ran into the kitchen. "There!" she said and pointed at the earthen porous *kulleh* which kept their drinking water cool. "That'll do for now."

Her mother stared at her, then shrugged. She thrust the flowers into the water-jug, then went to the faucet, filled her mouth with water and started to spray the flowers.

Aisha laughed. "Where did you learn that trick?"

"I've seen the gardener next door do that a couple of times before he took cut flowers inside. Smart, eh?"

At eleven sharp, Ibrahim arrived in full uniform, a box of candy in his hands.

The minute Zakiya set eyes on him, she literally dissolved. She watched admiringly every expression that crossed his face and every gesture of his hands. Each word that he spoke overwhelmed her. Once or twice he turned and smiled at her and little Fatma, and their happiness soared.

Then her mother excused herself to prepare some coffee for their guest. The minute Aisha stepped into the kitchen, Zakiya grabbed her by the arm. "If you have any brains in your head, you won't let that man get away from you."

Aisha laughed.

"Go ahead and laugh all you want, but this man was born for you, Aisha."

"We hardly met him. How do you know?"

"I know. I'm your mother!" she said authoritatively, as if there was no argument when it came to that. "Look at him. He's a man, not a butter-ball. He's kneaded with hardships, just like you are. What you need, daughter, is a man with nerve, a man like him to keep you in line, not one you can push around like a puppet."

Her mother was not the only one to fall under his charm. Little Fatma was immediately infected, too. "He's so handsome and so nice, Aisha. Can we keep him here with us?" she asked as they were getting into the car Ibrahim had borrowed for the occasion. She promised Fatma she would think about it and Fatma seemed happy.

Ibrahim drove through the clogged streets of the ancient city, which in itself seemed a difficult task. Cars, trucks and donkey carts pried through the crowds, while men and women, carrying incredible weights on their heads, dodged and darted in every direction.

"This is the medieval part of the city," Ibrahim explained, as the car rolled through the better sections of the city, marked by wider streets and grassy parks. "There's a European Cairo, another side of Arabian Nights, and a Cairo of heavenly elegance and silver-service teas."

"How old is the city?" Aisha asked.

"Very old. It was built in A.D. 969 by Tunisia's Conqueror Jawhar, and was named *El Qahira*, the Victorious, which the

English pronounced as Cairo. Like so many other capitals, it has become overcrowded."

"Look! There's hanging room only!" Zakiya said, pointing at a battered old bus. Outriders hung from its open windows, doors, and fenders like grapes on a vine.

They laughed, seated comfortably in their private car.

"Tell us about the history of the city," Aisha urged.

"Well, following the line founded by the Kurdish conqueror Saladin, the Mamluks ruled Egypt from Cairo for 267 years. Then, in 1517, the Ottoman Turks stormed into the country, hanged the last Mamluk sultan, and nailed his body to one of the gates in the city wall."

"Allah, have mercy on us," Zakiya said.

"It all happened a long time ago," Aisha reminded her, and they all laughed. He was so cute when he laughed, which wasn't too often, she thought.

Her mother apologized. "I thought it happened now."

"Who was next in the conquering line?" Aisha asked. "I know so little. You see, at school they made me study French history instead."

"Guess what," Ibrahim said with light mockery in his voice. "Your friend, Monsieur Bonaparte, the Frenchie, was next. He came to Egypt in 1798, together with 55,000 troops and an armada of nearly 400 vessels —"

"What are these ... vessels?" Zakiya asked.

"Boats, mama. Ships. You know."

"Oh, yes, I know. We were there when they came. We saw them! Yes, haven't we, Aisha? Why don't you tell Ibrahim how they bombed the city every night with their vessels."

Ibrahim looked at Aisha who felt a wild fit of laughter about to seize her. He was just smiling, so she fought her laughter down.

"It's beautiful," he said. "It's just like being home and

listening to my mother. We should get those two together. They'll have a ball!" When he smiled that way, with all weariness gone from his face, his eyes relaxed, he was truly handsome, she thought.

"Go ahead, son, tell us more," Zakiya said.

"I forgot. Where was I?"

"With Bonaparte," Aisha reminded him.

"Ah, yes. Well, the French stayed for about three years. Up to 1882, Egypt had four rulers, all descendants of the Turk Mohammed Ali, who almost bankrupted the country to build a mosque of alabaster on the Muqattam Hills. We'll go by and look at it if you want."

"Yes, I'd love that," Aisha said.

"You do know when the British came, don't you?"

"Well, not exactly."

He went on. "In 1882, Egypt was weakened by internal strife, so the British marched right in and occupied the country." He frowned. "They came to protect their trade route to India. This was an overland route across Syria and Iraq to the Persian Gulf. To keep this route open and safe, the British backed the Ottoman Turks as rulers of the country, and in exchange for this, the Turks guaranteed the British right of transit."

"But didn't we have the canal?" Aisha asked.

"The digging of the Suez came later, and the British opposed it at first. But then Disraeli bought forty-four percent of company shares held by Egypt's spendthrift ruler, the Khedive Ismail. This began England's involvement in Egyptian politics for three-quarters of a century!"

He paused, lit a cigarette, and concentrated on the road. "You'll notice now that we're going through a different Cairo," he said, as the car rolled over the bridge and into the wider streets of a park-like island, Gezira.

Extending from the Nile banks and shaded by endless rows of palms, the imposing villas of the wealthy Europeans gave a viewer the impression of being suddenly somewhere in the gardens of Allah. Ibrahim explained that Gezira was joined to the mainland east and west by four bridges. Two of these opened at regular intervals to let the river craft through.

They drove by the Gezira Sporting Club, a 150-acre recreational jamboree of color, elegance, and perfume. Bougainvilleas, jasmine, roses all in full bloom surrounded the vast manicured turf of the polo fields, the tennis courts, and the swimming pools.

"Membership is for British and Europeans only," said Ibrahim grimly.

"You sure know your history," she said.

He laughed. "It's really ironic."

"What is?"

"I was first exposed to the political history of the Middle East while I was at Staff College, as part of military training. My instructors were British!" After a brief pause, "And now you'll see the Cairo of Arabian Nights. Every woman visitor wants to see the famous Khan el Khalili bazaar." The car left the island and headed toward the old part of the city. "It dates back to the late fourteenth century."

The bazaar was crowded with natives who came to buy essentials, and tourists who searched for treasures, bargains, and souvenirs. The temptations were all there, waiting for buyers.

They wandered through the alleyways, jostled by the human traffic. They heard radios blaring the latest twangy tunes, the sound of money-changers clinking coins, the shouts of the hawkers selling everything from gold to water brought down from Mecca, the arguing and the bargaining of sellers and buyers.

A hundred shops side by side competed for customers and offered everything from Oriental treasures to junk. Rich fabrics, satins, brocades, Persian rugs, leather belts, leather purses, suitcases, handcrafts, copper trays, jewelry, silver, gold by the ounce, by the piece, by the dozen.

They found spice shops with every herb from the four corners of the ancient world. The smell of burning frankincense, the aromatic fragrance of saffron, cinnamon, clove, ginger, cardamon, cumin, coriander, *kuzbarah* and the smell of freshly roasted coffee filled the air. A sweetmeat vendor kept the flies off his cart with a palm-leaf whisk.

Aisha bought a blue bead bracelet for Fatma, to ward off the evil eye, and a golden bracelet for her mother. In the silver shop, she purchased a lighter with the head of the beautiful Queen Nefertiti engraved on it, and a bracelet for herself with the head of Rameses II.

She gave Ibrahim the lighter. "For selfish reasons," she said. "Every time you'll be lighting a cigarette, you'll be thinking of me."

He seemed touched by the gesture. She showed him her Rameses. "And this will remind me of you."

His eyes sad, he smiled. "I bet you didn't know that Rameses' favorite consort was Nefertiti."

He was right. She did not know.

He bought Fatma and Aisha sugar dolls in colored paper clothes, and for Zakiya a miniature sugar horseman in bright costume.

The smell of the frying *Ta'amia* reminded them they were hungry. They stopped by the small shop that sold sandwiches made of *fuul* and *Ta'amia*. The *fuul*, the staple brown beans that the Egyptians thrived on, and the *Ta'amia,* small round patties, the size of a shilling, made of crushed haricot beans with parsley, green coriander, onions, and a teaspoon of bicarbonate of soda. Prepared like meatless meatballs and fried in hot oil, they were delicious.

When they left the shop, little Fatma could not walk any farther. She complained her feet ached. Ibrahim scooped her in his arms.

Aisha felt her mother squeezing her elbow. "See? He loves children." She winked at her suggestively.

They had seen more of the bazaar. Then they came across a fight. Two Arabs holding each other by the throat, their noses an inch apart, shouting at the top of their lungs.

"They'll kill themselves in broad sight and spoil a beautiful day for us!" said her mother, slapping her thighs.

A passer-by made a loud joke: "The tongue of the wise is in his heart, the tongue of a fool is in his arse."

The bystanders roared with laughter. Instantly both fighters relaxed their grip and started to laugh. The battle was over.

They returned to the car. "Next stop on our tour, dear ladies, is the Citadel," Ibrahim said, imitating the voice and manners of the tourist guides. "Are you ready?"

"As ready as we'll ever be," Zakiya said, holding her shoes in her hands.

"Mother!" Aisha screamed with embarrassment.

'They're new and they're killing my feet. I'll put them back after a while. Don't fret."

Ibrahim smiled. "Let her be. She's having so much fun."

Their next stop was the Citadel.

"Saladin ordered the Citadel to be built on a hill during the thirteenth century as part of the fortification of Cairo," explained Ibrahim as they entered a long, narrow street of the old city. Soon they found themselves in a courtyard completely overshadowed by the Mosque of Mohammed Ali.

"Tourists seldom miss a visit to the Mosque," he said, and

went on to explain that it was considered the most magnificent of all Mosques. The alabaster structure was surmounted by a large dome in the middle, with four smaller ones in each corner. Two slender minarets thrusting upward pierced the blue, clear sky.

They pulled soft slippers over their shoes before they entered the carpeted interior. A few men prayed on their knees in earnest meditation. There were warm, white alabaster walls, and hundreds of suspended lamps like myriad stars which flooded the void from above. They saw Mohammed Ali's tomb, next to the Minbar, a raised enclosed pulpit, golden-scrolled, where the Koran was read. The beauty was breathtaking.

It was late afternoon when they left the Mosque and walked on the outside parapet. The entire city was before them with its beauty and its sores extended below, encircled by the Nile, beyond which the pyramids glittered in the silvery haze that began to descend from the day's heat.

Aisha felt the deepest sadness for her country, the land that had its humble beginning before the birth of the Western civilization; the land of many wonders and more contradictions. In the foreground rose the minarets from the tombs of the Mamelukes, resting place of many rulers of Egypt, the City of the Dead, surrounded by the sprawling Muqattam Hills.

As she stood there gazing, the entire city seemed extremely distant, like a picture made of mist and fancy. Suddenly she felt overwhelmed with love and bitterness. Why was it, she wondered, that people had never learned to live together in peace. Was fighting the only way that life could renew itself and advance? But advance to what? Surely, there must be another way by which men could find justice.

A pair of doves sailed through the air and came to perch above the parapet, cooing.

Startled, she turned to find Ibrahim looking at her. She had forgotten he was there, but she was happy he was.

"Welcome back," he said.

"Nonsense!" She fought the desire to turn away.

He extended his hand. "Care for a cigarette?"

She nodded.

He came closer and struck a match. Then a second. "When I fill my new lighter, I'll have no use for these darn things."

"Look at them," he said, pointing.

Zakiya and Fatma sat on a rock, their shoes on one hand, the sugar dolls on the other, playing puppets. They saw the two approach and started to get their shoes on.

During the early afternoon rush hour, Aisha noticed squadrons of American sedans that jostled and honked. Strangely, the ear-splitting noise perturbed neither the bold-breed Cairo pedestrians nor the laden donkeys.

On the way back, they drove by Opera Square, which was set around the equestrian statue of Ibrahim Pasha. The street in front of Shepherd's Hotel had the usual hawkers in *gallabiyeh*, trying to sell their souvenirs to the tourists. On the hotel terrace, which was raised from the street, sipping their tea sat the wealthy travelers who came to mingle with the luxury-loving elite Egyptians.

They found a sidewalk café overlooking the magnificent square and ordered a *cassatta* ice cream.

"It is elegant inside," said Ibrahim, pointing to the Opera House. "Khedive Ismail built it with forced labor in less than six months, when the Suez Canal opened in 1869. Ismail commissioned Giuseppe Verde to write a work with an Egyptian theme, which gave birth to *Aida*. This was to entertain the French Empress Eugenie, who was his honored guest for the inauguration of the canal. Ismail, the big spender, had a road built from Cairo to the Pyramids so that Eugenie and the other notables like Emile Zola and Ibsen, among others, could visit the ancient monument in comfort!" Ibrahim explained this all in a low, sarcastic tone, rolling his eyes.

Overwhelmed by what she had seen and heard all day long and for no apparent reason Aisha started to laugh in brief little bursts of giggles. Her laughter infected the others. Soon little Fatma joined in, and then her mother, in a high-pitched giggling fit. In vain she tried to see the joke responsible for this sudden outburst. Then she realized it was the reaction to the nervous strain that had racked her all that day, searching for some kind of relief.

Ibrahim smiled. "Feeling better?"

She gave him a nod and a smile. "It was a memorable day."

"Oh, it was but a glimpse of the old city."

"No, my dear. It was more than what a tourist will ever see. It was an emotional, revealing experience. One I'll never forget. It showed me who I am and where I came from. Thank you ever so much."

There was a gleam in his dark eyes. For a moment or two they stared mutely at one another. Her hand went up. He held it and gently brought it to his lips. Then he looked away shyly and studied the traffic on the street.

CHAPTER XIV

Before long Aisha found herself deeply involved with both men. As different as Ibrahim and Robert were, they both seemed to share one thing: her.

They both visited the club where she worked, at their own pace and their own convenience. And yet it seemed that whenever she wanted them, they were never there.

Each resented the other. Ibrahim hinted that Robert Fawzi was an idle, rich playboy who never put in a day's work in his life, and Robert claimed that Ibrahim had a desk job and stayed in the army for security and the prestige that came with the uniform. And whereas Ibrahim felt unsure of himself and Aisha's feelings toward him, Robert was over-assured, over-confident, to the point of being impudent.

She knew Robert was a cynical rascal, but he courted and wooed her as she had not been courted before, with small gifts, flowers, and compliments. He could be as serious as a judge when dealing with business or political matters, but he could also be fun and full of laughter as if life was a great joyful game, which for him it probably was, a game to be fully enjoyed and savored.

And yet, for the life of her, Aisha could not feel the emotional attraction and connection she had felt from the beginning with Ibrahim. At times, she would get angy with Ibrahim and vow she would have nothing more to do with him. He was an enigma, buried behind an impenetrable wall she could not penetrate. Every time she missed Ibrahim, who did not show up for days at a time, and she felt lonesome and miserable, she ended in Robert's company.

"How long has it been this time since you've seen him?" Robert asked one night.

"Too long."

"He may have lost the address," he joked.

She was annoyed. "I don't have to talk about him with you," she said.

"No, you don't have to and I'd rather you didn't. Maybe he was promoted to a higher rank. Army promotions are passed out like candy these days."

She stared at him. "Robert Fawzi! I won't stand here and have my friend sneered at."

"Friend? I see. He loves you for your mind."

She was furious. "You have a lot of charm," she said. "But you also have a dirty mind. Why, there's never been anything wrong with us."

"Wrong?" his eyes opened. "I never said it was wrong, in which case, he's stupid or sick."

"Don't be so nasty. I don't like nasty men."

He gave her a narrow look through the curling smoke of his cigarette. Then he placed his hand on her wrist, speaking softly as one who had secrets to impart. "I like you, Aisha, and I like you mainly because you know what you want and you go after it by the shortest route. You're like me, in a way." He stopped, puffed on his cigarette. "On top of that, you're devilishly beautiful, very, very desirable," he said, and held her hands.

"Are you asking me to marry you?" she asked and laughed.

"By Allah, no! Didn't I tell you I was no marrying man?"

She jerked his hands away. "Let's keep our love pure then."

A mocking smile curled the corners of his mouth. "The mere thought of it scares the hell out of me. But there's always a first time for everything."

"You mean you don't believe in platonic friendship?"

He looked down at her. Then he put his hand under her chin and lifted her face. "Platonic? With you? Why, I'm only human, my dear, impossible girl. Damn you! You're a fool! It's like trying to quench one's thirst with salt!" he said, his eyes wide and blazing.

She thought of Ibrahim. Oh, how she had missed him this past month. His half-smile, his fiery eyes, the way he held her arm reassuringly, the way he kissed. And even though he had never said he loved her, somehow she knew he did, he had to, she wanted him to.

Robert bent as if to kiss her. He looked her straight in the eyes. She felt confused. "Damn you, Aisha," he whispered and moved back. "I honestly feel sorry for the poor bastard in the uniform, especially if he's in love with you, sugar doll." He looked disturbed, hurt and mocking. Then he clapped for the waiter and ordered.

She felt momentarily lost. Then she laughed. "My dear, what's bothering you?" she asked.

"You!"

"Oh, you're impossible! Give me a cigarette, please."

He took one out of a silver case and lit it. "And stop feeling sorry for yourself," he said. "Did you stop to think that the poor devil couldn't come, perhaps, because he might be out there fighting or helping or mourning for his dead friends who lost their lives in Falluga?"

The word Falluga sent chills in her. "But he didn't — I mean the army opposed the war."

"True, the high officers and the Prime Minister knew we had nothing to gain and much to lose in an open war. But the Muslin Brothers wanted field action and influenced the King for a *jihad*, a holy war."

She was aware that since the British had given up their Palestine Mandate in May 1948, Egypt's Nationalists regarded the newly created state as an open threat.

"But Egypt had nothing to gain," she repeated his words.

"Only as part of the Arab League," he said. "And of course, King Farouk saw this as an opportunity to back the demand of the popular party of Brotherhood and to shore up his fading popularity. So, he persuaded six other countries of the League to enter the war."

"What happened then?"

"Hell's fire!" he said with disgust. "We sent our men out there without supplies, no transportation and with defective arms, which our politicians bought cheap and sold to the army for a profit. Then at the height of the fighting, the Engineer Corps was ordered to build a villa for the King in Gaza, while our men took a beating with ammunition that either exploded in their hands or didn't fire at all! That's what happened."

"Oh, no!" she said and covered her mouth to suppress her scream.

"Oh, yes, dear."

"But we had a parade. We celebrated the return of the heroes from the war."

Robert raised his arms helplessly. "Yes, there was heroism in the siege of Falluga, where a small Egyptian unit was isolated and refused to give up. I know for a fact that a force of 150 men, led by a husky lieutenant-colonel, fought their way through enemy lines to bring relief. He was wounded, but his action encouraged the Falluga defenders to hang on till the Israeli-Egyptian armistice was signed."

She hesitated. "What's the name of the officer?" she asked and her heart pounded fast, her hands clenched tight.

"Gamal Abdel Nasser. It's not your man. I checked to make sure. I mean — I'm a reporter. I had to cover the story, so I met some of the officers. They're humiliated, sore as hell. I don't believe they'll ever forget the Palestine fiasco!"

She stared at him in utter disbelief. "So you did check. You rascal, I know why."

"Oh, God!" he whispered and turned his head away. "You try to trap me!"

"You fell into your own trap!"

He laughed and there was no mockery in his face. Just the free, exciting laugh that made him so appealing.

She held his hand. "Thank you, *cheri*," she said. "Thank you for checking."

He bent and kissed her hand. She was relieved to see his good humor return. A few seconds later, she decided it was a good time to bring up business.

"Did you also check on the property, as you promised you would?"

"Good God!" he cried. "Don't you ever think of anything but money and security?"

"No," she said frankly. "And if you'd been through what I have, you wouldn't either."

He shook his head as if to say how impossible, unbelievable she was. Then he sensed she was hurt. "I'm sorry," he said. "Yes, I checked. The Greek man who owns the building downtown will be happy to sell it to you, for anything you have to give him. He and his family are leaving for Australia."

"But it's a four-story building; it's worth more than I have to offer him."

"That's true, but all foreigners try to unload. They're liquidating what they've accumulated during a lifetime. They leave the country in droves. The exodus fever has gripped not only the enemy nationals, but every foreign community in Egypt. For any Egyptian with money, this is the chance of a lifetime to get anything at a bargain price."

"Are you buying?"

"Hell, no! What do I need more property for?"

"Would six thousand pounds be a fair offer?" she asked.

"Fair, no, but the man will be grateful to get it. Even if he gets more, he knows he can't get the money out of the country." Robert paused. "I feel sorry for the poor bastards. First the riots, then the abolition of the Mixed Courts, which restored a common law to which even Europeans would have to submit, and God knows what else."

He was silent for a while. She recalled the lovely Greek woman who made it possible for her to go to school. The thought that now in her old age she would have to leave and go to a new place to start all over again made her sad. Silently she offered her good wishes.

Robert guessed her thoughts. "Many older foreigners will remain in Egypt till they die. But they are sending their children abroad, first to study, then to live, and they do not urge them to return. You may not like me for what I'm about to tell you, Aisha, but Egypt for me is the way I knew the country growing up, with the foreigners and the cosmopolitan, romantic atmosphere I knew. I guess I'm not for drastic changes. I like improvements, but when it comes to major surgery, no." A smile flickered over his tired features. He recognized someone and rose. He waved and motioned.

She turned to see a tallish young man with a lean body and the unmistakable cropped head of an American. He had a pleasant face, a wholesome smile and gorgeous blue eyes that were alert.

"Hi!" said the man and thrust out a hand. "John Briggs." The two men shook hands.

"Aisha, I want you to meet a nice fellow and a colleague. John is from America," Robert explained.

She found the first part of the introduction intriguing, the last superfluous. "As if we couldn't tell," she said and laughed.

The American laughed, too. There was a sort of freshness and innocence about him. Nothing, she felt, had ever gone wrong in his life. He seemed to have abounding enthusiasm and energy.

While Robert ordered drinks, she took a good look around the room. No, Ibrahim hadn't come, and at this late hour she hardly expected him to show up. She leaned back, relaxed and observed her two companions. The American talked with some reserve, Robert made gestures. He must have said something funny, because John laughed good-naturedly. Then he looked apologetically around and saw that she was watching him.

"How do you like Egypt?" Aisha asked.

He shrugged and cleared his throat. "Egypt is Egypt!" he said.

Smart, she thought. Smart and bashful. She listened to them making conversation. John struck her as a proud man. It was a natural feeling that came out freely without any effort on his part. It was as if he wanted, with every part of his body and soul, to let others know that he was an American, and was proud of it.

He took a cigarette and she noticed that he returned the package to his pocket without offering one to anybody else. "I had a hell of a time at the Ministry," John was saying. "I couldn't find anyone who'll talk about political assassinations."

A singer's voice dimmed, grave, slowly lingering:
La mer

Qu'on voit danser le long des
golfes clairs —

Robert gave her a sideways, tender yet provocative stare. He reached out his hand and touched hers. His grip was tight, his eyes shone. It was the song they had danced the first night they met; he had called it their song.

An electrical current swept through her and she shivered. She felt a huge lump in her throat, choking her and she thought she was going to cry. Then she became conscious that the American was watching them. She pulled her hand away.

Robert bowed and his lip curled down in an amused smile. "Please forgive us," he said. "This is Charles Trenet's latest song. It's so nostalgic, so beautiful, about the sea, the clear gulfs, the silvery reflections, the summer sky. 'And with a love song, the sea lulled my heart forever'," he sang.

They remained silent for a long moment. Then it was Robert who spoke again. "You were saying, John, yes, the political assassinations." He ran his hand over his brow, as if smoothing away a headache.

"In a nutshell," Robert began, "the Prime Minister, Dr. Ahmad Maher, was murdered in 1945. In 1946, Amin Osman Pasha, who was Minister of Finance during the war had the same fate. Among the latest victims, we have the President of the Cairo Court of Appeals, followed by the Cairo Chief of Police, General Salim Zaki, outside the gates of the Medical School, and later Prime Minister Mahmud Nuqrashi — and we're still going strong."

"It's bad," said the American, in full control of his emotions.

"Bad? The country is sick, my dear friend. The force and hope that were seething in our young seem to veer into destructiveness."

"Is there nothing anybody can do?" Aisha asked.

Robert passed his hand over his eyes. "We're doing it!" he said. "We're all doing things! We may not know what we're doing, but, by Allah, we're doing a lot!"

"It looks as if you've got a tough way ahead of you," the American said.

"Our troubles have just begun. What's facing all of us is worse than war," Robert said, a pensiveness in his voice. He took a sip from his drink, lit a cigarette for Aisha and turned to John. "But American journalists fascinate me."

John fidgeted in his chair. "In what way?"

My! He's sensitive, Aisha thought settling back. She tried to recall the Hollywood films she had seen. Contrary to what they depicted, the man in front of her hardly glanced at her, as if she were an invisible woman. He projected himself so self-assuredly, and yet he did not care or did not dare to look at her.

Robert remained serious. He seemed half-lost in thoughts. "I can't judge you, of course, when you're dealing with internal matters pertaining to your own country. I'm not there and I couldn't possibly make a fair evaluation, right?"

"It's a fair assumption," the American said, with mock seriousness.

"But I know for a fact that when you're handling foreign affairs, let's say, you tend to judge other people or other regimes in terms of your own aspirations. Your editorials, for instance, well — there is an element of speed, how to say it," he fumbled for words. "When I read them, I get the feeling you're fast in making up your mind, taking sides that often express what your readers expected of you. Do I make sense?"

"Interesting, go ahead," John said.

"In my opinion, when you report on foreign affairs, you are too self-centered to be totally detached. And once an opinion has been voiced or expressed by your peers, you all tend to agree, as if all of you writers see through the same set of eyes! Take the European press — "

"What of it?"

"Well, it offers greater individualism, diversity of thought, opinion, and a more realistic understanding of facts and events of the international scene of our times. In a world crisis, the adequacy of a foreign correspondent is the key to a just and correct assessment of important issues at stake. Otherwise, it's like keeping your poor readers in blinders. And I believe in your country people don't read other than the American press, no?"

John nodded and she noticed he was frowning. "They don't, true. But don't forget that we have a free press, which outweighs other disadvantages or weaknesses."

"But that's why it becomes so vital that you use initiative and good judgment with total objectivity. Can't you see? If not, you end up being subservient to the interests of your peers, your government, or specific ideologies or political parties. Of course, the rest of us must fight sedition laws and stifling restrictions, and must live in terror of offending the powerful and the government," Robert said with resignation. He took a few hurried puffs and continued.

"Leaders of emerging nations today maintain that such restrictions are essential, to give the state an opportunity to establish its strength and bring about order. They argue that when a viable democracy has been established, the restrictions will be removed. But hell! John, you and I know that when the free flow of information is suppressed, no one knows what's been planned or what's happening. For all we know, we may not like the type of 'ideal' setting they're preparing to impose on us, right?"

"I can't agree with you more," said John.

"Well, this is the situation here in Egypt today. Since the outbreak of hostilities, we are under martial law."

It was late and Aisha was getting bored. Frankly, she didn't give a damn what the American or the Egyptian press did or did not do. But both men seemed to be enjoying themselves, as they were totally engulfed in what seemed an intellectual debate. Good for them, she thought, and rose to her feet.

Both men stood up.

"I must go, Robert," she said. "Can we meet tomorrow morning and close the deal about the property before I lose it?"

He laughed. "Oui, cherie," he said obligingly. "Of course."

She walked up to him and gave him a hug. "Thank you," she said softly. "I'll meet you around noon, at Shepherd's," and held out her hand.

Robert brought it to his lips and kissed it. "Tomorrow, then." She shook hands with John, asked him to come back and see the floor-show, and left.

Squatting outside her dressing room door, she found Ali.

"You're still here? You ought to be in bed, young man."

"Yes, Miss Aisha, but I kept an eye open, hoping he'd come."

She smiled. *Good God. Another supporter rooting for Ibrahim.*

Ali hesitated, "there was a civilian man who asked me if officer Ibrahim was here tonight."

"Did he say why?"

"No. He sat alone and waited. I'm sure I've seen that Arab here at the club a couple of times before when Ibrahim was here, but I never saw him speak to the officer. That man seemed suspicious to me. I have a bad feeling about him. I don't like him. I don't even think he knows Ibrahim."

She yawned. Suddenly she felt so tired she did not even

try to listen to what Ali was saying and dismissed his remarks.

"Ibrahim didn't show up tonight. But you run and get me a taxi, Ali, and you come with me young man. I'll give you a ride home."

He stood momentarily looking at her as if he wanted to say something but could not. "Yes, Miss Aisha. Thank you," he said and dashed out of the room.

CHAPTER XV

The following day Aisha went with Robert, and in less than two hours she became the owner of a four-story apartment building close to the downtown Opera House. It cost her every piastre she had managed to save, but finally a long improbable dream had become a reality.

Had she tried for a worse time, she could not have possibly done better. At the time, Egypt was full of unrest and misery, beaten down by riots, epidemic, war and anarchy; a nation doomed to perish. In fact, the future had never seemed more hopeless.

But she could not ignore life. She wanted to live it even if it was too brutal, too hostile. The world was changing. She wanted to be prepared to meet this new world on secure grounds. In her mind, land was the only thing in the world that lasts, the only thing worth working for.

"Let others hail the rising sun," she said to Robert. "All I care is to get enough security so I won't ever be hungry again."

"At least you're frank about it. I hate hypocrites and pseudo-patriots."

Of course she knew they were sitting on a volcano, but until the volcano erupted there was nothing anyone could do. Any reader of the *Ahram* or the *Balagh* was confronted daily with the picture of a crazy and suspect world. The news media were in a feeding frenzy. Writers critized the women who squandered their money in beautifying themselves, at a time when a lipstick was worth 20 to 80 piastres. "Even working-class girls have begun to use powder on their faces accordingly to fashion, instead of following the example of their Palestinian sisters who sacrificed all their pocket money to equip their troops with arms," the writers reminded them.

Aisha was still making good money, and she felt she had no immediate cause for concern. But as many items became scarce and prices rose higher and higher, she found herself unable to save, no matter how much she earned. She had two costly apartments to maintain, she was buying expensive clothes for work, she paid for Fatma's private school, and she regurlarly mailed small sums to Uncle Youssef at the village.

In spite of all that, she was happy with the purchase she had made. No matter how things turned out, she would have security now. With the rental income from the newly acquired property, she could easily pay the taxes and have some money left for the upkeep of the building, she thought, and she could not curtail the profound feeling of ownership which stirred in her heart.

That night at work, she had picked up a cup of coffee from the restaurant kitchen, and was returning to her dressing room to change into her costume. In the dimly lit corridor she saw two men near the telephone booth, talking. She stopped on her tracks, and listened.

"He's not in uniform tonight," the one said. "Did you put a tail on him?"

"Yes, sir. We have a number of men. They follow him closely."

"Don't let him suspect us."
"We're very careful. Don't worry, sir."
"All right. Cover him when he leaves from here."
"Yes, sir."

She waited until the men left, then went to her room. The scene of the two men in the semi-dark corridor bothered her for a while. *There is always someone being followed these days,* she thought, and dismissed the incident.

When the show was over, she saw Ibrahim in a grey suit, waiting for her. She was angry. She had rehearsed and knew everything she was going to say, and had decided to give him hell. Then she took a good look at him and knew he had been there already.

"I'm so glad you could come tonight," she said, and it took a great effort on her part to hold back the *Your Highness* which waited at the tip of her tongue.

"I'm sorry," he said.

She was instantly ashamed of her meanness. As she looked at his sallow face her heart was wrung with pain.

"Please forgive me for not showing up sooner," he said, averting his eyes from her. "But I had no heart. I just couldn't come to the nightclub while my friends were drenching the desert with their blood. I know it was rude of me. I even thought of calling you at home, but then decided you'd be better off without having me around to spoil your fun."

Then he spoke about Ghalil calmly, in the same voice. He had been wounded, but now he was convalescing and was getting better.

She heard him and tried hard but could not understand him. She was puzzled. There was the way he looked at her at times, when he thought she wasn't looking. Often she'd catch him watching her, a tender, waiting look in his eyes.

"What made you come tonight?"

He took a sip and gazed at his glass. "I missed you. At first I thought I'd stay away for good, that I'd forget you or something, but you haunted me. Wherever I looked, I saw your eyes looking at me, and I had to see you again. I thought you'd help by calling me a louse, a brute or something."

He drank slowly, watching her over the glass. For a time, his face did not change its expression, but finally he smiled, still keeping his eyes on her.

"You don't know how close you came to the calling game."

He laughed. "I can guess." After a pause, "I have the car. Would you like to take a ride — I mean, can you leave?"

"Yes, I'm through with the show for tonight."

"Get your coat. I'll meet you out front."

She hastened to her dressing room, her heart pounding with excitement. *He might talk, he might explain*, she thought as she changed into her street clothes.

"Were are we going?" she asked, pulling a cigarette out of the package he held.

He lit it and smiled. "To the pyramids."

"The pyramids! In the desert? At night?"

"There's a moon."

"It's crazy! Everyone goes there in the morning."

"We're not tourists, and I have no intention of taking any pictures either. This way we'll avoid the tourist crowds, the guides, the souvenir vendors, and the hot sun." He paused. "Besides, seeing the ancient relics by the dim moonlight will be something you'll never forget if you live to be a hundred."

"Let's go then," she said and took hold of his hand.

When they reached the exit, Ibrahim stopped and carefully scanned the parking lot. Suddenly, in the dark, a man stepped from behind a tree. He stared at Ibrahim, then started to walk in the opposite direction.

"Everything all right?" she asked.

"Oh, yes."

They held hands and walked quickly through the parking lot to his car.

"What are you thinking?" she asked after they drove a while.

"You. I feel stupid, empty-headed. Like a schoolboy on his first date."

For a moment, their eyes met and held. Then he looked out the window. When they arrived, Ibrahim locked the car. In the distance, behind a moat of darkness, the city of Cairo showed itself with a million twinkling lights.

They walked along a narrow paved path. On both sides the desert stretched for miles. It was a desolate, arid, treeless land without a blade of grass.

In this inhuman solitude, the nearness of the man beside her became much keener. She wanted to feel close to him, to touch him and kiss him, but something held her back. She reached for his hand, and held it tight.

As she became accustomed to the darkness, she began to distinguish at a distance a great mass of grey stones. When they reached the whitish, huge structure, the moon hung round above them, shining brightly on the pyramid.

There was an eerie feeling. The silence was disquieting, almost unbearable. Only the faint distant roar of the busy city reached them. Around them was boundless, hopeless sand that glistened in silvery mauve shades.

He pointed. "There, to the left, is the pyramid of Cheops." She heard Ibrahim's voice as if coming from another world. "And here is the world-famous Sphinx. Man's work, built with man's labor. These relics have survived time, space, the elements, and have entered infinity."

She stood spellbound. Then they walked and came to stand facing the half-beast, half-human Sphinx. Its enormous grave eyes stared ahead, surveying the wide horizon.

"She's beautiful. So majestic and beastly. I wonder who conceived the idea of carving this huge stone? And what does it really represent?"

"The Greek historian Herodotus was the first to name the Sphinx. I don't think we know the creator of this masterpiece, for the simple reason that his name is not engraved on it. Or at least no one has been able to find a name yet."

"What does *she* represent?"

"Why *she*? It could be a *he*, you know." Ibrahim laughed.

"I've always heard people referring to the Sphinx as a woman, at least they compare it to one."

"Well, then I've heard people say that she, if you prefer, represents eternity, life with no beginning or end." He avoided looking at her.

"And to think that this motionless structure has witnessed every single sunrise and every moon-washed night for thousands of years."

Ibrahim just stared at the Sphinx.

"And people come from every corner of the world to look at her enigmatic face, only to depart more puzzled than before. If she could only talk, how many things we would learn from the wisdom of her words!" Then she noticed the broken nose. "Do you know how it was broken?"

He laughed, a short, nervous laugh. "There's a legend that Napoleon's soldiers used the nose of the Sphinx as a shooting target."

"What an atrocity! Then perhaps it was her curse that put an end to his glorious victories and made him lose his shirt out here in the desert," Aisha said and felt happy with her wild interpretation.

"Perhaps you're right," he said and smiled. Then his face became serious. Taking his cigarettes out of his pocket, he offered one and lit it for her.

They sat on a step at the base of the Sphinx, intensely aware of each other's presence. She looked up at the dark sky with the galaxies of shining stars.

She laughed and pointed into the dark sky. "There goes a *shihab*, a falling star. You know what we were saying when I was a kid?"

"What?"

"That a *shihab* was a dart thrown by God at an evil genie."

He laughed. "You won't believe it, but that's what we suspected in my village too!"

She caught his persistent look. "Why are you looking at me?"

"You are so beautiful, Aisha. I wish —"

"You wish what?"

Ibrahim leaped to his feet. She went and stood facing him. In the moonlight, his face looked haggard and drawn. She had never seen him look so tired, so shaken. Her hand went up to remove a streak of hair from his forehead. He held her hand and gently brought it to his lips. His face hardened suddenly. His eyes anxiously searched her features. The muscles around his mouth tightened.

For a stricken moment, they dared neither breathe nor move. The silence was so intense it seemed as if time itself had stopped. Then she tried to speak, but his mouth, hard, determined, shut her out.

Her lips were on his, hungry and demanding. She felt her knees give way and before she could prevent herself, she threw her arms around him. His strong, tough muscles engulfed her. A cold anxiety began to throb her breast.

His eyes flickered with desire. Little drops of sweat stood on his forehead. Every vein in her body was screaming as his hand went up and down her back. He drew in his breath.

"God! I never thought I could love anyone this much," he whispered, his warm breath close to her ear.

With urgency, he began tugging at her coat. She helped him untangle the clasps. Then they were lying on the warm sand.

In her mind, the moon, the stars, the sand intermingled with the Sphinx and the pyramids into a divine whirlwind, which grabbed her and lifted her up, high. In that void, she felt their burning bodies and souls coupled in an exhilarating, stunning harmony. Awakened in her was the surprising realization that she truly loved him and wanted him like she had never desired another man before. He stroked and touched her body, exploring gently at first, then fiercely, desperate. Fully aroused, their bodies joined together, comfortably, naturally, as if they had been designed to fit together.

After a while, they both lay there, spent, breathing hard.

"I've been dreaming a lifetime for this moment. It was wonderful, darling," she whispered stroking his damp face. And as she looked at him, lying beside her, she knew why making love with Ibrahim was so different, so fulfilling. She loved him. The realization was dizzying, and she became conscious of a chill in the air.

"You're shaking, love. Are you cold?" he whispered shifting his weight from her and smoothing her dress.

She nodded.

Ibrahim straightened up, brushed his pants, then picked up his jacket and threw it around her shoulders, kissing her gently on the cheek. Then searched his pockets for cigarettes.

"Aisha ...."

"Yes, darling?"

"Aisha, I love you, but I feel ... I have to explain."

There was a long, ghastly pause.

A loud alarm rang in her head. "What is there to explain?"

"Us. This."

Her heart began to swell. Pleading, obscure voices rose

within her. "You mean that I shouldn't take you seriously?" she asked, not knowing just then if she should laugh or cry.

"Not exactly," he said unhappily. "I'm serious, very serious, in fact. I love you."

"Then what?"

There was another pause. "It's hard to explain. You see, I'm not entirely free to do as I please." His voice stopped, and for a long, quiet moment, he contemplated his hands.

A wild thought crossed her mind. Stunned, she stared at him. "You mean there's another woman?" Suddenly she was sick to her stomach.

He exploded from the ground. "No! it's not that."

"Then what the hell is it?" she asked, looking at him dumbly.

"I just don't want you involved. I can't explain now. Please, don't ask me to, I meant every word I said to you." He squatted by her side. "Just have faith in me, Aisha, be a little patient. I'm sure that soon I'll be a position to explain everything. You'll realize then my reasons. You'll understand then."

As she stared at him, she tried to think. He was not a man given to whims, and the explanation eluded her. Whatever else she thought, he was not like anyone she had ever met. The look of happiness fled from his face and a kind of bewildered, conscience-stricken worry took its place.

"Why can't you tell me now?"

His mouth twisted. "It's a long story."

"Makes no difference."

"I'm not trying to excuse myself for the way I acted just now because I love you. In all my life, I have never said these words to another woman."

She swallowed hard and racked her brains to think. "I see," she said, even though nothing made sense.

"No, you can't see. You can't possibly. How could you? You're upset, and you're imaging all kinds of things."

There was another pause.

He took her hand. "Just give me time, Aisha. I mean, wait until I'm in a position to explain."

"Let go, Ibrahim. You're just not ... easy to reach, you keep to yourself, you're never open for me to get in and perhaps see or feel what you carry inside you. Let's go." And pulling her hand from his she turned to go.

His hand caught her arm and pulled her around to face him. "Wait. You can't leave like this. You've got to listen to me. You're angered."

She looked up and saw he had tears in his eyes. "What's the use?" she said. "You won't tell me what I want to hear anyway."

"Couldn't you please be a little patient? It's only fair."

"All right. I'll accept that. Now, please," she said shakily, "let's go," and started toward the car. As she walked she could still feel the pressure of his hard body, his strong arms around her, still hear his breathing and words of endearment in her ear.

In the stillness, Aisha heard the howl of a dog and she felt the dark presence of a strange feeling, almost an intangible foreboding.

The ride back was speechless. She had neither the strength nor the will to discuss the matter any further. *How can one be one minute in heaven and the next in hell,* she wondered. But she did not desire to find an answer just then. She felt as though all her senses had been paralyzed and she was unable to take in what was happening to her.

The narrow streets blurred past. Fearfully, she tried to imagine what the future held for them, if there was one, and a new fear crept into her heart. And yet, in her sorrow, she realized that it was impossible to imagine life without him.

The stars grew dim, and the sky grew light. When they parted, dawn was breaking.

CHAPTER XVI

"There are no fans in hell," Aisha decided with bitterness.

The first few days after the night by the Pyramids, she felt indifferent, then she was restless, and after that stage came and passed, she became vulnerable. As the days passed and Ibrahim did not call, she went wild with fury, hurt and humiliation.

In the weeks that followed, Aisha's anger reasserted itself. *All right, if that was the way he wanted to play, she could live without him.* Only she did not believe it.

Night after night she lay sleepless for hours, trying to establish order over the chaos of her imagination. She lay down to sleep, but she could not find peace. Her whole life paraded like a dream and came to a halt with Ibrahim.

As the days passed and she did not see him, she saw him in her dreams. She could feel his strong arms around her, his soft touch as he rubbed the tightness behind her neck. The desire to be with him burned inside her and left her restless, hollow and in pain. In her heart she knew he loved her, and was sincere, but his sudden periodic disappearances and enigmatic excuses left her confused, angry and despondent. So she fought back at the slightest opportunity, which made matters worse.

Meanwhile, she was seeing Robert regularly, and she found herself drawn to him. Together they took long rides by the Nile, danced at the happiest places and mingled with well-dressed crowds of men and women who, in the winter of 1950, flocked the nightclubs, partly to seek distraction, partly to see their own life dramatized, and partly to have fun.

But was that was she really wanted? The nagging question was always there torturing her. At times Robert sat looking into her eyes and she felt an intense feeling of love coming from him that made her uneasy. *But I'm in love with Ibrahim. Sure, I'm terribly attracted to Robert, but I'm not the right woman for him,* she thought.

One night Aisha was at the nightclub with Robert, when John, the American journalist, joined them for a drink. She was feeling depressed, and tried to drown her sorrow with whiskey, which she was not accustomed to drinking. Before long, the liquid fire had gone to her head. She felt tipsy and the room began to reel. She laughed and talked loudly, holding her glass in the air, when she saw Ibrahim standing by the bar.

She felt as one must feel when he is caught stealing. Shock, guilt and panic overwhelmed her, until she thought she was choking. But then the panic left her and she became hilarious.

"I hope he took a good look at me," she said, mostly to herself. Then, in a sugary voice she asked Robert, "How about another drink, darling?"

He stared at her. "Why, yes. Are you sure? You usually don't — I've never seen you —" and then he saw Ibrahim.

"He must have thought I'd go running into his arms," Aisha said. "Ha! The hell I will!"

John looked confused. "Who you're talking about?" he asked, spilling his drink before it reached his mouth. "Who's got your dander up?"

She saw Ibrahim take a stool at the bar. "No one in particular. Don't mind me. I'm talking to myself."

John and Robert exchanged glances. Suddenly, the fun was gone. They sat looking at each other, wrapped up in their own thoughts. Then Aisha saw Ibrahim leave the bar. "Why, the brute!" she croaked angrily. "He's leaving without even speaking to me!"

Before she could say another word, she saw Ibrahim start in their direction. He came and stood for a second looking down at her with expressionless eyes. "I hate to interrupt your fun," he said rather abruptly, "but I'd like to have a word with you."

Robert stood up and John followed. *Please God! Don't let them fight,* she thought, sobering up in a hurry. *At least not in here,* she prayed.

"Sure, officer. Wouldn't you like to join us?" Robert introduced himself, then John, and offered his hand.

"Thank you. I'd rather talk to her alone, if you don't mind." His tone was hostile, and he ignore Robert's hand.

Good! she thought with wild satisfaction. *He is madder than hell. I'll see that he gets worse.* Anger bubbled up, pushing aside good intentions. Turning around, "Why, officer! Can't you see I'm with company?"

"It won't take long," Ibrahim said. "I'll be very brief,"

"Some other time maybe, eh?" she said and tried to look calm.

Ibrahim swallowed hard. "It can't wait, I'm afraid."

"Oh, come off it," she began, getting more furious by the minute. "And who do you think you are!"

Ibrahim seemed embarrassed. "Aisha, you're drunk!" he

said with difficulty, glancing around to see if he was overheard.

"For the first time you make sense. I believe I am," she said. "But that's my damn business and not yours." There was a pause. "How dare you reprimand me." She spoke in a rage and then forced herself to laugh. "You don't object to drinking by any chance, or do you?"

Ibrahim's eyes mirrored his surprise. "It's hard to believe it's really you!" he said.

She saw sadness, anger and contempt on his face, but she continued defiantly. "It's me, all right. Your eyes and ears don't deceive you, friend."

Robert's face hardened. "Aisha, it'll be perfectly all right with us if you wish to talk it out with the officer."

"No. It's not all right!" she snapped. "I have nothing to discuss with this man, believe me. Besides, he bores me. He bores me stiff!"

Ibrahim turned about. His lips twitched. "People are watching us," he said in exasperation. "Where is your sense of respectability and decency?"

She laughed. "How lovely! Look who's talking of decency and respectability."

Ibrahim blinked, then stared as though waking from a dream. "Have it your way, then," he said sharply and left with hurried steps. As she watched him walk away, she noticed an Arab drop some money on the table, then quickly followed Ibrahim out of the nightclub.

She sat paralyzed with shock and disbelief, then she became conscious of Robert looking at her quizzically, knowingly. John sat, his head bowed, staring down at his drink. Then she became aware of people at the surrounding tables watching her.

"Let's get out of here," she said and stood up, knocking over her chair. "I need fresh air."

Robert finished his drink with one swig. John rose, pretending to be amused by the whole affair. The three of them linked arms and marched in unison towards the exit of the club. Robert whistled for a taxi and the three got in.

"I was willing to — I tried to help, give you both a chance to talk things over," Robert said. "You're sure you know what you're doing?"

"Yes, I wanted to hurt him."

"Oh, I'm sure you've done a good job!" he said flippantly.

"I don't even want to see him again. To lie to me after ... deliberately lie and then brazenly resume —"

Robert turned her face to the light and looked for an intent moment into her eyes. "I don't understand you," he said. "Can you tell me, John?"

"Tell you what?" asked the American with mock innocence.

"Why do women often act so contrary to their hearts?"

John drew on his cigarette. "How would I know? I've never been a woman!" he said, uncomfortably.

Robert turned to her and let go of her chin. "You're crazy about the man."

"I'm not!"

"Darling, it's written plainly on your face. It's no use denying it, at least not to yourself."

She sat listening, paying little heed to what he was saying. Suddenly Robert was no fun anymore.

"A man needs his vanity soothed."

"Oh, Robert!"

He made a helpless gesture. "It's no use." Then he turned and started to talk with John.

When the car reached Shepherd's Hotel where John was staying, he asked them if they cared to join him for a drink.

"No, thank you, Aisha said. "I'm terribly tired and I'd like to go to bed."

"Let me take you home then," volunteered Robert. "I'm still your friend."

She was deeply moved. "There's not the slightest need to see me home. Stay with your friend. Thank you."

He bent and kissed her. "Don't take it so hard, darling. In love and war, things work out somehow," he said soothingly as he got off the car. "Will I see you tomorrow?"

She nodded. "Good night," she said and sent him a kiss with the tip of her fingers.

Robert paid the driver and, with a generous tip, instructed him to take her home.

The house was quiet. Her mother and little Fatma had long since gone to bed and only a small light burned in the hallway. She went straight to her room, pulled off her clothes and lay down on the bed. Her mind whirled in every possible direction.

She tried to sleep, but the memory of the ugly scene and Ibrahim's face haunted her. She lay limp thinking of him, warm, sad and strong. His melancholy eyes seemed to pierce the darkness of the room. She had shamed and humiliated him. She had torn his pride to shreds, she knew, and was desperately ashamed. He would never return, she thought, and felt a terrible wave of guilt that swept over her. She did not want to lose him.

Two weeks later, John said goodbye to Aisha and left the club early that night. He had to pack and catch a midnight plane for Syria and Robert was taking him to the airport.

Aisha was sitting alone, lost in her own bitter thoughts when she felt a hand on her shoulder. Startled, she turned.

"May I sit for a moment?" Ibrahim asked. Dressed in civilian clothes, he looked pale. His mouth was tight.

"I ... I don't mind," she whispered weakly, taken by surprise.

"I see your elite friends have deserted you."

"In my kind of business, it's not unusual. It happened before. Of all people, you ought to know."

Ibrahim pulled up a chair and sat. "I'm sorry, Aisha. I really am," he was silent for a moment. As he spoke, he gave her repeated glances of appeal, as if he was trying to hold himself together and needed her cooperation. "I didn't mean to sound cruel, but it hasn't been easy for me."

"I understand," she said, with remnants of pride and anger.

The light went out of his eyes. "But you don't! You couldn't. That's why I asked you to trust me and be patient."

"Yes, I remember you did!" she was sarcastic again. "As a matter of fact, I remember everything you said that night by the pyramids, all the lies you told me — "

"Lies?" He gasped. "I never lied! I meant every word I said."

"So you did, eh? What's with you, anyway? Wait for what? For the peaches to bloom? Why are you so evasive, so ... so elusive? Is this the way people who're in love behave? Is it?"

He shrugged. "How should I know? I haven't been stricken so badly before. It's the first time for me. Anyway, I doubt I could survive a second time like this."

She tried to hold on to her sanity and remained silent.

"Aisha," he whispered gravely, taking a firm grip of her wrist. "Stop being sarcastic and please listen to me. Better yet, go fetch your coat, we're leaving this place. We must talk. Go," he ordered.

Her first impulse was to resist. "I'm too tired, Ibrahim. Why don't you leave me alone?"

"I'm not leaving you alone until I make you understand."

"And where are you taking me? Not to the Pyramids, I hope."

He smiled. "No need to worry yourself. My intentions are strictly honorable. Besides, I'm not in the mood to make love to you, not in the state you're in, anyway."

She was ready to burst out something hateful.

"Don't," he said and shut her off by placing his finger on her lips. "Don't say any more that you may regret later. Go get your coat. I'll wait for you at the exit."

His voice had taken a commanding air now, and in a strange way she was glad he had ordered her. Had he left the choice to her, she knew she would have refused to go with him, even though she understood she could no longer separate herself from him.

As soon as the car was on the road, she asked him again.

"Where are we going? Can't you give me a simple answer? Have you lost your tongue or something?" Not that she really cared to know, but she was not ready to give in, and besides, she couldn't stand the dreadful silence.

"You'll soon see, just be patient. Surely, you can wait a few more minutes."

Ibrahim drove for a while in complete silence, but he kept a constant eye on the rearview mirror. Then he stopped the car, and they got out. They walked through an empty alley and came to another street. She was aware they were somewhere in the suburbs but she did not know exactly where. The dim gas light of the street lamps cast a dusty yellow veil over the walls of the houses.

It was late, and the streets were empty and quiet. At the end of the street, they stopped. He put his arm around her, and motioned her to remain silent. He looked around and waited for a few seconds. "Come on," he said and hurried toward the front of a pink house. Ibrahim rang the doorbell twice and waited. The door eased open and they slipped inside.

"Ghalil!" she whispered.

"Good evening," said the officer, offering his hand. "It's been a long time, Aisha. No?"

"Yes, it's been a long time," she repeated, totally unprepared.

He grinned. "Ill health, for one thing. Come in, come in. Make yourself at home. My wife is upstairs, she'll be down in a minute."

"Of course," Aisha said and she realized the late-hour visit was not a total surprise to him. She became curious. Before long, Ghalil's wife entered the room. She gave Aisha a pleasant smile and a civil nod. She appeared to be in her late forties. Her eyes were sharp, worried, inside dark circles. She looked exhausted.

The two men exchanged a few hurried words and then Ghalil's wife excused herself and left for the kitchen to prepare some coffee. To Aisha's astonishment, Ibrahim volunteered to help and followed her, leaving her alone with Ghalil.

"They'll be back," Ghalil said, stretching himself on the sofa in a comfortable position and lighting his pipe. "Besides, I wanted to talk to you alone. It's about Ibrahim and you."

"There's nothing between us, much less to talk about," she felt her body stiffen.

"Oh, yes, there's plenty. Ibrahim loves you."

"The coward! He asked you to intervene?" she leaped to her feet.

Ghalil swung around on her so fast she thought he was going to climb the wall. Then he gave a sudden laugh that sounded very much like the edge of hysteria. "You're wrong, my dear. Ibrahim doesn't lack courage. It was I. I've asked him to bring you over. If anyone had to do any explaining it had to be me."

For a few seconds, she just stared at him, puzzled. "I don't understand."

"As you'll soon see, I'm responsible for Ibrahim's, let's say, irrational behavior."

"You?" She stared in wide-eyed disbelief.

"That's right. And I am also to be blamed for not letting him communicate at times with you."

She returned to her chair. Ghalil spoke in very good Arabic, but somehow she was incapable of grasping the meaning of his words. She tried to remain calm.

"You see, my dear girl," he said, "although there wasn't the slightest doubt in my mind that you were worthy of our trust, yet, as a senior officer, I felt it was my duty to be cautious. We had to be sure that you could be trusted."

She tried to think. *Trusted for what? What was he talking about? Why "we?"*

"We checked on you," he said in an undertone.

She laughed. "You checked on me? You mean you spied on me? What in the world for?"

"We had to. We simply couldn't take any risks at times like this," Ghalil paused. Then with an abrupt movement of his hand he wiped the sweat off his brow. "We have too much at stake. We can't take any chances. It means our lives. But more than that, long years of hard work and planning, perhaps the only chance for our country's rebirth."

"But —" she fumbled and stopped. "I don't have the slightest idea what this is all about. Are you trying to tell me something?"

He waved her to silence and went on. "You'll soon see the connection," he said, frowning. Then he drew on his pipe. "Ibrahim and I belong to the secret organization of *Zubat el*

Ahrar, or Free Officers. In joining, we have sworn on the Koran to guard its secrets with our life. Secrecy among the Free Officers is solely maintained on our military honor. The Free Officers is by no means a religious organization," he hastened to add, "although the great majority of our members are Muslims, like the majority of the Egyptian people. We do not act as Muslims, but as officers, sworn to defend the honor and dignity of Egypt."

Ghalil's wife returned, carrying a tray. On it were two cups of coffee and a decanter with two thin finger-like glasses with liqueur. She placed the tray on the table and left the room. Ghalil handed Aisha a glass, and then lit her cigarette.

"To our health," he said, raising his glass in the air, and took a sip.

She played with the stem of her glass. "Please continue. I'm listening."

He poured himself another drink and started to pace the room, holding the glass in his hand.

He spoke of corruption and the political scandals; the officers' humiliation in Falluga, and how the King and his entourage made a fortune out of the sale of defective weapons. "He sells his friends more easily than the brethren of Joseph sold him!"

But all this was common knowledge, she thought. At the time, King Farouk was not simply debauched, but an exhibitionist into the bargain. He had abandoned all decorum. He went from one nightclub to another, and sang and danced till dawn, especially after 1948, when he divorced the Queen and mother of his children, a fact which shocked the people and set them talking.

"And how does the army figure in all this?" she asked.

He took a sip from the coffee cup and looked searchingly at her. "Ours is not a guerrilla band to kill," he said.

"What is it then, and what can you do? You said yourself the people are outrunning the government."

"Our principal objective is to liberate our country from the octopus of feudalism which, throughout the ages, has symbolized political bondage. We want Egypt for the Egyptians."

Ibrahim entered the room and took a seat.

"And how do you plan doing that?" Aisha asked.

Ghalil raised his hand. "By a peaceful social revolution. A real revolution of the people — not merely a coup d'etat — one that will shatter the whole system of feudalism and semi-slavery."

She felt he wanted to say more than he allowed himself to say. Out of caution, he was alert and guarded, as if he didn't want to reveal something on the spur of the moment that he would regret later.

Momentarily, she remained silent. She felt her stomach grow tense. How absolutely irrational he was! She wanted to scream: *You're all crazy, or something?* Instead, she said, "Revolutions are not fun. People get killed."

Ibrahim chuckled but it sounded as though he was strangling. "We're not counting on having fun. What we're planning on doing is necessary to regain our lost dignity, to provide our people with the strength to keep their heads up and their knees unbent," he said looking at her with sad, dark eyes.

A rasping voice came from Ghalil. "After the Palestine fiasco, we became convinced that the King and his government were not interested in the nation's or army's welfare."

"But a revolution?" she asked with a shudder, as her mind traveled fast to the bloodiest pages of the French history books that she had read at school.

Ghalil leaned forward. "Why not? It'll be part of the worldwide movement for social justice. How else did you think we can accomplish what we're trying to tell you? Surely, not by teaching the peasants the rules of democracy!" he laughed. "Not only it's not practical, but you know it's impossible, no?"

Was it? she wondered as she rose and came to stand by the window overlooking a small backyard. Her conscience nagged her. Perhaps she should be more patient, more understanding. She tried to remain calm.

But she felt oppressed by the immensity of the game played, feeling its weight. Were they sane or mad? How could she tell, she wondered, as she looked about her. Both men smoked silently, sipping their coffee. Her rotten luck, she thought. *Of all the men, I had to hitch my wagon to an ambitious fool! Of all the men, I want and love him!* She felt as if she was sucked into quicksand. If anyone was crazy, it had to be her. And she was wondering if it was a mistake to talk about this at all.

His face expressionless, Ghalil spoke. "Ibrahim didn't want to expose you to any risks, but found himself on the horns of a dilemma. It's like having to choose between the devil and the deep blue sea," he said, and laughed. "On the one hand he loves you and wants to protect you; on the other hand, he can't marry you and have you implicated, but doesn't want to lose you, either! You see, we are all suspects."

"Suspects?" she asked with a start. She must have looked funny, because Ibrahim burst into laughter.

"What's so funny?" she asked angrily.

Ghalil answered. "The police and the palace spies watch our every movement. Just the other day, a posse of military police descended on the home of a suspected officer —"

"You mean Nasser?" asked Ibrahim.

"Right!" Ghalil said. "Luckily, their search revealed nothing, so they let him go free. But they're trying to discover at least one weak link in the chain, and although they've laid many traps for us, they haven't been successful so far."

"What if one is caught?" she asked lamely.

Ghalil shrugged. "A palace informer trapped one of our Free Officers, Lieutenant Hassan Allah. He was caught writing a revolutionary pamphlet."

"Was he?" she interrupted anxiously.

He nodded. "Yes, but we were forced to abandon him to his fate, so as to safeguard the future of the rest of the officers," Ghalil shot her a quick glance. Ibrahim remained silent.

They stayed a while longer. Then Ibrahim stood up. "It's very late. We better get going and let you and your wife have some rest. We all need it," he said.

On the way to the car, she asked Ibrahim, "Aren't you pushing things a bit?"

"How can you say that?"

"Well, I mean, is all that crazy notion about a revolution necessary? And why now? We're safe and secure. More people have money and I'm sure they feel secure. Why make things worse? I've never felt more secure and never had more than I have now."

He looked at her in astonishment. "And you think money will give us justice and security, when the rest of the masses continue to go hungry? You really believe you're *safe* and *secure?*"

"Yes!" she said, without hesitation.

Ibrahim's face had a look of sour disapproval. "But, my dear girl, we live on borrowed time. I can assure you, no one is safe because there's no law, no justice and no freedom. You seem to have the staggering belief that freedom, security, or integrity is like ... candy that we can receive or buy from foreign hands. Well, Aisha, it's not! It is something we must earn. We must earn it with tears and blood. That's our destiny, my love. That's every man's destiny."

CHAPTER XVII

For months, life had been turbulent and uneasy. In spite of Ibrahim's reassurances, Aisha felt nervous and in a constant state of worry, suspicion, and fear. Anything could happen.

It was Monday, and she didn't have to work. Ibrahim had promised her an evening all to themselves, full of fun and excitement, and she looked forward to it with anticipation.

He arrived in uniform and on time. He bent and kissed her mother. "You look younger every day," he said, and she laughed happily. Fatma ran to him. He knelt on one knee and put his arms about her. "How's school? I hear you're doing really good," he said. He always made a fuss over the little orphan. Aisha could see he loved children.

Fatma grinned. "I guess I'm doing good."

Ibrahim laughed, and swooped her into his arms. "If you're nice and learn to read, I may bring you a toy," he said.

"A toy?" Fatma's eyes turned bigger, darker. She looked at Aisha, then at Zakiya, who nodded approvingly. Without any hesitation, Fatma flung her arms about his neck and kissed his cheek.

"I'll be right back," Ibrahim said, and put the little girl down. He walked to the door and went out in his car. A few seconds later, he returned with a box which he handed to

Fatma. "Why don't you open it and see what's inside?"

The women went close as the child tore the wrapping. With hesitant hand, she flung the top open. There lay a beautiful doll, dressed in an elegant pink gown, shoes, and gloves.

"A doll!" Fatma exclaimed. "For me?"

"Aisha is too old to play with dolls. Of course it's for you!" he said.

Delirious with happiness, Fatma ran up to him and kissed him again. Then with caution and tender love, she lifted the first doll she ever had, and held it in her arms. Just then, Aisha wondered how different life might have been. Oh, why did he have to be involved? Why did it have to be him!

Ibrahim turned about swiftly. "It's time. Let's go."

By Cairo standards it was early in the evening, and the quaint restaurant was only half-filled with customers but already noisy. Sitting at a small table that was set against the trunk of a live palm tree that grew in the middle of the floor, she looked about.

"Well, how do you like the Royal Palms?" asked Ibrahim.

"I like it fine. I've heard people talk about the place. Have you been here before?"

"A couple of times."

"Alone?"

He smiled. "By Allah, Aisha. Let's not start that again."

"Well? Did you come here alone?"

The smile broadened. "If you mean with another woman, no. I think Ghalil was with me. Satisfied?"

"For the present."

"How about a drink?"

"A beer will be fine."

He summoned the waiter and ordered. When the drinks arrived, Aisha raised her glass in the air. "Do you know what Americans say?" she asked, remembering John.

"What?"

"Down the hatch!"

He laughed. "It makes no sense, but if that's what it takes to get Lady Luck on our side, then down the hatch it is!"

She laughed and glanced around the dining room. She caught a glimpse of a man sitting alone, four tables away. He was a stocky Arab with bold black eyes, thick heavy brows, and a thin moustache. He wore a fashionable British gabardine, but the suit was wrinkled and rumpled, as if he had been living in it. His face and eyes held her. His eyes had been fixed on Ibrahim until they suddenly swung around to her, and he became aware of her scrutiny.

"Ibrahim?"

"Yes, darling?" he said, lighting a cigarette.

She asked him to check the man. "I can't help feeling there's something unnatural and unpleasant about him. He's been watching you."

"You're imagining things," Ibrahim said and smiled. Apart from a tightening of his lips, he did not appear the least disturbed.

"But I'm not imagining," she said with apprehension. "And what really bothers me, is the feeling that I've seen that man before. He looks so familiar, and yet I can't place him. Take a look, please."

Ibrahim turned casually and looked about. Then he frowned. "I have the impression that I've seen that Fairbanks moustache and the gabardine suit before. But where in Allah's name have I seen him?"

"Could he be someone you know? An officer perhaps?"

He shook his head. "No. He's not an officer, I'm sure. When our eyes met, he seemed perturbed and lowered his head. Why, his nose almost touched his plate. Obviously, he's avoiding me."

"Could he be spying on us?" she said in a low whisper.

For a moment he didn't reply, that narrow gaze still intent through the smoke of the cigarette. "He could be working for anyone as an undercover man. Our enemies suspect that the officers are up to something, but they don't know what. Every day that goes by, the circle of spies tightens more and more around us. I wish to God we could get it over with before —"

"Before what?"

He shrugged. "Before we're discovered. What else?"

She stared for a moment in silence.

"For Allah's sake, don't look so serious," he said. He reached across the table and gently took her hand. There was a hard, driving fear in his face. "Aisha, you haven't talked to anyone about us?"

"How dare you! Me? An informer? Why, the nerve!" She leaped out of her chair.

He pulled her back to her seat. "I'm sorry, darling. Please forgive me. I guess we've reached the point where we can't trust anyone. We no longer know whom to trust. Tonight of all nights —"

"Tonight what?"

"I'm sure I'm being followed very closely. Most of the time I don't care. I go about my business. Tonight is different. Damn! I have an important meeting."

"Meeting? But you couldn't have." As much as she wanted to, she was unable to control her disappointment. "This was going to be our night together. Dinner, opera, remember?"

"I remember. I'm sorry, but it couldn't be helped, darling. Try to understand. I have a paper I must deliver."

"Understand what?" she said with bitterness. "You're wasting your time and mine, and we ran the risk of getting caught and rotting in prison for nothing."

"For nothing?"

"Yes. Nothing will ever come out of this mess. The others are strong, they always were, and you know it!" Suddenly it occurred to her that she was repeating Robert's words. She thought she must be going crazy.

If he was waiting for an answer, these were not the words he wanted to hear. His face hardened slightly, and his eyes became blank. He reached for another cigarette.

"I forgive you because I love you," he said. "By the way, our man is gone. He moves fast. He must be working on me, I'm sure." He paused. Then looking at her, his voice came out flat. "I think I know where I've seen him."

"Where?"

"Where else? At the club where you work. He was there the night you were drunk and we fought just like now." He pursed his lips tightly. "Let's get out of here," he said briskly, dropping some money on the table.

At the exit an old man dressed in gallabiya with a cane, inched toward them. "Be careful. You're followed," he whispered and wobbled away. They walked out of the restaurant towards the parking area. There was no one around, and the place was quiet. Ibrahim unlocked the car, helped her in, then got behind the wheel. They had driven for a minute or two in complete silence, and then he spoke.

"Do you want to come with me to the meeting?" he asked.

"I might as well. I made no other plans."

"What I can't figure out is how in hell's name that man could've known where we were going tonight when I wasn't sure of it myself. I only thought of this restaurant after we left your house. That's it!" He slapped his forehead. "There's no other explanation. He must have followed us from your place!"

"Oh, no!"

"Oh, yes," he said and made a sudden turn with the wheel.

"I bet that son of a dog is following us right now. That is, if he's really after me. Can you check the car behind us?"

"It's a Mercedes, a black one."

"A Mercedes, eh? He expects me to take you home and then follow and see where I'll go from there."

"In that case, you'd better not go to the meeting."

He shook his head. "It's imperative that I go, Aisha. They'll be waiting for me. It's important."

Ibrahim drove the car over narrow roads. They bounced over the unpaved streets and swayed around treacherous turns, sending up a trail of dust and jolting them unmercifully. But wherever they went, the headlights of the black Mercedes followed keeping a discreet distance. She lit a cigarette and gave it to him. Her nerves were raw with strain. She sat at the edge of her seat, leaning toward the dashboard.

Ibrahim stared out of the moving car. He turned to her and his hand reached for hers. "That's why I've tried to keep my secret from you as long as I could. I didn't want you involved. And if it wasn't for the fact that you were so suspicious and hard-headed, I wouldn't have let you in it at all. But you're my whole world. I love you, Aisha. I don't want to lose you. It would mean fighting for nothing." He paused. "Why is it so difficult to understand such silly notions?"

He seemed to concentrate on his driving, battling the wheel, an eye on the rearview mirror. Then they came to the better paved streets of the city and Ibrahim jammed down the accelerator. The little car smoothly gained speed.

"Did we lose him?" she asked.

"No. I didn't try to. It's better if he thinks we are not aware of his presence. This way I can keep an eye on him. By the way, is there a door leading to a back alley at your place?"

"Yes. Why?"

"There is something you could do," he said.

She waited.

"Reach down. Inside my right sock you'll find a folded paper. Take it and while you're bent, try to hide it. Fasten it on your bra or somewhere. Can you do it?"

When she finished, she kissed him on the cheek.

"Good!" he said approvingly. "Now we'll see how smart that son of a dog is."

They stopped a short distance from the entrance of her house. The street was empty and dark, except for the pale street light. In the darkness, the old house silhouetted in a thinning mist. They left the car and crossed the street. She opened the front gate and they shuffled into the courtyard. Ibrahim's hand tightened around her arm and he pushed her flat to the ground. Shocked, she lay still and watched him.

He was lying flat, only his head raised, trying to watch the street. He started to crawl, and she followed suit. The soil of the flower beds was damp and smelled of manure and jasmine. When they reached the far corner, he stopped, straining his eyes in the dark. Then he pointed at the black Mercedes parked a few meters from the street corner, outside the native café.

"He's waiting in the car," Ibrahim said. "He hasn't even taken precautions to conceal himself. He must not think we suspect him."

In the dim light, she could see the familiar husky back of the man from the restaurant. "What now?" she asked.

"Keep moving," he said. "And don't make any noise, or your mother will come out and scream robbers."

They broke into a crouching run. "Where's the back gate?"

Before she could open her mouth to answer, she heard the thump of a heavy body falling. She shuddered. A long second passed. Her mother came out and turned on the porch light. Aisha remained hidden behind a bush, while a cold sweat ran down her spine. How in the world would she explain to her their strange behavior without revealing Ibrahim's secret? Not only that, but their plans to escape their follower's attention would also be ruined. She saw her mother glance around casually, then she went in, turning the light off.

She exhaled slowly in relief. "What happened? What was that noise?" she asked in a low whisper, searching beside her for Ibrahim.

"It was me! I stumbled on something and fell," he said quietly.

Suddenly she was struck by the odd realization of the entire scene. Two grown people on their knees, playing peekaboo in the dark, and she in her new green satin dress! She started to laugh, a jeering, unstable laughter. "It's ridiculous," she said.

He came close and laid a finger on her lips. "Shush!" Then he threw his arms around her and they kissed. "I wish I didn't love you the way I do," he said, holding her tight. There was sadness in his voice. His muscles relaxed. "Let's get moving."

She laid her hand on his arm, and they walked in step, stride for stride. They reached the back wrought-iron gate, and she pulled the latch. The gate opened softly, and they slipped into the narrow alley.

She took a deep breath. "Let's run," she suggested.

"Nothing of the sort," Ibrahim said with a firm grip on her arm. "You just put your arm around me and we'll take a walk."

"That's not bad," she giggled. "As a matter of fact, I'm beginning to enjoy this game in the dark."

"Aisha, behave! This isn't as romantic as it may appear to you." He squeezed her hand and kept his voice low, but there was a discernible note of alarm telling her he was worried.

They moved without apparent purpose through the narrow trash-filled back alley until they came into a larger street with traffic.

"Is the man still following us?"

He shrugged. "I doubt it. I imagine he's waiting for me to return to my car. But we better be cautious, just in case there are others posted around. One can never tell."

He whistled at a passing cab. The driver turned around in the middle of the street and came to stop in front of them. They stepped in and he took off.

Just then, she realized how tired and exhausted she was. Unconsciously she brought her hand to her chest, to make sure the paper was still there. Ibrahim's worried eyes met hers. She nodded. He leaned back with a sigh of relief. His face was pale, and he looked tired.

"If anything happens to me," he whispered, his eyes closed, "I want you to see that this paper gets safely into Ghalil's hands. It's very important. It contains the names of influential people who are out to get us and who should be watched closely." He paused briefly. "It also means treason and death if caught in an officer's possession."

Her surprise left her silent. Ibrahim looked back over his shoulder still checking on the road. "Cigarette?" he asked, flicking open his case. As he lit her cigarette, she thought he had meant to change the subject. She was wrong.

"They might attack me and make it look like robbery. But I wanted you to appreciate the importance of the paper you carry, and know what to do if the occasion comes." Then he asked her to memorize Ghalil's address.

The feeling of confidence that had come momentarily at the thought of having escaped their pursuer quickly evaporated, and she felt frightened again. He looked impatiently at his watch, then asked the driver to stop. "We better walk the rest of the way. If anyone's followed us this far, we can see or hear him before we reach there."

But everything was quiet, and all that could be heard was

the echo of their footsteps on the asphalt. They got to the house and Ibrahim glanced about casually, then knocked two times at the door. The door opened, and they slipped in.

Ghalil approached, extending an arm. "Well, I'll be —" he said, and then he took a good look at them. "Come in." They followed him through the entry and into the sitting room.

"I've been shadowed," Ibrahim explained. "I figured it would look better to bring her along. I hope you don't mind."

"It's no problem, my friend. Let's join the others. They're waiting," Ghalil's eyes moved from Aisha's face to her ripped dress, which showed big patches of caked mud and dirt. He tried to smile. "Are you all right?" he asked with concern.

She nodded and started to giggle at how ridiculously filthy they both appeared.

"Nothing that a good brandy won't fix," Ibrahim said.

"I'm sorry," she apologized. "I'm all right, really."

They passed into another room. Six men stood up. Some were dressed in uniform, others in civilian clothes. Ghalil introduced them, and the men greeted the couple in unison. Then one by one, left the room and went into an adjoining spacious study, where they took seats around a table.

"Now you can hand me the paper," Ibrahim said.

Without thinking, she thrust her hand in the opening of her neckline. Then she became aware of the two men who stood looking at her, smiling. Embarrassed, she turned her back and completed the search.

"I must say," Ghalil laughed, "I can hardly think of a safer hiding place!" The men laughed and left the room as Ghalil's wife came in. Her face drawn, her eyes showing rings of sleeplessness beneath them, she smiled kindly. "I'm so glad to see you," she said. Then she noticed Aisha's dress. "Why ... are you all right?"

After Aisha explained, Ghalil's wife raised her hands.

"Praise unto the Lord, the Great! Wait. I know what you need." she said and left the room. She returned quickly with a glass, handing it to her. "Drink it. It's good cognac."

Aisha took it obediently and had a long swig. It was smooth and hot. The heat went all through her and made her feel warm and safe.

"Got your wind?"

She nodded. "I needed that. Thank you." She saw a comfortable armchair and sat.

There was a double knock at the door, followed by the doorbell. "I'll get it," Ghalil's wife called out.

"Good evening, officer. How are you tonight?" Aisha heard her greet the newcomer.

"Very well, Madame, thank you," replied a strong, husky voice. "Have the others arrived?"

"They're in the study."

When the officer came in, he looked at Aisha disapprovingly, then nodded, and walked straight for the study. She had a quick glimpse of his face. He had a dark complexion, with a serious, determined expression. Dark, inquisitive, piercing eyes and a small moustache. He was a tall, thin, handsome man.

"Who's he?" Aisha asked as soon as Ghalil's wife returned. "I don't think he approves of my being here."

"I'm sure he doesn't. But —" She shrugged and raised her eyebrows. "He's Lieutenant-Colonel Gamal Abdel Nasser."

"Never heard of him."

She went on to say that the officer was in his early thirties, was married, and had two daughters and three sons. As she spoke, she picked up her knitting from the nearby table. "I have a feeling, he's the big leader behind the movement."

"Young, isn't he?" Aisha said cautiously.

"They've got to be young for this kind of involvement," she said. "Young and daring."

"True."

"He's a real *baladi* from the village of Beni Mer, in Assiut. He knows well the plight of the *fellah,* and he recognizes that no matter how much prosperity comes to Egypt, it never trickles down to the peasant."

"I know that too well."

"We all know it. The difference is he and the others want to do something about it. You see, his mother died when he was eight and his father, a postal clerk, raised Nasser and his two brothers alone. He is a graduate of the Military Academy and served in Alexandria, Alamein, and in Sudan. He has also seen duty in the Palestine campaign, and the siege at Falluga."

"Oh yes." She remembered Robert telling her about the officer's heroism at the time.

"Nasser is smart," the woman continued. "In 1942 he went to the General Staff College where he's now a lecturer. He's non-violent, but he's a proud man. He's cautious, deliberate, calculating."

"He looks the part."

"Yes. He's bright and liked by most. I believe the tragedies and scandals he witnessed during the Palestinian war, and of course the episode of Al Majdal, where the army was ordered by Farouk to surrender, filled him and the others with anger against the responsible authorities." She hesitated and glanced toward the door. "Well, now my dear, they seek revenge."

The study door opened. "Wife," called Ghalil, "be a darling and bring us some coffee, please."

"Sure, Ghalil." The woman obediently got up.

Aisha offered to help.

"No, my dear. I'll be right back. You try to relax. And don't open the front door for anyone." She patted her on the back and ducked out for the kitchen.

Aisha looked about the room. There was a magazine on the table, and she picked it up, but she found it impossible to concentrate. *What in the world am I doing here?* She wondered. What Ibrahim and the other men wanted was beyond her comprehension. *Are they anarchists, rebels or heroes who were trying to change and improve the life of the common man? They risk their life for what they believe in. Are they brave or crazy?*

Round and round, thoughts darted in her mind, offering neither solution nor relief. But why could they not see how futile their efforts were? They kept dreaming of miracles, endangering their lives. If only she didn't love him. If only he wasn't as proud and as concerned about causes and revolts. Of course, there was always the possibility of changing his mind. Perhaps, if things got worse, they would perhaps have a change of heart and give up the whole foolish scheme.

And Aisha felt her heart leap with hope. Yes, she could play along for a while longer. Time worked miracles. Besides, she was still young.

"Those brothers we lost in the Palestinian disaster did not die in vain," said the angry voice of the speaker from the opened door.

Then came a second voice. "But let's remember that ours is an Arab people, and our destiny is tied to the unity of the Arab Nations."

Ghalil's wife stepped out of the room, an empty tray in her hand, and closed the door behind her.

The two women were making small talk when the door of the study opened again and one of the men came out, heading for the bathroom. It was obvious he knew his way around because he didn't ask for directions. From the partly opened door, they could overhear the men arguing.

"Communism is not a solution to our problem. We struggle and fight to get loose from the lion's jaws, only to fall into the bear's paws!" the speaker said in a strong determined voice.

Another voice began. "We will befriend those who befriend us and be hostile to those hostile to us. We will return blow for blow, slap for slap."

Ghalil's wife looked at Aisha, and their eyes met and held for a minute. "Nasser," she whispered.

"But he's a Communist," shouted a second voice.

"We all know that, but now is not the time to raise trouble among ourselves. We need every man we can count on. If we succeed with our plans, then we can take care of him and the others who obstruct our work." There was a short pause. Then the same husky voice. "As for the Muslim Brotherhood, join if you like," he said, "but beware, they're a sect of fanatics."

The man had returned, shutting the door behind him.

The woman put her knitting down and looked instantly at Aisha. "Are you scared?"

"I guess I'm too frightened to be scared."

She smiled. "Can I get you anything?"

"Do you have an aspirin?"

She nodded and left the room.

How had she ever fallen into such a hopeless affair Aisha wondered, numb and tired. She had lost the capacity to feel even the thrill of danger.

It was 1:30 A.M. when the door of the study opened and the men started to leave, with regular intervals between departures.

From where Aisha sat, she concentrated on the tall dark officer, the one Ghalil's wife had suspected as the leader of the movement. Nasser was talking to Ibrahim, and she had the uncomfortable feeling they were talking about her.

Then Nasser nodded and looked at his watch. He leaned to snuff out his cigarette and for a minute Aisha had a glimpse of his face, a hard, young, masculine face in which heavy worries had already left the first traces of premature wrinkles.

"Goodnight," he said hoarsely, not looking at anyone. Then he opened the door and was gone.

CHAPTER XVIII

From the beginning, the year 1952 showed that it was going to be hard and decisive.

During its first weeks, Cairo went through a period of disturbances. The unreal and the unbelievable became commonplace. Hunger and unemployment became commonplace too. There was no order, only men filled with anger and despair.

Some 40,000 Egyptians employed by the British in the Canal Zone were forced to give up their jobs in return for the Wafd's promise to employ them elsewhere. The new year found them hungry and unemployed, and the steady rise of clashes and incidents between British and Egyptians kept everyone on edge.

From day to day, the situation grew worse, and everyone felt the tension in Cairo's streets and in everyday life. The skeptical natives on the streets gathered in groups around the newspaper stalls or cafés that had radios. They listened to the inflammatory speeches made by leaders of Wafd, and the Socialists, and Communists, and the Muslim Brothers who advocated the setting up of a state under the sovereignty of God.

Meanwhile, Ibrahim called at the nightclub as often as he could. But as the days went by, he grew tense, tired, and more preoccupied. His work had become the central factor of his life, a true obsession. Everything else was thrust aside. The revolution became the hub upon which all Ibrahim's thinking was centered.

"To hell with improvements and a better world for the future," Aisha screamed at him. "What about now? What about us?" She fought and argued, one night when he appeared briefly at the club.

"The time is crucial Aisha. We're having problems even among ourselves. Some of the members of our secret organization are becoming impatient waiting, and want to rush things. But the head of the council does not think the time is proper to act as yet," Ibrahim tried to explain.

"And when will be the right time? What will they do if they catch you?"

"Execute me." He said calmly.

"You call yourselves freedom fighters, but the government calls you terrorists, rebels."

"It all depends on who is in power at the time, between a patriot or a rebel." He studied her for a moment.

She just looked at him.

"Right now we have the British to contend with. The British have 80,000 men in the Canal Zone. All Egyptians going in and out of the zone must be searched. Even Egyptian judges entering on official duty have to submit to the humiliating search on Egyptian soil, and the government can do nothing about it. But of course, you're not concerned with any of these things," he said gravely, and then was gone.

And Aisha thought: *Am I concerned? If not why am I attracted like a magnet to him?*

All these events were played up in the local press, and Aisha, like everyone else, lived in a nerve-straining atmosphere, watching and waiting for the slow fuse to light the powder.

And then, it happened. Injury was added to insult.

On the morning of January 25, the newspapers carried stories that more than 70 Egyptians had been slaughtered at Ismailia, the halfway point on the Canal. According to the press, 1,500 British soldiers had surrounded the governorate of Ismailia and commanded the Egyptians to surrender. The commander-in-chief of the 200 or so Egyptian policemen inside the governorate refused, and the British opened fire.

The Egyptians returned the fire with old-fashioned rifles, and the battle started. Arab civilians and policemen against British soldiers, entangled in a battle that lasted for several hours. More than 70 Egyptians were dead, and around 100 wounded, on Egyptian soil.

News of the massacre spread over Cairo like a prairie fire. They all felt that a climax was approaching. They were now conscious that the political situation was about to break loose. People everywhere read newspapers, commented, criticized, suggested, reacted.

Usually the corner café by Aisha's house was full of peaceful Arabs who played backgammon or smoked their water pipes. That Friday morning, the place was swarming with restless men who sat on their haunches in circles and listened to the news and screamed for revenge.

Aisha had hoped to see Ibrahim that night at the club. He did not show up. *Another meeting*, she thought disgustedly. *Oh, damn him! Why must he be such an honorable fool? Why does he feel he has to be the savior of his country, the freedom-lover!* Why? *If I could only feel like him and his friends.* They were whole-hearted and sincere in their devotion to the revolution, she was sure. Or, *if I could be like Robert, who took things in stride and very seldom, if ever, had reason for unhappy introspection.*

But she realized she could not be like either of them.

Aisha left the house early the next morning. She had promised Fatma a pair of red shoes, like the ones mother had bought her at the village bazaar. Downtown Cairo looked no different than usual that Saturday morning, January 26, 1952. By eleven o'clock, she had made her purchase and was walking to the left of the equestrian statue of Ibrahim Pasha, son of Mohammed Ali the Great, which dominated the Opera Square.

She contemplated the idea of stopping at Shepherd's Hotel for an ice cream. In front of the hotel was the usual crowd of dragomen and tourists. On the terraces and balconies sat the wealthy foreigners and the elite Egyptians who spoke French.

"*Baksheesh,*" asked a beggar, his arm outstretched.

She fished into her purse for some coins and was ready to drop them into his can when she noticed he was blind in the left eye. She brought her hand to her mouth to muffle a scream.

"Allah be with you," he said.

"*Inshallah,*" she mumbled. "Oh, God, bless our lord Mohammed," she said, and spat over her left shoulder three times to prevent an evil result.

By the time she reached Shepherd's she had lost her appetite for ice cream, so she walked past the entrance of the hotel and kept going. She thought that perhaps she would stop by her property, which was not far from there, and check with the doorman to see if any repairs were needed. All four apartments were rented, and the building was in good condition.

She heard a great commotion from behind. Startled, she stopped and glanced over her shoulder.

At a distance of a few meters from where she stood, was a frenzied mob of thousands, it seemed, who filled the street and the air with hysterical screams, waving their banners in the air. They marched toward the square, chanting.

Looking about, she felt as if the earth had cracked wide open and started to heave up the scum of the earth. Like enraged rats, the rogues, hoodlums, addicts, and riffraff of the city of two million inhabitants crawled out of their holes and ran to join the demonstrators.

Drivers abandoned their cars in the middle of the street and ran for shelter. Store owners rolled down their shutters with staggering speed. Doors and window-blinds slammed instantly.

She stood there as if hypnotized, unable to pull herself away.

Then she felt someone pull her by the sleeve. "Run, *Yia Sitt.* Find cover. They mean business. Run!" It was the one-eyed beggar who hopped briskly on his way to join the mob.

She knew she had to get out of there, but go where? Her heart was pounding, drowning out every other sound. She saw an apartment building and dashed for the door. It was locked and barred. She banged and beat. "Help! Somebody open, please!"

A window on the first floor cracked open and she saw a woman's white head. "Please, open the door and let me in, please," she screamed hysterically.

The woman went in and shut the window. What if she won't come, Aisha thought, what then? The rioters, clad in torn shirts and *gallahiyeh,* chanted closer. Now she knew a fear that she had never known before. Then she heard footsteps. The door eased and she pushed herself in quickly.

"We have a porter to protect us, but instead he ran to join the crowd," said the elderly woman, with a strong foreign accent. "Do you live in this building?" she asked.

"No. I happened to be out. I had no place to go."

"Then come up with me, child. You can't stay here. This *mouzahra* looks serious today. It won't be just another demonstration." The frightened woman wiped her eyes.

They climbed the stairs and went into the woman's apartment. Then she bolted the door. The blinds had been pulled and the room was semi-dark. In the light of a burning candle, she saw the old woman's face lined with worry, as she silently wept.

"Are you scared?" Aisha asked.

"Not for me, child," she said. "I don't care for myself. I'm old, and I've lived my life. It's my grandson, Yannis, that I'm worried about. He's only eighteen. If anything happened to him, I'd blame myself to the day I die."

"Why?"

"For months now he's been trying to persuade me to let him go. But I wouldn't listen. Australia seems so far from here, a strange country, and we have no one there. Yannis' parents are dead." She paused. "Then, of course, I always hoped things would settle down here. It's not easy to leave the country where you were born and spent all your life, and go places starting from scratch among strangers. This is the place we know, Egypt was the country we considered our own."

"What nationality are you?"

"Greek," said the woman. "We've had a thriving community."

"It isn't fair."

The woman stared at her. "Life isn't fair. There's no logic." A silence fell between them.

The screaming grew closer now. Aisha ran to the window and peeked through the drawn blinds. All the unchecked energy of the mob brought such havoc as she had never witnessed before. Now the angry men, armed with iron bars, broke down store barriers and went in shouting like wild animals. Looters carried merchandise, which they tore to pieces and threw in the gutter. Cans and bottles with gasoline passed from hand to hand, and soon black smoke and flames leaped high, burning everything in their path. The screams of the victims trapped in the blazing buildings were agonizing to hear. Unable to stand it any longer, Aisha turned away from the window.

The woman, on her knees, eyes closed, seemed to be praying in front of the candle and two icons. Aisha dropped by her side and tried to pray as she had seen the girls do at the Catholic school, years back. But the prayers would not come. Could it be, she wondered, that God had forsaken them?

"Revenge for our brothers in Ismailia! Down with England! Long live Egypt!" the mob chanted.

"To hell with all of you bastards!" Aisha shouted angrily and leaped to her feet. "If you want revenge, you don't have to kill us to get it. Go fight the British! Don't burn us like rats."

The woman stared at her with a look of perfect incredulity, but she remained silent. Aisha returned to her observation post by the window.

The raving mass now had gathered in the nearby square, arms waving in the air in a roar from thousands of voices. Behind them the buildings were still burning, while cars and buses lay wrecked in the middle of the street. There was no sign of the police, and the frenzied mob, thirsty for more blood and action, surged ahead. The leaders, who were carried on the shoulders of the stronger men, continued their oratorical speeches, demanding that the massacre of Ismailia be avenged with blood. The mob agreed and cheered as they slowly swarmed toward Shepherd's.

"It's terrible. It's sickening!" Aisha groaned in pain. "They've gone crazy and no power on earth can stop them now."

"Where is the police?" The woman asked.

"I can't see them. They must be praying in the mosque, or they're having a strike!"

"And the army?"

"The army? The army?" Aisha repeated stupidly. *Yes, where is the army to restore order? What are they waiting for anyway? To see us all dead?* "There's no army, either," she said. "The entire city is burning like a candle, and nobody seems to care."

"Are they coming closer?" asked the woman from her corner.

Aisha nodded. "They're outside Shepherd's Hotel."

"Oh, that beautiful hotel. It's been there ever since I can remember. It's been the pride of Egypt. I hope they don't ruin it."

"I don't believe they'll go that far," Aisha said. "I see officers of the tourist police. They're trying to stop the crowd from attacking the foreigners staying at the hotel."

She had not finished talking when the raving mob surged into the hotel, dousing furniture and people with gasoline. They threw flaming torches, setting the biggest bonfire she had ever seen. Guests stampeded toward the exits, only to fall into the hands of the enraged crowd.

The world had become an inferno of noise and flame. Through the nerve-wracking sounds, Aisha heard the screams for help of the people trapped on the upper floors of the blazing hotel. Two frightened pigeons soared from the roof, seeking safety.

She turned her head so the woman couldn't see her cry. Impotent rage quelled what little fear was left in her heart as she stood helpless while her fellow men plundered and killed like savages.

"What happened to them? How could passive men change like that?" Aisha asked. "These are not the Egyptians I've known."

"In a crowd, emotions are apt to break loose," the woman said. "Don't upset yourself, child."

"Long live the Germans! Long Live Rommel!" chanted the mob.

They stared at each other. "The Germans?" Aisha croaked.

"Rommel, now?" the woman said, and they both returned to the window.

Leaning over the third-floor window were three blond men who had been trapped. The mob cheered and was trying to save them.

"They love the Germans now, because they hate the British," Aisha said.

In a matter of hours, the luxurious hotel with the red carpets and the heavy crystal chandeliers was no more.

After the walls of Shepherd's Hotel caved in, the mob moved across the city, burning, looting, and destroying other establishments. A dark smoke hung over the old city as the wave of flames billowed up from street to street. By mid-afternoon, it looked as if the entire city was destroyed.

There was no phone in the house, so Aisha could not call home. The worst part was not knowing what was happening elsewhere. She realized it was not safe to leave her shelter yet, so she sat and waited a while longer. The woman prepared and brought her a cup of coffee. "Drink. It'll do you good."

"You must really hate us after this mess."

The woman raised her head and looked at her. Her eyes softened. "No, I can't say that I do. Surely, I cannot condone today's behavior, but I try to understand." She took a sip of coffee. "Your people want food because they've gone hungry for so long. They want clothes because they've had none. They're furious. If now they seek revenge, it's because they have been neglected and mistreated. It's a human reaction."

She paused. Then spoke again. "We, the European residents, have always felt great compassion for your poor. But then, we've had no political or other power in our hands. We couldn't interfere with the basic structure. We are foreign subjects, and even though born here, we've maintained our foreign nationality. What they've done today, it's terribly wrong. It's unfair. On the other hand, your landlords' approach to squeeze the *fellah* and squeeze him again to get the last drop of profit from him wasn't fair either. Yet, when land taxes went up, your wealthy landlords simply passed the burden on to the *fellah*. As a result, even if he slaved, he ended up not having enough to support his family. This is only one of many wrongs."

"You understand us, yet you wish to leave the country and go elsewhere."

"That's true," she said, with a turning down of her lips. "But we'll always remember the happy years we've spent here, years that'll never come back. Egypt was good to us. Gave us shelter, peace, and comfort when we needed it. No one who ever drank the water of the Nile will ever forget this land." She shook her head. "But we must realize, my dear, that the time has come for us to leave and let others take over. Others who, perhaps, have more rights than we do. Hospitality sooner or later must come to an end, and the guests must eventually depart and return home — or elsewhere, if they're wanted."

"You're such a fine lady," Aisha said, and before she could contain herself, she went over and threw her arms around the woman. "I sincerely hope you find happiness wherever you go." Then she bent and kissed the top of the woman's snow-white crown.

"Thank you, child. I hope you and your people find happiness, too. You deserve it." She appeared deeply touched.

"But you don't have to leave, you know. We don't ask for the foreigners to go."

"True. No one has asked us to leave — not yet, anyway, but can't you see there's no room for us? No nation under the sun can live forever in darkness and suppression. In time, the people see the light of truth and revolt. And that's what is happening in Egypt today. A sleeping giant has awakened and needs room to roam. We, the foreigners, are in its way." She stopped for a minute to catch her breath. "To survive now, we must all adapt ourselves to the changes. That's all there is to it."

It was late. Aisha was tired and depressed. The streets below were deserted, except for some natives and very few Europeans who walked hurriedly on their way home to hide.

She rose to leave and the woman held her hand. "Take care." On her pale cheek was a streak of tears.

Aisha's heart beat fast and her stomach churned crazily as she stepped out and into the street. She felt beads of sweat break out on her forehead. She started to walk, not knowing where she was going. She saw a group of young Arab boys painting over European signs of street names and stores with Arabic letters.

Suddenly she was less frightened, as if life had taken on the quality of a dream. It almost didn't seem possible death was so close. It wasn't possible that within hours the quiet pace of life could have changed so much. The whole thing seemed unreal, grotesque, brutal, and imaginary.

A European man walked by, and some native boys chased after him, yelling offensive remarks. She moved briskly and crossed the street. On the corner was a parked taxi. She opened the door of the car and got in. The Arab driver stood at the nearby café talking. When he saw her, he left his friends reluctantly and came and stood by the car.

There was a sinister look on his face and a sarcastic smile on his lips that she hated. But she tried to remain calm. She gave him her address and asked him to hurry and take her home. He didn't budge an inch.

"If you're not interested in this fare, just say so. Don't stand there glaring at me. I don't scare easily."

He laughed. His black eyes flared. "It amuses me," he said. "All of a sudden, everyone now talks Arabic! It makes it hard for us to distinguish a foreigner."

"How dare you! How dare you call me a foreigner when I'm as much an illiterate peasant as you are!" She erupted as if the mere thought that she could have been mistaken for a European was an insult. She flung him a vindictive glance.

He met it with cold contempt, impervious as stone.

"By Allah, haven't we done enough damage for a day?" she asked.

He laughed raucously. "That's only the beginning. There'll be more, and much worse."

"Take me home, please."

The man pondered for a moment. Then he scratched his head in perplexity, as if wondering whether he should get mad or obey. Finally, he walked around and took his seat behind the wheel. He started the engine and the car took off.

"So you say you're *baladi*. One can't tell these days," he said after a while. "Even the Jews now wear crucifixes around their necks."

"Why would they do that?"

"Why? To save that neck! That's why!"

"But I thought you were mad at the British?"

"British, French, Jews. What's the difference? We're mad at all them bastards." He snorted and spat out the window.

"And where are your friends, the demonstrators, now?" she ventured, shakily.

"Hell, the army dispersed them and restored order," he said in a disapproving way, and spat again. "They should have let us burn all them bastards. The army shouldn't have interfered. What business is it for the army, eh?"

Thank God they did, she thought with relief, and her mind ran to Ibrahim. Then she felt depressed. Somehow, the thought that men like Ibrahim, Ghalil and the others, who endangered their lives for the betterment of people like the destructive riffraff she had seen that morning, did not make sense. She was sure Robert would have agreed with her on that. He usually did.

CHAPTER XIX

When Aisha reached home, she was relieved to find her mother and Fatma safe.

"I'm so glad you're not hurt," Fatma said hugging her doll.

"I'm glad, too, darling," Aisha said. And the thought of how close she came to being trapped at Shepherd's Hotel sent shivers up her spine.

It took her a while to convince her mother that all the foreigners were not slaughtered and the city was not entirely burned, as she had been led to believe by Ali, the café owner. Then Aisha was interested to find out what else Ali, the neighborhood's unofficial Reuters News Service, had to say.

It seemed that after the rioters burned Shepherd's, they swarmed across Abdin Square to the King's Palace, which was some four blocks from the hotel. There, the tens of thousands hurled offensive insults at their king. Never before had a mob overtly challenged the monarchy.

"They shouted at Farouk to show them the new-born baby who had teeth in his mouth! And they chanted dirty slogans at him!" her mother explained.

"What do you mean?" Aisha asked.

"Rumors have it that the king made sure his new Queen

Narriman could bear him an heir before he married her. Which means Farouk's son was born prior to his official and much-celebrated wedding!"

There was a series of sharp raps at the door. Aisha leaped to her feet and ran. Standing on the steps and looking like a ghost was Ibrahim, with another army officer, supporting a half-conscious man in uniform. The man's head hung to one side, his mouth distorted from pain. She brought her hand to her mouth to suppress a scream.

"I'm sorry for bringing him here," Ibrahim said, "but I was around the block. Besides, I was anxious to see you. I've sent for the doctor."

"Why, yes," she whispered and swallowed hard. "Bring him inside. Don't just stand there."

They laid the unconscious man on the spare bed, and Aisha pushed a pillow under his head. Then Ibrahim opened the man's jacket. The spot of blood on his shirt was bright red. She closed her eyes and reached out for support. Ibrahim helped her out of the room, leaving the other officer with the wounded soldier. Zakiya prepared some coffee and brought it to them in the living room.

"What in the world happened to us?" Aisha asked Ibrahim. "Have our people gone out of their minds?"

"It sure looks that way, doesn't it? It's terrible." His eyes swept the room. "The biggest mess I've ever seen." He lit a cigarette with shaking hands.

"But what bothers me, and I can't understand, is why someone didn't try to stop them. Why? Where were you all? Having a political meeting or something?"

He looked at her calmly, a blank expression on his face. "We could have restored order easily," he said. "Just a resolute action on the part of the government or the palace would have prevented the whole disaster. But no action of any kind was taken." He turned around, and she could see the pain in his face. For a second, she felt sorry.

He went on with the gruesome account of the day's results. More than 100 foreigners and Egyptians had been killed. Schools, clubs, scores of department store, 18 banks were looted and burned to the ground. Twelve Englishmen at the British Turf Club had been disemboweled. Barclay's Bank was set on fire and clerks trapped in the basement were asphyxiated. Close to Opera Square, few buildings were spared when the mob set fire to cafés, bars, and cinemas.

"And while all this was taking place, where was the king?" Aisha asked.

"Four blocks away! He didn't have to be told, he could see it from the palace windows. The prime minister as well as the rest of our high officials were all guests at the Abdin Palace where Farouk had a banquet in honor of his son — the son Queen Narriman Sadek had borne him ten days ago. It wasn't until four o'clock in the afternoon that the army was finally permitted to restore order."

There was a knock at the door, and Aisha got to her feet.

"The doctor is here," Zakiya announced from the door.

They joined the others in the hall. The elderly man with the brown leather bag introduced himself and then followed the men into the room where the wounded man lay. The women waited outside.

"How did the man get hurt? You haven't told me," she asked Ibrahim when he came out and closed the door.

"Some officers got impatient and attacked the mob. It shouldn't have happened. It was a terrible mistake. I found him wounded not far from here and brought him over as soon as I could. It's not serious, I hope. He only lost consciousness minutes before we reached your place."

She hesitated. "Could today's incidents hasten the plans for the uprising?"

"There is no doubt that we must act before any foreign power intervenes. If they do, it would be too late then."

"Is there a chance they might?" she asked, holding her breath.

"If we have another riot like we had today, foreign governments may intervene to protect their subjects. That's why today we were so anxious to act fast and restore order, which we could have very easily done so when the whole thing started this morning. But we had no authority!" He spoke bitterly and banged his fist into his palm.

"At any cost, we must protect the foreigners and avoid any bloody disorder." He continued. "We can't afford to give the British any excuse whatsoever for acting against us, as they did against our revolutionary predecessors back in 1919. Can't you see this is exactly what the British and the palace wait and hope for?" His voice was choked with outrage.

She stared at him, unable to understand.

"That's what they pray for," he said. "the opportunity to return and restore order, proving we are unable to handle a self-governed country. They've done it in the past."

"And if they do come? What then?"

His eyes flared. He frowned and gave a gasp of dismay. "If they come, we might as well forget our precious dreams about revolution, dignity, and freedom. It's that simple."

She remained silent. *Revolutions could be good, but peace was better,* she thought stubbornly. *Wars, riots, and revolutions were men's business, not a woman's. Why should he expect her to understand or be interested in such things?*

The bedroom door opened, and the doctor came out. He explained that the man was now conscious, but should be taken to a hospital. He offered to take him in his car. Then he greeted everyone politely and left in a hurry.

Ibrahim helped carry the wounded man to the car. He returned and assured Aisha there would be no more trouble for a while. The army had restored order, and a curfew was imposed. He kissed her hurriedly and went down the steps and into the street.

Fires still glowed in the dark sky. The evening breeze carried the smell of burning, death, and destruction.

Zakiya came and stood beside her. Aisha saw her shake her head, slowly. "Life, like a fire, begins in smoke and ends in ashes," her mother said.

Early the following day, Aisha received word that her four-story building had gone up in flames during the riot. One of her tenants of the third floor had fired a few shots from his window and killed a couple of demonstrators. The frenzied mob took their revenge by setting fire to the building.

Until the moment she heard the news, the thought of losing her property had never entered her mind. How could anyone dare tamper with her security! After years of hard work and saving, she suddenly found herself flat broke because she had invested all her money in the building for *security*. Now she had no building or security because others, insecure themselves, decided they had nothing to lose by depriving her of hers!

As she looked at the blackened stones of the burned building, she was reminded of the remnants of an old carcass of a cow she had seen when she was a little girl in the village. Just like then, the vultures had left nothing but the skeleton, she recalled. She couldn't believe that so many years of hard labor and sweat could have gone up in smoke in a matter of minutes.

"It isn't fair," she said coldly. "It just isn't fair!"

"No, it isn't," her mother said, tears in her eyes.
"This building was my, our security — Why?"
"As long as the masses go hungry, and there is no justice, no one is secure."
Wasn't what Ibrahim was trying to tell her, over and over?
"We've lost everything. Everything." Aisha cried.
"Not exactly. We still have our lives, daughter. We're safe and have a roof over our heads. It's more than we ever had."

How well she remembered. The hot sun that beat fiercely on their heads in the summer, the muddy, cold streets in the winter, and the stinking hovel they called home, she thought. Her heart ached.

"I'll never be cold, hungry, and ragged again. I'll never be poor again!" she swore.

"I know we'll survive, child," Zakiya whispered.

At that moment Aisha remembered the elderly woman who had offered her shelter the day of the big riot. "We're not the only ones, you know. Many people like us will have to make a new start," she said.

Her mother wiped her tears. "That's my Aisha! That's my girl! We made it once, we can do it again. I know we can," she tried to reassure her.

It was two days later, early afternoon when Aisha was returning home. From the bend of the road, she heard the bloodcurdling cries of lamentation, *welweleh*, the signal of death.

"My God! What now?" she mumbled to herself and started to run. Pushing through the throng of screaming women who pulled their hair, tearing at their own clothes and flesh, she reached her courtyard.

"What in the world is going on?" she screamed. "What is it?"

"Oh, our misfortune!" said one. "They've killed her. The beasts, killed her!" The woman moaned and joined the earsplitting chorus of the other mourners.

Fear paralyzed her. For a second, she remained powerless, as if glued to the ground. She looked about, then grabbed a screaming woman who tore at her cheeks.

"They killed who? Why?" Aisha shouted.

The woman let out a long, quivering, ragged moan. Before the woman could answer, Aisha shoved her back.

"Let me pass!" she screamed, as she pushed her way through the crowd and in a frenzy climbed the steps.

Her living room was filled with more wailing women who came to unite in the melancholy task of mourning. Aisha found her mother in a corner sobbing. As she approached her, a new outburst of the tongue-trilling shrieks filled the room. "Oh, my flower! Oh, my joy," they uttered, rocking backward and forward, their fists clenched as they beat their breasts and tore at their clothes.

"Mother, what is it? What's happened?"

Zakiya wailed miserably. It was several moments before she could speak. "It's the child. Fatma. They killed her! My little angel is dead!"

"Dead? How could she be, she's a child!" Aisha dashed for the girl's room. "Fatma, baby," she screamed from the door. Clapping her hands over her ears, she fell shuddering to her knees. "Oh, no!" she cried.

The child lay lifeless, a smile on her tranquil face. "Talk to me, darling. Talk to Aisha who loves you so much." She kissed the girl's hand. She cried and caressed her and twisted her fingers in her hair.

Then Aisha became aware of the smell of rose-water and camphor which filled the room, and she knew the body-washers had already been there. She looked about the room. Above

Fatma's bed was her favorite talisman, the imprint of a palm with outspread fingers to ward off the evil eye. On a chair was her school uniform. A dark blood stain had spread into an ugly dry circle. Her knapsack was nearby, and Samira, the pretty doll Ibrahim had bought her, sat looking at her.

Then her eyes fell on Fatma's feet. She wore her new red shoes, the shoes Aisha bought for her the day of the big riot.

For a moment Aisha's heart stood still, then fear began to beat in her breast. "She can't be dead. Let's call a doctor. Don't just stand there!" she screamed hysterically. "Call a doctor!"

Her mother cuddled her in the cove of her arms and held her tightly against the spasms that racked her body until her sobs quieted and her hysteria passed.

"The doctor has been here, Aisha. It's no use. It was an accident." She paused, more composed now. "As long as there's hatred and bitterness in the hearts and minds of men, there'll always be sorrow and tears for all of us," she said flatly and covered the little body with a sheet.

"But mother, the little orphan never had a chance — a chance to grow, to learn, to love and be loved. Who's to say what a child may grow up to become. My God, why? Why?" Her voice broke. "This senseless bloodshed has to stop!"

"Yes," Zakiya whispered, wiping her tears.

Suddenly, Aisha felt as if the weight of a huge mountain came crushing down on her. She tried to maintain an equilibrium between the forces that battled in her heart, breathing heavily and fighting nausea. *My whole world is falling apart,* she thought trying to hold on to her sanity.

"Why don't you get some rest? I'll take care of all the details." Zakiya's lips were white as if all the blood had been drained from her body, as she helped her to her room.

Aisha went into her bedroom, shut the door, and passed out.

She was told later that all the students had been dismissed early from school that day. Fatma had been playing in the street with some neighborhood children. Suddenly, there was a squabble between an Arab and a European man. In minutes, what had begun as a relatively minor incident came to involve a bigger group of clashing opponents. Shots were fired. A stray bullet hit Fatma, killing her instantly.

Nobody seemed to know what caused the dispute or who did the shooting. And the police, preoccupied with more serious matters than the murder of a little Arab girl, made no investigation.

It was not until after the child was buried that the two women realized how much Fatma had meant to them. The house was never the same again. They missed the feeling of warmth and happiness she had brought with her when she came to live with them. They missed her childish questions, full of innocent curiosity, her happy laughter which filled the house. They missed her every minute of the day and night, and Aisha knew it would take them a long time to recover from the shock of her sudden death.

Her mother put up a good front, but Aisha realized with pain that, in the space of a few weeks, she had aged. Even the brightness of her black eyes had faded.

CHAPTER XX

That night, Robert was drunk and showing it. As long as Aisha had known him, she had never seen him show his liquor before. He stood by the bar, laughing and gesturing with a glass in his hand.

Since Black Saturday, as the day of the big riot came to be remembered, hardly a day would go by that Robert did not pay a visit to the club. He was not the only one. Many of the elite class came to use the premises constantly. For Robert and the others, the nightclub was the most convenient of places where they could transact their lawful as well as illicit transactions, make necessary bribes and contacts, and exchange profitable information.

At the time, money was flowing out of the country like water over the dam. Partly because of his business associations and partly because he could afford it and was capable of employing the greatest talent available, Robert Fawzi came to be one of the best known and best informed men in the city of Cairo.

Although February and March passed with no more major incidents, a hysterical alarm and angry pessimism swept the nation.

Property owners, most of them foreigners, had begun liquidating their assets at great financial loss. Then they were faced with the difficult task of how to send their money out of the country, since they were not officialy permitted to do so.

Houses, stores, and commercial buildings changed hands rapidly. Everyone who owned anything of value was preoccupied in smuggling it out of the country, hiding it, or selling it to the first interested party.

Hopeless claims that piled up at the minister's office, amounting to millions of pounds, found their way to the already swollen government files of previous unpaid claims. Business had come to a standstill, for no one was in the mood or felt secure enough to do any business while the terrified city was swept again and again by spasms of alarm and terror.

As a result of the chaotic anarchy and the riots, the European residents started to leave the country by the thousands, like a terrified flock. Most of them, highly educated and skilled laborers, were eagerly accepted by countries like Australia and Canada, which needed new qualified settlers. Even old Europe could not very well reject those who had maintained their foreign nationality, and therefore were legally subjects of the country of their origin.

Aisha used to think that Robert, of all the men she knew, was the least concerned or disturbed by this upsetting situation. But Robert had changed, too. Now, as she looked up at him, she had the impression that the drowsy aloofness had gone from his dark eyes and in them, at times, she came to detect a fear that matched hers.

He saw her sitting alone and walked over.

"Hi, beautiful," he said. Then he called the waiter and ordered two drinks. When the drinks came, he raised his glass. "Let's drink to the beginning of a beautiful friendship," he said with sarcasm. Then he leaned over and kissed her gently.

"Why, I'll be —" She laughed. "I believe you're drunk, darling."

"And I believe you're right, love. You know what?"

"What?"

"I intend to get worse before the evening's over." He glanced at his watch. "It's only ten thirty." He drank slowly, looking her over, then laughed, still keeping his eyes on her. "It's almost as if you were in love with me!" he said, half amused, half apprehensive.

"You're crazy. You're the most ... the most arrogant devil I've ever met! Besides, you're an aristocrat, my dear. And you're sleek like quicksilver."

"What's wrong with that?"

"I'd be crazy to be in love with you. We have nothing in common, *cheri.*"

"You mean I'm filthy rich. But I had nothing to do with it. I was born into it. And what's so bad about that? Most fights are money squabbles, my dear. The tragic part is that so few people admit or realize it. There's nothing wrong with having lots of money. I rather like it."

She laughed.

"What's so funny?" he asked.

"I was just wondering whether the French aristocrats thought and talked along the same lines until they climbed the steps of the guillotine."

"The thought has occurred to me," Robert said and took a long drink. "You're heartless, my love. But then again, that's part of your charm. And you're not a hypocrite. You're a woman who looks on the practical side of matters without phony moral issues or pretenses. You're wrong, though, about one thing."

"What's that?"

"We have a lot in common, you and I. We're both selfish rascals. Neither of us gives a damn whether the whole world goes up in smoke, so long as we're safe, comfortable and yes, secure! We differ only in one way."

"Please tell."

"You are an opportunist with a conscience. I have none!" His eyes sparkled wickedly. "You're a fool with a conscience, and that, my dear, can't go hand in hand. You're wasting your life over a man you cannot understand and never will."

He didn't have to spell it out. She knew he referred to Ibrahim, and she became furious. "How dare you, you of all people, talk about an unselfish, honorable man."

He raised an arm. "I know he's honorable, which is more than I can say for the two of us. But I'm not a fool, Aisha. Don't you suppose I know that you're always thinking of him while you're with me, and that you only seek my company when he's not around? But I'll give you some friendly advice because I'm your friend."

"I'm listening, friend."

"Let other women be proud that their men belong to secret organizations. Let others rot in jails for planning and scheming against the government." He was standing, looking down at her, faintly amused. "Don't you get mixed up, dear. You're not the type, and watch out. You're been watched."

"Get out of here. How do you know?"

"I have my contacts — "

"Spies, you mean."

"Something like that. Have you ever seen anyone or suspected that somebody was following you?"

"No. I don't believe I have," she said sobering up instantly.

"Well, I know for fact that you are."

She looked at him worried. "Am I in danger?"

"No, no. I shouldn't think so. But watch out."

Suddenly she was left speechless and her heart skipped a beat as she realized for the first time that there was very little he didn't know. A cold anxiety began to throb in her breast. She tried to think.

Robert had always admitted he was a staunch royalist, not for any love or respect he had for the king, but because the present corrupt situation fitted his purpose best. Yet, he seemed to take pleasure not only in affronting the ever-faithful royalists and land-owners, as she had often seen him do, but he could not resist pricking their vanity.

Time and again she had seen him attack men in high places, even though it was always in his subtle, courteous, elegant way. His victims never knew if they should get mad at him or defend themselves against his blunt accusations. But then, Robert had class and he could get away with murder.

"Too bad, because I love you," he said, uttering a deep sigh. "But no matter what, you can count me as a friend. Remember that."

She stared at him and somehow found comfort in the blank inscrutability she saw there. She had no idea why this should be, for he was so unpredictable, but so lovable. *Oh, damn him!* she thought angrily. *If I could have the courage to order him off. If only Ibrahim, that idealistic fool, wasn't so involved with his political dreams about revolutions and plotting schemes. If he could be around more often when I need him.* Her entire life seemed full of ifs, she realized, and became depressed.

Robert lifted her chin and looked her in the eyes.

"If you're waiting for your noble officer, forget him!" he said bluntly. "He's not coming tonight or any other night after that."

"You're crazy or something?" she asked, trying to keep from showing her fear. "I'd rather not discuss him, please. It's not amusing."

"I didn't intend to be amusing!" His eyes had become somber. Then he removed the silver case from his pocket, extracted a cigarette, and offered her one. "Listen. The officers have been under suspicion for some time now, only they've been too clever. That is, until tonight."

"What's happened?"

He hesitated, pushed his chair closer, and lit her cigarette. "My dear, at precisely twelve o'clock, the police will have them in their hands, with enough incriminating evidence to hang them!"

"And how come you know all about this?" *He is bluffing, that's all,* she thought. *Or, he is trying to trap me into admitting my involvement.*

"Let's say I've heard it from a very reliable source. I don't pay my spies for nothing, you know. This time, the fools have walked into the trap. Even if they get them without incriminating evidence, the police will supply them adequately!"

For a second it was as if she had received a heavy blow, but something kept her from leaping to her feet and screaming.

"Why are you telling me all this?"

He lowered his eyes. "Aisha, I came here tonight to talk to you before I go away — "

"Away? Where are you going?"

"To France, Switzerland, to hell. What's the difference?" He paused. "I'm leaving Egypt. And I know you're flat broke, having invested everything in your real estate venture — which was a stupid mistake, my dear, but then, you were determined to buy *security.* I also know you're involved with the secret organization. Let's say your name is on the list of undesirables, which doesn't make you a very popular number with the opposition."

"So?" *Oh, my God, he knows everything.*

"So, I came to you with a proposition." He sat very still for a while, then drew a quick breath as he spoke. "My plane is leaving tonight, precisely at one A.M. Ironic, isn't it?" He laughed. "Since I'm accustomed to traveling in style and good company, I'm giving you the chance to come with me. We can spend a whole summer abroad, and have some real fun, away from all this mess. I'll give you all the money you need. I'll take care of you, you won't have to worry. I have lots of it and it's all in banks where no one but me can touch it. I guess you know — I love you. In my crazy way, I love you. Damn you, I do! Are you interested?"

She thought of Ibrahim. She saw him as vividly as if he stood beside them, tired, full of courage and dignity, so utterly different from Robert. And painfully, she realized she could never belong to another man.

"Aisha, you're such a fool!" he said as if he read her mind. "It's only a matter of time. If it's not tonight, it'll be another time. They'll be caught, and they'll hang. They're dreamers, that's what they are. Dreamers and fools! Others have tried before them, only to fall flat on their faces."

Before she could withdraw her mind from its far places, Robert's arms were around her. She felt a rush of helplessness, a sinking yielding, yet a warm feeling. Then he bent and kissed her, softly at first, and then violently with an intensity that sent tremors along her spin. Before a swimming dizziness spun her around, she realized that she was kissing him back.

"Stop it!" she whispered weakly, fear sweeping her.

They remained silent, facing each other. His breath came in heavy gasps, as if he had been running.

"Go then. Why don't you go to hell and leave me alone?"

He laughed. "I've been sent there so many times, but they won't have me! They're afraid I might corrupt their subjects." The frightening glow had gone from his face, but somehow she could not meet his gaze while her mind whirled in a tingling confusion.

"You're not in love with me enough to marry me, are you?" she asked.

"Devil take me, I wasn't thinking of marriage just now, Aisha. I'm all confused. I can't promise, but anything is possible." His eyes sparkled wickedly. He was tempting and stimulating.

She felt a hot, sudden rage and she shuddered.

"Well?"

"Well what?"

"I have to finish my packing," he said. "I'll wait for you at my hotel until midnight. If you decide to join me, come as you are. You'll only need your passport, nothing else."

He rose, and his eyes met hers directly. It was an eloquent look with an unabashed challenge. Then he leaned over and slipped a piece of paper in her hand. "With this, I'm actually giving you two choices. Take either one, darling." He stood tall and lean and smiled. "I'll send you a card from the Riviera," he said and smoothly turned around and was gone.

Through misty eyes she watched him leave. He was the best friend she had ever known, and he was gone.

She opened the slip of paper. There was an address. It seemed familiar, and she tried to think. With a shock she realized it was Ghalil's house! "That's where lightning will strike at midnight," read the brief message.

The information took her breath away. She glanced at her watch. It was 11:05, and suddenly she felt struck by panic. *Oh, my God! What shall I do?* she asked helplessly, looking about for some help.

Am I losing my mind? she wondered, and held her throbbing head that felt as if it would explode. No, she was just dazed by it all. But she was the only person who could save their lives. With Robert, she would have everything she wanted, and yet, her mind fumbled and pulled two ways.

She looked at the time. It was 11:10 PM. For a moment, she stood irresolute. Then suddenly, she had the feeling that the crowd of people came surging up to her, like the roar of a huge wave that tried to engulf her, to swallow and drown her. She felt out of breath.

She grabbed her purse and started toward the exit. An alarm went off inside her head and she stopped on her tracks. She turned around and hurried through the kitchen. She reached the back door and she stepped to the back alley. She paused for a second, then turned toward the main street. She did not stop running until she reached the taxi stand. Only then did she realize that she was dressed in a low-cut long formal dress and had no wrap around her shoulders and bare back. She shivered in the evening chill, but she was too scared to bother about catching cold. She gave the driver the address Robert had scribbled on the paper.

"If you hurry and get me there fast, I'll pay you double," she said to the driver.

"Yes, madame! I bet I get you home before your husband gets there." The old man said and started the engine.

She almost laughed. "Yes, yes. Please hurry!" She whispered and leaned back exhausted.

A block from the house she stopped the car. She paid and tipped the driver and asked him to wait for her. She got out and started to walk.

There was an isolation about the street that chilled her. She started to run faster, her body shaking with fear, her heart beating loudly in her ears. The house numbers ran in sequence, and she knew Ghalil's was at the end of the street. The silence seemed to surge in, frightening, thick, cold. Then from somewhere came the sound of music. From an open balcony came a love song and the laughter of people who seemed to be having a good time. But the rest of the street seemed deserted, and her steps sounded incredibly loud.

Suddenly, the door of a car opened and closed with a bang. For a split second, she stopped in her tracks. Her heart began to jerk, then she heard footsteps approaching quickly from behind.

She continued to walk, not daring to look over her shoulder. *What the devil am I doing out here? What business do I have to get involved in political movements and counter plotting schemes?* she thought angrily.

There was a strong grip on her left arm. She turned around, drew out her right arm, and with the velocity of a coiled spring, her hand struck a man's face.

The man took a step backward, his hand going to his face. "Well!" he said with a gasp, and for a moment they stood facing each other in the darkness. "I shouldn't have worried about you. You're quite self-sufficient. I'm sure you can take care of yourself!" he said and rubbed his face.

"I'm so sorry, but you scared me. I thought it was that man," she floundered helplessly, struggling for breath.

He tucked the corners of his mouth into a little smile. "I'm sorry, too, if I scared you. I didn't mean to. I thought you were in trouble and needed help. I'm a police officer," said the man clad in civilian clothes. He offered his hand.

Terror paralyzed her and she could only stare into his face as if she had never heard the word before and had no comprehension of its meaning. She tried to laugh. "Oh, my! I'm so sorry. I mean, it's nice to know we are so, so well watched — protected, I mean."

He smiled. "You shouldn't have left the party and wandered alone in the streets at this late hour. It isn't safe you know, not any more."

"Party? Why yes." She remembered she was still in her working long dress. "It got stuffy in there, and then I had a fight with my boy friend. I thought a walk around the block would do me good, and forget the jerk. The nerve, flirting with another woman," she mumbled. Her throat felt dry, like leather, and her stomach turned over and over. She had never before known this type of fear.

She looked away and noticed Ghalil's house that stood only a few feet away.

"I thought you were that drunkard that's been following me," she said quickly. "That's why I slapped you. Sorry. That man almost got hold of me around the corner. He might still be there for all I know." She tried to appear calm and convincing. "I may have kicked him hard, I don't know. I had to defend myself, no?"

"But of course," said the policeman.

"When I hit him, he fell on the ground, but by Allah I'm not going back to check if he's dead or alive!" She suddenly realized she had been a fool to take such a chance with a whale of a lie.

"You go back to your party, miss, and don't worry yourself about anything. I'll take care of the man. I'll have him put where he belongs. Run along." Then the policeman turned around and briskly walked towards the direction she had indicated, where her imaginary aggressor lay hurt.

Her anger reverted to Ibrahim. *Damn him! he deserved to be caught. He's never been anything but trouble for me.* Furious, she picked up her long dress and ran the short distance that separated her from the house. She climbed the few steps and, maddened by terror, beat at the door.

A man opened and before he could utter a word, she pushed herself in and closed the door behind her. The hallway was in semi-darkness, but she noticed on the coat-hanger two officers' hats. The house was quiet, and the stillness soaked into her heart and frightened her.

"If there are any officers here, get them out," she demanded in a hoarse whisper as the man looked at her, bewildered, his dark eyes wide, searching, hunting for a logical explanation.

"Officers? What officers? Are you crazy?"

"Crazy I am, I can assure you. But we have no time to discuss that just now. Where's Ghalil?"

The man's eyes glittered at the mention of the name but he did not respond.

"In minutes, the police will raid this house. Some policemen are already cruising the neighborhood. Can't you understand me? Get your men out of here. Swallow them if you can, but do something, don't just stand there! I can't do anything else."

When she stopped talking, only the sound of a clock could be heard in the room.

"What are you waiting for? Hurry!" she cried, for he stood staring like one stunned. "Hurry!"

The man's face changed. He took an alert look. Swiftly, he pulled her by the hand and motioned. "There's a back exit through the kitchen. Get out of here, fast!" Then he raced down the hallway toward the study.

As she stepped out of the backyard into the dark alley, she was thankful she had told the driver to wait. The strain which had given her strength suddenly snapped. She felt no fear. She was tired, more tired than she had ever been in all her life. Then, in the darkness, she saw the shadows of men as they scurried away in all directions. She knew they were safe, and for the moment she could only feel a sense of relief and release.

She started briskly up the street, breathing the crisp, misty air with the strong jasmine scent, and she felt almost happy. Two unmarked cars passed by. Then another.

At the curb she got into the waiting taxi. "Hurry, please. To the Metropole Hotel." She leaned back. The time on the dashboard showed midnight. If she could only see Robert once more and thank him. He would understand. He always did.

When she reached the hotel, it was 12:30.

"So sorry, but Monsieur Fawzi has checked out, madame," said the night clerk.

"I'm late, I know," she said and started to leave.

"Monsieur Fawzi knew you'd be. He left a message for you." The clerk handed her an envelope.

"Thank you," she whispered and picked it up.

Slowly she walked out of the hotel lobby while her fingers mechanically tore open the envelope. His message was brief: "To a fool with a conscience. Love, Robert. P.S. I knew you'd come to say good-bye. Take care, R." Folded neatly were five bills, a thousand pounds each.

Her tears choked her. She thought of all the things she had intended to tell him, but there had been no opportunity. She knew now that she would never have another chance.

"Allah be with you, darling," she whispered.

CHAPTER XXI

It was long after midnight when finally she nudged Ibrahim. As he lay across the couch, he had dozed off, exhausted from many sleepless nights and the July heat. At first, he stared dazed and transfixed, then he looked up at her with the full glance that saw everything.

"I thought a little rest would do you good," she said, kneeling beside him.

He laid his hand on her shoulder, and gently it began to travel down the length of her back with firm, intimate knowledge. She quivered as she felt his hand groping softly. She bent and kissed him between the eyes that looked unspeakably warm and beautiful, and she could not help putting her hand on the defenseless nape of his neck.

He trembled with a deep shudder. Then he looked up with that awful appeal in his dark eyes. Just then she realized how incapable she was of resisting him. In all her burning dismay, deep in her heart, she knew that she loved him.

"Has anyone called for me?" Ibrahim asked. Then he rose and went to the window.

She looked up at him. "No. Are you expecting someone to?"

There was a brief silence. Then he came and sat beside

her on the sofa. "Any hour now. We've been alerted to expect telephone calls at night until further notice."

"Which means?"

"That time has come. The time is ripe now that the heat and sultry weather have lulled the king and his entourage into a false sense of security." He reached for his cigarettes.

Then he went on to explain that, as usual, most of the foreign diplomats had left Cairo for Alexandria and the cooler weather, and the king had already moved into his summer residence at Montazah Palace. Also, the troublesome students were gone on vacation and dispersed.

"Besides, everyone jokes that nothing ever happens in Egypt in the summer," he said.

"I suppose this makes things easier."

"Why, yes. Our chance is to act now, before the king has the time to appoint another cabinet. The last minister just resigned." He lit the cigarette he held, and then stared as if trying to visualize the impression his words had on her.

Their eyes met for an instant, and they both looked a little abashed.

"Why, Ibrahim? I mean, is it necessary to revolt?"

His gaze sharpened. "We're not idealists and we're not mixed-up or dazzled. We are realists, my dear. With our actions, we do not seek to destroy the integrity of others. What we want is to regain and establish our own integrity and self-preservation. It's as simple as a,b,c, really. You strip a man's dignity and integrity and you debase him to the level of a beast. And that's what happened to our people. We can't just let it continue, can we?"

"Yes, I understand," she said quickly. "I'll get you a cool drink."

She rose to her feet and returned a minute later. He was pacing up and down the room. She put the glasses on the table. He came and sat on the sofa and crossed his legs. He sat for a long while silent, his chin on his hands. Then he gave a sigh and shook his head sadly as he looked at her.

"What is it? What's bothering you?" he asked.

"I was just wondering. What will the foreigners do? Could they interfere? Could they stop your action?"

"The foreign powers suspect us already. But they have no right to interfere. I hope they realize that. If not, well ... then hell! It'll be impossible to avoid bloodshed." He paused and took a long sip from his drink. "By the way, why did you delay your trip to Alexandria? By July, you're usually there."

She hesitated. "I just couldn't get away now, now that you need me the most."

"Perhaps you should've gone, get away from this infernal heat." he did not look at her.

"At this point in my life, I can take the heat. Weather's the least of my worries."

He grinned and pulled her into his arms. "You've been through so much, darling, since we've met. Why?"

"I guess because I'm crazy, and because I'm in love. What else?"

He lifted her face and looked at her reassuringly. Then they began to kiss feverishly, desperately. The thought that this could be the last time together sent shivers through her.

A church clock struck three.

"Aisha," he whispered softly. "I must go now. I hate to, but I must."

"Yes," she said, burying her head in his chest. "I know you must."

He got up and straightened his uniform.

"When will I see you again?"

He was quiet for a moment. "I don't know, Aisha. I can't tell." There was a slight tremor in his voice. "Where is your much vaunted courage?" The muscles of his arms stiffened. "I'll be thinking of you. I'll contact you just as soon as I can."

Then he suggested that it would be better for her mother if she went for a visit to the village for a while.

The thought had preoccupied Aisha. Her mother needed a change, she needed to forget Fatma. Zakiya was still holding on to the girl's clothing and toys. It was as though something in her had died with the girl.

"Won't you be lonesome?" Ibrahim asked.

"I'll manage. I wouldn't want to add to her worries when she eventually learns of your involvement. And I'm afraid if mother stays here, I won't be able to keep my secret from her much longer."

He drew her to him and closed his arms around her. She clung to him in sudden terror. "Don't! Don't go, Ibrahim. Please don't," she whispered in blind frenzy, clinging to him with all her might.

"Aisha! What's gotten into you? You know I must. I can't stop now. I've gone this far, I can't change in midstream." Softly, with the gentle caress of his hand, he stroked the slope of her back and she melted in a flame of desire.

As he held her, she noticed he had lost weight, and she made a mental note to tell him later, and do something about it.

He pulled himself away then swiftly looked at his watch. *"Ashoofak bel Kheir.* I'll see you in good health," he said in a hoarse whisper. Kissing her forehead, he turned on his heels and left.

She stood there for a moment with her arms open as if trying to bring him back. She heard the outside door close, and she was alone.

Maybe it was only a bad dream, and she would wake up. But it wasn't a dream and she knew it. His cigarette forgotten on the ashtray was still burning, his empty glass was there next to hers. *Will I see him again?* she wondered. With sadness, she realized that she had never cared for anything or anyone except herself until that moment. With Fatma dead and Robert gone, all her love was transferred to Ibrahim. Nothing else mattered now, only his safety.

She could not and would not sleep. She thought of nothing. She felt a certain maturity. She could almost see the change in herself. Crouched on the sofa, she tried to understand the causes and effects of this miracle of growing up. Was it the sorrow and pain she had gone through? Or was it the miracle of love? Having made up her mind and chosen the path she wanted to follow was part of her old self. But then, resisting Robert's tempting and easy way out was not. She was a different person, she knew. Was it perhaps because of her love for Ibrahim? It had to be, she reasoned. Nothing else mattered now.

The minute she became aware of that, the strange wretchedness and heavy burden that hung over her suddenly left and the nagging doubts disappeared. For the first time in a long time, she felt calm, peaceful, with a sense of deep and wonderful contentment. Just then, her mother's favorite proverb came to mind: 'Were it not for fractures, there would be no pottery'. Yes, it now made sense.

Two terribly long days went by with no news from Ibrahim. The third day, Wednesday, July 23, 1952, she was awakened at dawn by the vibrant sound of flying airplanes.

She grabbed a robe and ran to the front yard. The sky was covered with bombers and jet planes that flew over the city. From the street below came the rumbling of passing armored cars and tanks. Her heart pounded with excitement and uncertainty. An Arab boy stood by with his shoeshine gear under his arm and looked up at the sky.

"What's going on?" Aisha asked. "Have you any idea?"

"Sure," replied the boy excitedly. "The army has occupied the city!"

By then more people clad in bathrobes came out of their beds and into the street. The woman from the next yard overheard the boy and asked, "The army? Which army, son?" Then, turning to Aisha, she said in a lower voice, "Hell, he's doped."

"Our army, of course!" yelled the boy. "This is our air force, woman. Look at them. Just look how they fly!" The boy pointed toward the sky.

The neighbor stared at Aisha. "I'll be damned if I know what it's all about. The army and the air force took the city from whom? Who had it before them? Why, the whole thing's absurd. It doesn't make sense."

Ali's radio at the corner café was going full blast, and Arabs had gathered around to listen to the news. Aisha ran back into the house and turned the radio on.

"To my brothers, the sons of the Nile," said the speaker. "You know that our country has been living through delicate moments and you have seen the hands of traitors at work in its affairs. These traitors dared to extend their influence to the army, imagining that it was devoid of patriotic elements.

"We have therefore decided to purify ourselves, to eliminate the traitors and weaklings, and thus record a new and honorable page in the history of our country.

"These who engage in destructive activities will be severely punished. The army will cooperate with the police in maintaining order.

"In conclusion, I would like to reassure our brothers, the foreigners who live among us, that their interests will be respected. The army will be fully responsible for their lives and property."

The speaker identified himself as Lieutenant Colonel Anwar al Sadat, speaking in the name of General Mohammed Naguib, Commander-in-Chief of the Egyptian Armed Forces.

Then the radio announcer explained that the proclamation would be repeated every half hour until General Naguib was able to appear in person and address another message to the people, keeping them fully informed of the proceedings.

The general's name was new to Aisha and she made a mental note to ask Ibrahim the next time she saw him. She hoped he was one of the Free Officers and working for the same goals. She thought of Nasser, Ghalil and the others. And suddenly she longed to see Ibrahim. Closing her eyes, she prayed. She prayed God to enlighten the minds of her people so they would cooperate and assist the Officers in their work.

"Please, God, don't let this turn into a bloody massacre. Forgive our sins and help us," she begged from the depths of her heart, while warm tears ran freely down her face.

Even though she was terribly lonesome, she was happy her mother was not there. She would be safer at the village, Aisha knew, and she would be spared the anguish and turmoil of the unfolding drama.

At eleven o'clock, Anwar al Sadat broadcast another statement on behalf of Lieutenant General Mohammed Naguib. The speaker repeated most of the previously made statements, asked for the people's support, and reassured the foreigners as to their safety. "I consider myself personally responsible," he stated.

The only thing that hinted of any trouble was the announcement pertaining to the arrest of "some officers." The speaker promised that no harm would befall them, and that they would be released "at the first opportune moment."

She tuned the radio off. How silent the house was! How

dreadfully still. She felt as if the walls were closing in on her. Her thoughts buzzed like a swarm of bees and would not let her rest.

She changed clothes and set off across town. All of a sudden, there seemed nowhere in particular to go. Every impulse, every desire, had faltered and faded. She felt empty.

Cairo was sweltering in a heat wave. Normally the streets were empty during the noon hours of the hot summer months, but that day, most of the people were out. Everywhere, men gathered in knots, formed groups on sidewalks, around kiosks, in stores, and discussed the news of the day, spreading rumors to the extent that it was hard for anyone to form an opinion or distinguish between lies and truth. There was, of course, always a shred of truth, or at least of inspiration, in each one of the rumors.

At the European grocery store where she went, the foreigners were positive that within hours the British would invade Egypt. They believed that the aristocracy would influence the dissatisfied portion of the Egyptian population to revolt against the rebels of the army and that a successful *coup d'etat* was impossible.

The Egyptians, with exultation and pride, watched the daring manner with which the airplanes performed, and had some faith that the revolution might succeed.

The newspapers had no news, except for the proclamations already broadcast, but passengers from trains, buses, and cars brought news of events from other cities. And the news spread from mouth to mouth and neighborhood to neighborhood, only to result in biased, distorted reports about the movement. There were more tales than Aisha could fit together.

Some people had heard that the British forces had already landed in the Canal Zone, while others denied it, claiming the armed forces were Egyptians placed there as a precaution to prevent a possible British invasion.

There were rumors that King Farouk had escaped the country aboard a British ship. Another version had it that the palace had been surrounded and the king had been shot to death, together with the other members of the royal family. Others went as far as to claim that they had seen American warships come to rescue the king, while not a few strongly maintained that the warships seen in Alexandria harbor belonged to the British Navy, which, having saved the king, bombarded Alexandria!

By Thursday evening, July 24, the air was so full of rumors that Aisha thought she would lose her mind. If she could only hear Ibrahim's voice. If she could only know if he was safe. And then she realized what he had said: "Do not listen to the wild rumors. We'll try to keep the people fully informed by radio messages."

She turned on the radio, and the first notes of a classical piece of music, sad like a funeral march, filled the room.

She was tired and aware of a heaviness in her chest. Her stomach was empty, the kitchen was full of groceries, but she was not hungry. Nothing in her stock of foods looked edible.

She poured herself some brandy and drank it at a gulp. She shuddered, but it steadied her nerves. Then she lit a cigarette and stretched on the sofa, waiting. In the quiet room, she waited anxiously for the ring of the telephone, the husky tone of his voice telling her he was safe.

For the first time she saw how things really were and dreaded what might happen next. What if the revolt failed? What then? The officers who engineered the coup would be shot as traitors, no doubt, and that would leave her with a tag around her neck, the inscription too legible for anyone to read. And yet, she had been warned of the outcome. Had not Robert repeatedly warned her?

She served herself another drink. The brandy felt warm as it went down her throat. She felt a little tipsy but still she could not get the thought of Ibrahim out of her mind. For the first time in her life, she was regretting things she had done, regretting them with a sweeping superstitious fear ... fear and remorse, and the torment of a suddenly awakened conscience.

She thought of the times she had made Ibrahim unhappy, when she could have been more understanding, more patient. What if God chose to punish her for not having been nicer? She shivered at the thought. In her heart she knew that nothing else mattered, neither friends nor money.

The music was suddenly interrupted, and she heard the familiar voice of the speaker. "To my brothers, the sons of the Nile," he began. "May the Almighty guide our steps and purify our hearts to the end, that Egypt may once again attain a position worthy of its name."

Naguib's speech made her cry, but it also revived her hopes and gave her new strength. After all, she thought, it may be that everything is going fine, and it's only rumors circulated by malevolent people who wished to stir up trouble.

In the stillness of the night, the telephone shrilly jangled. She jumped to her feet, her heart pushing against her ribs. The phone rang again, persistently. She tried to control the wild beating of her heart as she snatched up the receiver and tried to sound calm.

"*Allo, Allo?*"

"Aisha? Aisha, is it you?" It was Ibrahim's low voice.

She nodded. "Yes, yes, darling, it's me. Are you all right?"

"I never felt better. Listen, I don't have much time. I'm calling from the airport."

"Airport?" she repeated feebly.

"Yes. Everything's under control. We're getting ready for the big fish, the shark. You know what I mean, no?"

She knew he meant the king and nodded again as tears came down her face.

"I love you very much." He paused. "Do you think you could come to Alexandria?"

"I'll take the first train."

"I'll see you at your place then. As soon as I'll be able if all goes well —"

"Please, be careful. I love you. May Allah be with you."

Then she heard a click and the line went dead.

Hearing his voice was a great relief, and the possibility of seeing him again soon filled her heart with new hope. Nothing could happen to him. He would be all right, he had to be, she wanted to believe.

CHAPTER XXII

It was four o'clock before Aisha fell into a restless, thrashing sleep. In the morning she was depressed, her face drawn and her eyes showing rings of sleeplessness beneath them. Only the hope of seeing Ibrahim again gave her the strength she needed for the trip to Alexandria.

Panic-stricken, mad for speed, she almost screamed at every train halt. Finally, in early afternoon, she reached their apartment in Alexandria. She was relieved to find that, except for a few army tanks and armored cars that paraded in the streets of the city, there had not been a sign of disturbance or warships of any kind.

She was fixing herself some coffee when she heard the rhythmic booming of cannons. "Oh, my God!" she cried, running to the balcony.

"It's only the customary twenty-one gun salute," said her next-door neighbor, leaning over the rail. "It can only mean one thing."

"What?"

"That King Farouk of Egypt and Sudan has abdicated! For sure, this will be his last official salutation!" The woman burst into joyous laughter.

The day wore on. It was past midnight when she heard

footsteps outside, then a sharp rap at the door. She ran and opened it.

Ibrahim stood before her with a pale, grave expression of expectancy. He looked tired and strained. The very sight of his face frightened her. He came in and she shut the door. They were kissing at once, pressed against the door. When she felt his arms about her, all her doubts disappeared. There was only a deep sense of relief.

"We've done it!" Ibrahim said with exultation in his voice. "By Allah, we've done what everyone said could never be done!"

"Darling, I never believed it possible. Not for one moment did I think it was possible," she whispered. "Forgive me."

He laughed. "I didn't believe it either, darling!"

She stared. "But, taking such risks —"

"Aisha, nothing worthwhile was ever accomplished without a certain risk. The only thing we had going for us was hope. Hope! It was the only weapon we had. But a man with hope and courage can still win."

She asked him if he cared for some food.

He shook his head. "No food, please. A beer will be fine."

When she returned with the beer, he sat slumped low on the couch, as though every muscle was tired, but he gave her a faint smile.

"Has it been bad?" she asked, taking a seat beside him.

"Bad? Not at all," he said, shifting uncomfortably and reaching for his glass. "I believe very few, if any, revolutions have accomplished more with the loss of fewer lives."

"You mean you didn't encounter any resistance at all?"

He shook his head. "In spite of the fact that hours before the *coup* an officer betrayed us to the palace and we were expected everywhere. When we arrived to take over the vital communications center in Cairo, we found the building ablaze with lights and full of officers who had been alerted to put down our coup. They surrendered after putting up a token resistance."

"What about here, at the palace? We heard the king was shot."

A smile flickered over his tired features. "My dear, we are not murderers! We had decided to get rid of Farouk, yes, at the earliest possible time. However, he was entitled to a fair trial. Since we didn't wish to keep him in jail and preoccupy ourselves with him, there was only one thing left, exile."

He paused and pondered. "Nasser put it so well. He said that history itself will sentence Farouk to death."

As he spoke, Ibrahim began to loosen his collar. "Besides, justice is our goal. We can't commit murders in the name of justice. We are rebelling against the lack of justice."

He rose and restlessly paced the room, making a distraught circuit from the kitchen to the door and back to the sofa. There was so much anguish in his voice that her heart was wrung with distress.

"I don't know what life is all about," she said, "and I don't even want to try to find out. I know and accept that life is incomprehensible, but I also know that life is beautiful and has meaning and purpose. I know that life has its limit, which is death. So, I want to live to the fullest with its suffering and pain, and its moments of joy and happiness. Is that wrong?"

He was somber. "No, my dear. That's man's greatness. That's exactly why we were ready to die, if we had to, to attain our goals."

He was silent for a while and somewhat distracted, drawing on his cigarette.

"Did any of the foreign powers intervene on behalf of the king?"

He grinned. "Farouk asked for American help. I happened to be at the army barracks when the First Secretary of the American Embassy, Joseph S. Sparks, came to see Naguib."

Ibrahim went on to explain how the American told Naguib that his ambassador had been requested by Washington to inform the Egyptian prime minister that the U.S. government was prepared to regard the *coup d'etat* as an internal matter, concerning only the Egyptians.

"However, the ambassador wished to have our promise that we would not harm the king or the other members of his family, and that we would allow them to leave Egypt with the appropriate honor granted to a monarch."

Ibrahim spoke softly, a cold, dry smile on his face. "I was at the Palace when Farouk was forced to sign his abdication. It was a historical moment. I guess the whole thing was painfully embarrassing. I'll never forget how Farouk's hand trembled. He had to sign twice!"

Ibrahim paused and ran his hand through his hair. Then he leaned back and wiped his wet forehead with a handkerchief. "General Naguib was there, and all of us were gripped by a mixture of emotions that brought us close to tears."

Then he laughed. "When Farouk left the royal palace, the palace servants, in accordance with our custom, set up a wail of lament that could be heard a quarter of a mile away."

"How were they dressed? I mean Narriman, the king?"

Ibrahim blinked and shook his head as though emerging from a wave. "Dressed?" He grinned. "Oh, woman, be reasonable." But he went on to say that the king had on the uniform of an admiral and the queen wore a traveling suit. Farouk's mother, the former Queen Nazli, was not there. She had been living in America since Farouk banished her from Egypt.

"Farouk's last words were: 'It isn't easy, you know, to govern Egypt.'" Ibrahim stopped and looked through her, far beyond.

Then he spoke slowly but clearly. "Farouk is right. Egypt is not easy to govern." Ibrahim's voice echoed strangely in the stillness of the hot summer night. "The new discovery of what we've done is yet to come."

Aisha went out on the balcony. It was a glorious warm summer night. In spite of the dramatic events of the last three days, there was a peaceful feeling, as if time and life had come to a perfect standstill. Never had the ancient city looked so entrancing as in that pre-dawn silvery color that engulfed it. A light breeze made the palm trees sway. Millions of lights glinted here and there between the shadows of buildings, and the minarets seemed to hang from the clear sky.

Ibrahim came quietly and stood behind her. "I almost forgot," he said. "I have something for you. Something I've been carrying around for some time."

"For me?" she asked, taken by surprise.

He felt in his pocket and brought out a small box. He opened it, took out a ring and slipped it on her finger.

She stared stunned, totally unprepared.

"You better behave from now on," he said. "And let this remind you that the day millions of Egyptians won their freedom, you lost yours!" He laughed and pulled her into his arms. "Will you marry me?"

She nodded and felt the warmth of his embrace.

The stars grew dim, and the sky grew light. Dawn was breaking. In that pendant hour between night and day, she realized with relief that this was a dawn such as Egypt had never had before.

"I love you," she said weakly.

"And I love you more," he sighed heavily.

"You must be exhausted, darling," she said.

His arms tightened around her. "No, my dear," he said. "On the day of victory, it is impossible to be tired," and he held her in his arms.

EPILOGUE

OCTOBER 6, 1981

*A*s *Aisha applied the finishing touch of her makeup with a Chanel lipstick, she was reminded how lucky she had been to have kept her looks. The eyes that had dazzled men and audiences were still lovely and expressive; her strong cheekbones, full lips and black gleaming hair; all seemed untouched by time.*

Her fifty-fifth birthday was coming soon, but people always assumed she was in her early forties. Women still admired and envied her, even though ever since her marriage to Ibrahim, she had ended her dancing career. Not that she had wanted to, but it was not proper for an officer's wife to go on dancing in public places, even if she had become a legend.

But this was Egypt, full of traditions and contradictions.

That day was the country's proudest anniversary when the entire country, in spite of political or religious differences, joined together to celebrate the day in 1973, when Egyptian soldiers had crossed the Suez Canal to reclaim the land taken by Israel.

An hour later Aisha was seated at the top of the reviewing stand amidst wives of diplomats and dignitaries.

The military parade had started, but when the Phantom jets of the Air Force came in formation and started their aerobatics, everyone looked up with pride at the colorful spectacle in the sky. Then Aisha saw three army men running toward the front of the reviewing stand with machine guns.

"No!" she screamed.

But her scream was lost in the sound of an explosion, followed by the barrage of bullets, breaking glass, and the children's screams that filled the air.

For one heart-stopping instant she felt as if she were dreaming. Then she felt the strong arm of a bodyguard pushing her down to the floor, where ministers and wives of generals and government officials were huddled, behind the wall in the stands.

While the sound of machine guns continued, Aisha carefully raised her head to peek over the wall and she saw the beautiful face of Jehan, the President's wife, distorted by pain and fear as she tried to rush to her husband. But her bodyguard blocked her way, and pulled her to the ground protecting her and her four grandchildren, while reassuring her that the President was only slightly wounded on the leg and that he would be all right.

The whole scene seemed surreal, but Aisha knew she would remember it the rest of her days.

When the barrage of bullets stopped, and the wounded and the dead were transferred into ambulances, Aisha looked for Ibrahim but she could not find him. How many times had she experienced the same terror? How many times had she faced death and prayed for Ibrahim's safety? Fear for Ibrahim's life, being shot by a disgruntled assassin, was as much a part of Aisha's life as eating and sleeping. But at least they felt a sense of security among the members of the military. Until now. The day's assassins were army men.

Stop it, she told herself, you're thinking as if Ibrahim is gone. And he is not. No, he couldn't be. Please God, not after all we've been through ...

In the panic that followed, women and children pushed toward every exit. Feeling as if she were in a bad movie, a movie she was sure she had seen before, Aisha moved with the stampede to the street. An hour later she found herself back at home, not even remembering how she got there.

She turned the television on, but as soon as the firing had begun at the parade grounds, the television coverage had been stopped. Nobody knew the fate of the President. There was nothing else to do but pray and wait for Ibrahim's call.

In the late afternoon, the phone finally rang.

"Are you all right?" Ibrahim asked.

She couldn't hold back her tears any longer. "I'm fine and you?"

He cleared his throat. "Aisha, Anwar el-Sadat, the President, is dead."

There were a hundred questions she wanted to ask. She asked none.

"It's ironic," Ibrahim continued. "He was killed by the men he trusted, his military family, an army officer and two enlisted men." He sounded wrought with emotion.

There was a brief silence. Then "I'll be home as soon as I can. Be brave, my love." And the phone clicked dead.

It was not until 8 P.M., seven hours after the firing at the parade grounds, that Mubarak announced that Anwar el-Sadat, President of the Arab Republic of Egypt, was dead.

END